A Game to Play on the Tracks

A Game to Play on the Tracks

Lorna Jackson

The Porcupine's Quill

NATIONAL LIBRARY OF CANADA CATALOGUING IN PUBLICATION DATA

Jackson, Lorna, 1956–
A game to play on the tracks/Lorna Jackson.

ISBN 0-88984-231-0

I. Title.

PS8569.A2645G35 2003   C813'.54   C2003-904711-3

1 2 3 4 • 05 04 03

Published by The Porcupine's Quill, 68 Main St, Erin, ON N0B 1T0. www.sentex.net/~pql

Readied for the press by John Metcalf; copy edited by Doris Cowan.

This is a work of fiction. All characters are creations of the author's imagination and are not intended to bear relationship to living or dead characters; any resemblance to actual persons is wholly accidental. Likewise, the novel's British Columbia – towns, cities, and villages mentioned – is an invented province.

We acknowledge the support of the Ontario Arts Council, and the Canada Council for the Arts for our publishing program. The financial support of the Government of Canada through the Book Publishing Industry Development Program is also gratefully acknowledged. Thanks, also, to the Government of Ontario through the Ontario Media Development Corporation's Ontario Book Initiative.

Canada Council   Conseil des Arts
for the Arts   du Canada

Canadä

ONTARIO ARTS COUNCIL
CONSEIL DES ARTS DE L'ONTARIO

For Tonta, Selina and Hels

and

for David, our best man

Table of Contents

I
Arden

1. Where Do All the Shells Come From?

The shells in the sea are the houses creatures have made from their
own outsides. When these creatures die their bodies dissolve away,
but the empty shell remains. It is now much lighter, for its
inhabitant is not there to fix it to a rock or a seaweed, and so it is
cast up by the waves on the shore, where we find it.
   The Book of Wonder, Vol. v (1932)

Arden is one or the other – water or street. She'll flow and
flirt with shore – her hair and lips turbulent – or get hard and
twist ankles, send kids and their clean heads off bikes. Every
port town she works comes with a Water Street, the shimmer
of commerce at the bottom of a hell-bent hill. This is a lazy
name, a blurred tattoo of failed imagination. As usual, crows.
As usual, puddles and a drizzle so light it does not agitate
their surface. A radio from below some boat's deck chatters
out to the breakwater and echoes back to shore: *Here's what
I'm sayin', Mitch, the neutral zone trap means the end of the
game as we know it.* Mongrels – each with a white-tipped
trace of sheepdog – own the road and dance across it, change
partners, jump, splash and dance. Pulp, paper: stink. She is
rambling. On the water side of the road, beer parlours teeter
on creosote stilts out over the Pacific Ocean, and Arden could
walk into any one of them, take a window table, order a
pitcher of flat draft and watch the water darken, age and
disappear. Not now. In the illusional light of late afternoon,
the bars levitate across the harbour towards Grief Point,
neither here nor there, amphibious. *Next caller. Todd from
Port Moody. Your thoughts, Todd, about the Europeans and
their defensive trap?*
   On the town side of the road, slivered between Scandia
Bakery and Twice Nice Consignment for Ladies, is Granny

Baa's Wool Shop. Amber cellophane blocks ultraviolet rays and stains the booties and layettes like jaundice. A cowbell's dense music announces her. It is more chasm than room. Boxes and bags of yarn pile to heritage high ceilings. Shelves are invisible, no table legs. What's under all that suspension, the floating stock? One foot in front of the other – cautious, alert – Arden walks the thin, sticky carpet down the aisle like an outlaw's last sneak. She can hardly breathe. The air in a wool shop on Water Street: dust, septic bivalves, lanolin. A cigarette fidgets from the clerk's cedar-bark face. 'Something special?' The woman's hair is the colour of Mars and brittle as binder twine; her voice has cancer written all over it. 'What's the *project*, dear?' She wears an aqua Sayelle sweater set that adds twenty pounds to her skin and bones. Earrings the size of sand dollars: is that Queen Elizabeth's face? Elton John's?

'I need a pattern,' Arden says and already this feels like a confession to someone who has contacts, who can push the right buttons and make things happen. Pronto. 'I'm looking for – I think it's called – a bed jacket. Women used to –'

'Gimme a sec,' and she disappears behind a nicotined curtain, singing along to the surroundsound of country slime – *I don't care who's right or wrong* – she crescendoes a quarter-tone above the husky sizzle of 1970s Sammi Smith. She's back. She hurls and restacks stacks of printed matter and her cough cough hack cancer cells spread and kiss Arden's lips and then skitter across the puddled Water Street, to Grief Point, and over the Strait of Malaspina in the coastal version of remission. 'Nineteen fifties. "Beehive". One size, nicest they ever did. I made this up for my sister Enid out of the Paton's white sock yarn when she was laid up with her third. Three in four years. I'll let you have the pattern; now you need something special. Wool's itchy; I don't keep a cotton fine enough.' The clerk moves in and stoops for a close look at the name tag centred on the left lapel of Arden's

sensible, navy blue, knee-skimming, figure-fucking suit:
CERTIFIED PRODUCT DEALER COMMUNICATIONS SYSTEMS.
'You're not the synthetic type.' She bestows the pattern: baton
passed, tradition transferred. The music pauses around
Sammi and she's riding the groove: *Take the ribbon from my
hair.*

Even in yellowed black and white, the woman on the cover
is radiant. In the softlit distance behind her, the shadow of a
bassinet. The bedjacket uses a simple lace stitch – is that
cockleshells? – and has a wide satin ribbon and two pearl
buttons at the throat. The erotics of her breasts are both
stressed and played down: the white wicker, the hand-knit. Is
she expecting or recovering, breasts functional or decorative,
the bassinet half empty or half full?

If Arden follows up and down the aisles, there will be no
room to pass. The clerk hogs the stage, hoisting aside bags of
charcoal and red, counting clean pastel balls and skeins and
coming up short – 'Bloody hell.' Wheeze. 'I had more of that
at one time. Here's what happens when they put taxes up.'

The ugly air, the griping, push Arden down onto a child's
rocking chair at the front of the store. She rocks to the sound
system's mariachi horns and Fender Rhodes tremble:
signifying equal parts much and nothing. Granny Baa's
provides an orange crate of chipped toys and with each rock,
Arden flicks the wheel of a stainless steel steam train turned
turtle. *Train I ride. Sixteen coaches long.* She rocks faster and
hears Elvis, the Tennessee Three, the slap of brushes on snare
drum at the backbeat speed of steam, the glee of locomotion.
She monitors the stratus clouds of smoke above the clerk's
head.

'Whattabout Peach?' and she's motoring back, throwing
elbows at falling stock. 'See? It's a good natural shade. Sure,
you could go with the German sock stuff – but that's just
heathers and you don't want the woman depressed, for
chrissake. A kid on the boob's plenty. Tell her: guzzle water

and air 'em out. A little wool, a little cotton, and 10 percent plastic so it washes and holds. Twelve balls should do you, take thirteen. Need needles?'

Rockabilly has that hurt-by-history moan, and Arden is its victim again. Don't go, boys. Don't do me this way. Rock, flick and class the coloured beads along a wooden abacus from the toybox, calculate. She tells mostly this version: I have come without tools and I haven't knitted for years but my friend – Margaret – is at home, ill, not pregnant, not nursing – nursed. And I'd like to make her feel fixed. I want to sing spirituals, Appalachian primitive and clear and deep, but when I'm near her now my voice goes thin. I want to touch her twenty-four hours a day, but maybe if I just craft something to cover the small shoulders, and think of her with every stitch, it would be like an embrace, and the oils from my fingers would be a laying on, a healing. I had surgery early last spring – just a little operation – and she came for three days to read me Daphne Du Maurier and make sage tea and lemon mousse, and I showered so she could change the sheets, destroy the cells still leaking.

'Hoh, eh? That case, you'll need the pale green. Sea Mist. Just take me a minute to switch. Pick out a set of threes and a set of three-and-a-quarters. Those should cover your tension.'

A pale, perfumed and monotonic desk bunny gave Arden room 101, end of the hall beside the unruly ice machine. Room 101: Introduction to the Road. This trip has brought back an air-brushed rendition of her saloon-singer past. One glass of wine, and she is loose and nostalgic for 2 a.m. swamp drinks with the popluxe band boys from the cabaret – *The perfect recording is a document of a singular moment of sloppy intensity* – nubbly sheets, nevermade bed, cable piped in from hardcore Detroit. Back then, they witnessed the birth or backroom abortion of the music video. She was the city chick with smart talk, details, drunk but not stuck. She had the slap-and-pull rhythm on a caramel Fender Telecaster, an original style, into the red every night. Tonight room 101 has a test: remember this? Are these the empty hours you want again?

The fire door opens – the boom chicka boom of the stripper's first flaunt, her superior sound – and shrieks closed. The ice machine slides open and there is a bucket to fill, a scoop to clatter back into the cavern of the machine. The door rams shut and some salesman's sixth rye and water will perk with the chill. His so-called date will seem renewed, pleased, her lips shined up in his absence, the blouse gone one button south. The pantyhose rolled off, a drug of minor declension shared and the sex shaken out of garden variety: an unexpected insertion, obscure fluids mingle. 'There's that done. Let's go catch the singer,' he says from the bathroom, in lieu of post-coital chit-chat.

Tonight Arden drinks topnotch white wine. Puffed ankles crossed, suit jacket slung around the shoulders of the only chair, she sits up in bed and knits a sample swatch, twenty stitches by twenty-two rows, to gauge tension. She can't watch just now, but listens: a tender-voiced documentary about reindeer migration, its risks and triumphs, the long cold synchronized swim toward blooming tundra, antlers shed and regrown, velvet, the white babies and their myths. She thinks of her mother, a teenager in a 1940s New Westminster movie house, knitting ribbed socks for her POW fiancé in Germany, a crush on William Holden, so good she doesn't look at the stitches which are nevertheless even and smooth tight.

On the first ferry tomorrow, Arden will head home to Sapperton without a sale. And this time, no hard booze in the hotel's tavern, no flirt with the owner's son across the bar until closing, no liquored replay of the stripper's strut and stoop. Room 101 is both beginning and end.

* * *

Nichol calls after eleven, saving charges and taking advantage of everywhere's quiet. He is not angry yet – 'The work couldn't wait?' he begins – but there is going to be trouble, bony Arctic wolves are driving her into ambush. Beware the lone pine. She has knit two inches up the back. It is slow going with all the lace, the knit-three-togethers and yarn-overs, but she feels meticulous.

'You and Tom were handling everything. You weren't crying, so I thought it could just happen without me and I didn't want to wake you when I left for the ferry. I'll help with the service, that's more my strength. Parties, performance. When?' She brings a new ball of yarn to her mouth, rips away its paper band, and presses it under her nose. Is that lavender?

'I think "performance" is the wrong word for my mother's service. Are you drinking?'

'I didn't mean in the flirt-and-smooch sense.' Always the ruminant. Separated from the herd, she seems agitated but oblivious to the tracking wolves. She heads for the lone pine, for cover, and that will do her in. 'A glass of wine does not cause babies with two heads or third eyes or dangling bowels. The French know this. I am drinking French wine.' It *is* lavender; how French. 'The body is mine, Nichol, regardless of temporary boarders.'

'Margaret has died, Arden. You missed it. This isn't about you. It isn't funny. I'd like you home now.'

Home is temptation and danger. Home is brick fireplace heat and fresh apples and a dog-thick bed without springs or polyester. The tea there is black and strong. Hand-me-down white tulips frame the back porch. One small room – once a windowed closet next to their bedroom – has the clarity of childbirth: walls the colour of jonquils, a rag rug, a womanly rocker Nichol's father made, sanded and sanded and oiled and sanded and rubbed with more oil. There is a twirling mobile of thirty orca whales, black-and-white like the midwife counselled, a huge hung pod turning to look out across the nearby Fraser River when the window is open. Or is that mass hysteria?

The wolves chase her home, she swims the chop and presses that long head forward against the current, she undulates even with her girth. On the beach, she stumbles as they snap at her terrible haunches and knows they will rip off her face – even the velvet nose – and eat out her brain and leave the rest of her not yet skinned and bleached bones. As usual, crows.

The potential baby is their beachline. Nichol is shore, Arden the swells, tide rips, kelp beds. But shouldn't Arden be the vessel? He trusts she will stay and believes she needs to. His hands will wander her flagrant stomach at night, gently at first, and then at month seven he will poke and jab unkindly, find a limb or rising extremity and press with stiff fingers to submerge it, hold it under. Love me tender, she will tell him, babies know. 'The kid's safe,' he will snide, 'that's what your womb's for.' He will rub what he believes to be the baby's backside but complain of being too tired-cold-busy to do hers: muscles ache, spasm and lock. He resents the way she leaves towels on the floor, how her eyes pillow in the morning, the fridge crisper full always with green apples, green grapes and limes, her all-night itching skin.

She is trying to get at why she will leave him. Reasons seem concocted, dreamed up to excuse personal disability, liability. As usual, hormones. But Nichol's body perseveres while she is metamorphic. His body is the same as four months ago: vacant, all sinew and stress point. There has been no communion or coming together or significant cell division; no cleavage or honeycombed love. There's someone else living in her body. At night, the intruder roams, bumps door jambs, slips on scatter rugs, and comes up against night-belly resistance. Her patience lapses. She needs sleep but someone has her body for the night. 'Home. Now.' He is hard as a skillet, loud as a rotten mother.

Room 101: the phone in its cradle, the cool and smooth
wine glass at her cheek, Arden calls up the last clear sky
before Margaret's distortions, aphasia, the stupid urine. On a
day trip to Vancouver Island, Nichol's mother held her
forearm along a bark chip path through dank woods. The
hand, the bones: sorority. Also, harbinger. Their husbands
bulldozed ahead through fat tree trunks and super-ferns. Tom
wore corduroy slacks, their own fine bark whispering a
rhythm to the Douglas fir. Nichol wore canvas shorts, though
the month was October and full of a low pressure ridge. Their
big shoes rattled small bridges. 'Will you look at that,' the
men took turns saying, a silly song, a vintage recording before
high fidelity, before vinyl and its hereness. Their voices slid at
78 rpm, its dark glass surface. The creek ran, filling for
winter. That day, at the pace of an invalid, Margaret walking
was a long poem, echoed air, stanzas of flora and fauna:

> Madrone, bolete
> (bend, stand, rest).
> Salal, slough sedge,
> (bend, stand, rest),
> kinnikinnick,
> winter wren,
> (rest).

Long poem or samba, what's the difference.

The two women stepped down to the cup of Sherwood
Pond, its westering grass. 'This is a good idea to do,' Margaret
said. 'Look at the green.'

No sand, no softness, no wimp-ankled shell pickers. A
cobble beach. Beyond it, a tide ran out into Juan de Fuca
Strait – where does the water go? – its Olympic Mountains
and their summer-snow peaks. The whisper of little boats'
stops and starts, desperate men yarding crab traps. As

Margaret and Arden stuttered further down the last few steps, Nichol was already smoothing the blanket over what is smooth-proof. His father, Tom, straddled a cedar castaway, upright as horsetail. Tom rubbed one hand over his face, frisking himself for whiskers, and with the other hand he inspected a stash of pebbles, sorting them into equal piles along his log. Ramparts. Tom did not regard the space across the water and the sun-cleared sky above it. He did not fall for the towboat's allure.

Margaret and Arden strolled shoreline. The tide was out but nudging in. Margaret let go of Arden's arm and their shoes flew off, cotton cableknits and sundresses pulled up. Margaret waded in smiling like a Baptist or a spaniel, elbows tucked at her waist. 'Oh, this salt,' she hissed. 'This will do it. This should clear it all up.'

Most Sundays, she stayed underground in Vancouver, the Juan de Fuca Museum, to identify, clean, classify, and file seashells, 750,000 specimens recorded by her thin fingers. She was named Honorary Curator of Molluscs. Every Sunday, Tom had lunch baked and buttered and whipped and puffed for one o'clock when she came home quiet, whitened by her cold hours in the brick-walled basement. But she was pleased for new lists, curves and colours, new miracles of order. This Sunday, she wanted the weekend off. Her fingers, she said, felt stiff.

Margaret pulled her full skirt up more and sat at the water's edge, on the vacillating tide line. She allowed sand-warmed waves to reach the tops of her thighs, to wash over her huge ankles, the never-right knees and their garden calluses, to splash those purple veins. She buried her hands. Arden sat beside her, not flinching at the wet cold in her underpants. So what. Her ruby toenail polish, her beachcombed blond hair. Their thighs spread to rest against each other. Four legs, twenty toes extended to the Olympic Mountains, to Cape Flattery, where tidal turbulence extends for miles into the Pacific Ocean, where prevailing wind greets parent wind.

A long shriek came from just down the beach and behind them and then, 'Do you have a bucket?' Two barchicks – how to zip jeans that tight? – their melodramatic bent knees struggling against the pebbles. 'We need a vessel of some kind. Very, very quickly.' Any response was too slow and they shouted and bent their bodies in half as they came closer. 'Please.' The shrill of hard liquor. Their bras could not cope. 'It's beached, it's going to die, for fuck's sake. We have to wet it down. It needs water very, very badly.' Is that asthma or the legacy of Drum tobacco?

Margaret did not face them and scowl as Arden did. 'Is it a seal you're shouting about?' she asked quietly, the hard gloss of an emergency ward intern. 'No, it's a sea lion. It's huge. The poor stinking thing's going to suffocate if someone doesn't help it. It stinks like death. It stinks like death, right, Vonny? Fucking skunk of the world. Do you have a bathing cap even? A fucking beer bottle?'

Margaret did turn then, and she put a hand – stiff fingers – above her eyes to look. Where cobble evolved into coarse sand, two spindly young men stood smoking and tossing pebbles at the huge animal which was a curve, a stilled hump in the well it had made in the beach. Their chests glowed white and smooth, their almost-muscled arms bruised with the paisley of bad tattoos. The stones were getting bigger. 'Make your boyfriends stop that,' Margaret scolded. 'You there,' she called out to them, but the boys were upwind and laughing. The women looked at Arden to measure the older woman's chew-out. They looked back up the shore's incline at Tom and Nichol and their beer on the blanket.

'We want a cup. Or a vessel. We need to save its life.'

Margaret considered the water and pointed her toes at the United States. 'Leave it alone, better. That's an elephant seal doing what elephant seals do.' Which, at that moment, was to

lunge its huge blubbered body viciously and bare its teeth and
roar and provoke a waterfall of profanity and outrage from
the appalled skinny boys. The seal pounded and bounced to
the water's edge – growling, sighing – and slipped into the
low surf, disappeared and surfaced beyond a dark bed of
kelp, a dog's head above water, considered the assholes on
shore.

'Fuckin' dyke whale,' the boys not conversant with such
power and so the name-calling. And so their retreat – Buffalo
Gals bounce to catch up – down the beach, towards the
lagoon.

They didn't know anything demonic grew in Margaret. She
didn't seem interested in Arden's life, though. She didn't
respond to her leading questions: What would Nichol do if I
went back to the bars? What age were you when you had
him? Did you feel stripped and strangled with a baby? She
didn't respond, and Arden should've known.

'I have a terrific memory,' Margaret tilted her mouth
toward Arden, toward the now peopled lagoon. 'When Nichol
was a baby I washed him in the kitchen sink so I could look
out at the garden. It was late spring, I know, because I had a
mass of lily-shaped white tulips in a curved bed around the
Yoshino cherry. No deer that year. I can see it. Tom and I
argued before he went off that morning. It was about, I recall,
his mother pressing for early baptism. The morning's door
was slammed, I don't remember by which one of us, but the
sting lasted. I know so much.

'Look. Goldeneyes. No. Buffleheads.' She pointed her toes
at a floaty entourage of water birds showing off their heads. 'I
wanted the baby to soak while I looked at the trees and
flowers and cried a little because I was home and disregarded
and not loved enough. But Nichol kept shrieking to get out of
the sink and I became more and more annoyed and shoved
him back in again and again. Then I realized with a terrible
nausea – there it is, I feel it again just here – that the

plugged-in cord of the electric frying pan had slipped into the water and that the baby got a shock every time his lovelorn mother shoved his little shoulders back down. Is that possible? Have I made this up?'

And then a long sandy beach of silence until Nichol called them back for a thermos of sweet tea. 'Thank you, dear,' she said and took the blue metal cup, and mother and son smiled at each other with tender hearts.

The little tumours were spotted the next day, Monday afternoon, their dance and spark across the CAT scan, multiplying and metastasizing before their eyes, the diameter of pebbles.

She wants to sing at the service of Nichol's mother. *'We'll understand why, Lord, by and by'* was what had uncoiled in semi-sleep the three nights since Margaret's death. An echo from a dark choir loft, Arden will be every voice, a peculiar unison, life's hills and lonesome valleys. She's picked out a linen dress. The minister, Anglican and frayed, suggests: 'Is there someone close to the family who might contribute a solo?' Five of them in the small living room – the minister has brought his daughter, Ruth. Arden's black-and-tan dachsund, Mrs Kriegie, breathes and shifts in front of the dormant fireplace: she pretends it's still winter and takes comfort. Nichol and Tom blink to see possibilities and leave plenty of space before and after every word. 'I think the regular organist will be fine,' says Nichol. Nichol's father says, 'So long as he knows Bach. Maggie liked Bach at a service, doesn't matter what. Cheerful, but not syrup. Lots of notes.' Tom has not touched his wine, but repeatedly tips his glass to see just how close to the rim it will go without spilling.

Ruth is Nichol's age, a former sweetheart, the kind who supplies a lifetime of tarty flashbacks though the romance fizzled. She sits on Arden's loveseat, next to her father. She flexes and pulses her thighs to emphasize the silvery spandex around them; her blouse is a high-tech version of lace current teenagers save up for, the kind that poses the question: 'nipple?' Her toes cleave in matching silvery sandals, one tucked under her ass, one swinging in front of Mrs Kriegie's long Grecian nose. Arden's heard Nichol tell and retell and expand on the story of their first date: two in the morning, side of the highway into their pulpy home town on the Island, they fashioned campfires with their parents' driest kindling and set billboards on fire, they clutched hands and slid the steep bank to the train tracks to lose the cops and then duck the topple and crash of flaming plywood. They fucked on the tracks. Imagine the rush. What was she wearing that night? Has she always been several notches the wrong side of appropriate? Is that it, her appeal?

Arden sits on the low hearth stool, by the dog. Nichol is close, cross-legged on the floor, clutching her hand since the wine was poured; like a first-time parent at a crosswalk: proud and held. Nichol looks to her for unanimity. 'What about you,' he says and squeezes hard. For a few bars of internal sacred melody (*Farther along   we'll   un-der-stand why* she hears Emmylou's angel-speak and wants to sing like that), Arden blushes at being asked, included. Business acumen and false modesty keep her from accepting any job too fast. She tousles her own hair, trying to keep up with Ruth. 'Is Bach okay with you?' he says. 'You lost a mother, too. You should have a say.'

'What about me?'

'That's what I'm saying, Arden. Is Bach on the organ what you'd like?' In this moment they seem to be getting along better than ever. Tack together enough of these moments – when care is taken with her feelings as sun speeds through windows and Mrs Kriegie dreams of subterranean badgers – and she might feel permanence.

'I'd like me, Nichol. There's something I'd like to sing.'

The minister makes a steeple with his yellow fingers and stays out of it. Ruth bends down and scratches the dog's belly and gets her to dry-hump the air and wag simultaneously. 'What's wrong with this idea?'

Nichol addresses the minister or perhaps some larger, more formal audience. 'I was a jazz fan for most of my life, but Arden won't allow it in the house.' He doesn't look at her even when her name comes up. 'My mother loved Bach. My father is obsessed with what Arden calls the testosterone classics – Beethoven, Liszt, Strauss. She allows Stravinsky. Vivaldi makes her jumpy, she says. I have had so many people tell me what music to enjoy. Arden is a country singer. She is a good guitar player, but not a great one. Because she sings songs first performed by men, the keys are wrong. She gets shrill.'

Nichol lets go of Arden's hand to refill wine and take complicated sips. The minister helps himself to a homemade ginger snap. Fresh Jamaican stem ginger comes as a shock to a good Anglican. Startled by the taste, he puts what is left back on the plate. Ruth gazes out through the sheer curtains, long gone, Arden imagines, and back on the tracks with Nichol.

'Well, Arden,' Nichol takes a long time to say. 'I don't think the Reverend thinks we should hire a saloon singer.'

As if she planned a George Jones rodeo dance medley. 'It's a hymn.' The dog gives her a look, wags once. There's been a misunderstanding.

Nichol smiles and then chuckles, saving face. 'I don't think turning St Mary's into the Grand Ol' Opry is what the Reverend had in mind. People would take it the wrong way.' Tom burbles something about 'hard on people' and tilts his glass. Nichol, superior, getting a little red wine on his attitude, his wording. He stands and places his hands along the mantelpiece, his back to her now; he is a cliché whose origin she cannot place. 'And also, what about your own mental well-being and the safety of this pregnancy?' What Nichol means is, 'as opposed to the last one'.

Mrs Kriegie sighs, fed up with a tone she associates with

digging dahlia tubers, and stretches out even further into sleep. Her paws seem huge. Arden leaves the room, leaves the house, and no one tries to stop her. They mistake her decisions – the options she is considering and the unorthodox line of her mouth – for misplaced, undeserved, thinner-than-water grief. She was her mother, too. She was not.

She wants to sing.

The regular organist – Gord – resembles Liona Boyd – part lion, part Afghan hound – and there's Ruth, too. She turns his pages for the pre-ceremony medley of Bach's number one hits. Ruth's pin-up girl legs sparkle in the risqué candlelight. Gord's last number, Arden thinks, is really just 'A Whiter Shade of Pale' with more passing notes, and this doesn't seem right for a memorial service in the darkest wood of St. Mary's Sapperton. Just before the service begins, in the front pew between Tom and Nichol, Bach riffs niggling, Arden asks Nichol, 'Why would a man wear shorts to his mother's funeral?'

Nichol whispers without defensiveness, 'I am wearing shorts because I always wear shorts. It gets back to work versus play. I want to always be in play garb even though I may be working, or for that matter, bereft. I want to make someone say, "Hey, that guy's in shorts," even if I'm at my mother's funeral. Maybe that person will see grief in a more playful way.' Only a few months ago, Arden would have been jerked and jostled and pleased by this explanation. Now, she hears everyone through a toxic filter that steals all light and possibility. Tom falls to his knees, fists to forehead. 'Ode to Joy' is treacly at half tempo and the minister swooshes in. The Fraser River – just across Columbia Street – is brightened by spring sun and a good wind; it rumbles with commerce and muddied grief. It is a river road that leads everywhere and back, praise Gord.

2. Why Do We Get a Headache in a Crowded Room?

If the room were not crowded, the people could walk about and make a little breeze round themselves, and so escape from the heat and moisture accumulating under their clothes; but in a crowded room even this slight relief is denied them. The main cause is the wetness and warmness and stillness.

The Book of Wonder, Vol. xi (1932)

Tonight's poet at Doctor My Eyes is from Nichol's cycle club and this seems like a good junket for a pregnant woman: quiet, clean company, wordy without exhaustive interaction. Nichol says they need diversions to get their minds off baby's due date and false labour. 'They're nice people,' Nichol orders. 'I'll drive,' he says.

The walls are whitened brick and go up forever. A Philip Glass-y synth-boy squeezes through lousy speakers but the point is made: we are on culture's sharp edge here. We move with the groove. No: we *are* the groove. In hard chairs at card tables, women wear thrift store hats that hide something to do with their heads; the men flip Prince Valiant cuts away from their shirt collars and sit church-pew straight. Granted, some have ponytails, but really. Who looks like that any more? This crowd – *Wow. Excellent turnout* – is representative of nothing. It is Friday night, and they deliberately forgo other pursuits – they don't coach kids' soccer, don't flap their coated tongues at A-list strippers deeper downtown – and are impressed with that. They sip cottage beer from artsy bottles; they smoke and watch each other smoke and then smoke some more, desperadoes astride the groove. The ceilings are high, but Arden imagines herself crawling the floor on hands and knees, desperate for new and safe air and trying to turn the baby to the anterior position; the midwife says this must happen or else back labour and other tortures. Her pelvis tilts. Creep, breathe. The last two months have been one long obsessive grapple with what to do to guarantee a healthy baby, one long rant about the shit and insincerity in every human. She has tried to settle down. She has tried to cheer up. She has tried to smash her head against the French fireplace tiles and do permanent damage *but what about the baby?* and so hauls the camping mattress from the spare bedroom, inflates it just enough, and sleeps under a rough blanket in front of the never hot fire, Mrs Kriegie tunnelled in behind her knees. Her eyes are all puff, all the time.

Nichol's circle of chums hesitates – it is this way every time, even before her girth – and then they recognize her and take her into the fold. The added weight around mouth and breasts has created someone even more grotesque and yet familiar. Her skin has darkened and feigns aboriginality. They remember their own births and recoil, mother haters forever pissed off by the tight trip down that narrow canal, the bright lights, in love with the father who says deeply, 'I'll cut that cord.' No one offers a chair, but Nichol seems popular and welcomed and is chipper when he swings one over for her. He's got beer. He's got conversation. How nice. 'That's a great haircut,' the poet's wife shouts at Arden. 'I'm an artist. I know.'

Nichol's cyclist reads about opiated travels, about cynicism and cheap sixties politics. The crowd goes rapt. His poems seem to be about other continents, big islands with tribes and tribal problems of their own, but Arden can't find where she is; there are foreign words she doesn't know, but that's deliberate, right? The poems are about language, am I getting it? It is boys' adventure verse and lonesome cowboy mysticism set in a country that really likes Buddhism. Arden thinks the poems say he'd rather be there than here, but she's not sure where he is, where he's been: 'I need to look at a map,' she mutters before she counts her own breaths, measures the speed of her pulse and charts the rhythms of her irregular heartbeat. Since he fell for a young lover – Nichol told Arden one breakfast after he observed she had not shaved her legs for five months – the poet's sense of self has boomed, and audience members are outsiders to a private, obscure language that seems critical of Western or domestic whatever. Once a shrubby and nervous man, he is now sleek and impressed with his own words; someone with freckles and an ankle bracelet now hangs on every one of them. She lives a block from the Moodyville Bar. The hours they spend there, fingertips spliced over the dark little smoking table behind the dart boards, are good for his art. She's here somewhere.

At the start of the next verse – stanza? – he takes a wrist watch from his pocket and places it on the podium. It looks like a child's first one, tiny, with a black strap too small for a cat's ankle. His wife sits dumb-hatted at the table, and her left wrist is beside Arden, a band of fresh pink skin around it, flanked by a tanned and roughened small hand and its arm. The watch has been taken from her arm and there is a stretch of virgin fleshline to be rubbed or scratched or raped by sun. She has made a sacrifice. Like a kid with filched treasure, her husband looks superior and mad, and the poetry suffers or gets better. 'I need to see a map,' Arden mutters. '*Now* where are we?'

It was once a textile sweatshop and when Nichol's friend is finished and the crowd's hoots dwindle, the industrial heaters and fans come on and the room hums and rattles. We should all get back to our stations, Arden thinks, and make a living for some cost-conscious conglomerate. Her mouth is smart right now, and she can't stop it. In all the afterglow, the reader's wife tips red wine across the table, over her taupe kid gloves and Moroccan leather billfold; red wine creeps across the white Naugahyde tabletop and Arden thinks her bag of waters has ruptured, popped under all the social pressure.

Nichol scurries off and returns with a wet cloth and full glass of wine for the poet's wife. Complimentary.

Nichol puts his dark brown cyclist's hand on the poet's dark brown cyclist's hand, connects, and tells him a little story. All the women and their hats listen from behind their tiny lips. Nichol says, 'I stayed in a village in the south of Wales, outside Swansea, when I was twenty-three, where there was a small population of gypsies – they told me this – a lost tribe of castoffs from other bands. Some were Macedonian, others Romanian, Polish, others Lithuanian, and there were some resident Welsh women who, I guess, just wanted renegades. Beautiful women, dark hair, pale skin, sturdy builds. The one from Romania had hair to her waist, plated with silver coins; her left nostril was slit which is the punishment for adultery where she came from.'

'You must be joking,' says the poet's wife and laughs hideously. Arden has heard this one before and next time wants that part left out.

'Her breasts, after ten children, also hung to her waist. Though some of the gypsies have tried to work in the coal mines, most refuse to work, refuse education of any kind.'

The poet senses an opening and does not want to be left out. 'And prefer to steal from nearby peasants, right? This is grounds for romantic reverie, Nichol?'

'Should I continue, or have you lost interest?'

Go on, go on, yes, go on, the women plead. A man in shorts arouses them, some colonial residue.

'Those people don't think of thievery in the same way we do. It is not so much that they want what you have and so take it; it's more that property, the concept of it, has little value to them. They have not endowed it with cultural value. So the theft they do is the ironic embodiment of larceny. It's opposite, really.'

The poet brings out a Moroccan leather notebook, writes, and Nichol waits, pleased he's being robbed. The women make sure lipstick has not begun to leak across boundaries. They touch their own nostrils, trace the perfect contours.

'There was a list of foods to steal for the group, and each week they would rotate the list so no one would become familiar to certain clerks or farmers. I gathered apples, garlic, and celery from farmland. These are meals I will always remember.' The baby gets hiccups; Arden's stomach moves like a slow heart, or a war drum, or the Tennessee Three.

'I need to go, Nichol,' she says, rising, and places that symbolic ringed hand across the expanse of her womb.

'Fuck,' he says, drains his wineglass, drains his poet friend's, does not say goodnight to anyone as he stampedes out the door and down the wide stairs. 'Do it, Arden,' he shouts as the door swings shut. They regard her as the bitch she has become and mumble their goodnights to themselves instead of her.

It is late for this neighbourhood and dark. 'Drop me here,' she says. The bottom of the hill fronts the river's north bank. She wants to start at sea level and climb home with cold rain on her face and hands.

'Don't, Arden.'

'No, it's not like that. Just pull over.'

'Don't.'

'If I'm not there for tea and toast in twenty minutes, call the cops. Take my purse.' She is out of the car – a lime green Valiant, a name, look and price that pleased Nichol's aesthetic the week before they wed – and onto the sidewalk, the shock absorbers, she imagines, relieved to have her gone. A retro spin of angry tires, and then Nichol's taillights are vintage, too, and smudged by rain. At the crest of the hill, he signals left though he is the only driver at this hour on the wide hill. Arden feels touched by his dispatch, but maybe he's just being bossy. Pregnancy makes her scramble what's simple. Is that it?

Walk backwards and the pelvis pain shifts. The water is black but the river is lit. This is the first hill of New Westminster, where a hundred years ago 250 sappers camped and cleared the thick and steep forest so that gold could do its rush. Now ex-cons and mental cases work in huts on the docks and build stepstools and octagonal mirrors from import cedar and knotty pine. The river still works. The crowd is rough and worn down, but Arden walks the dog there on Sundays and pretends steamships and paddle-wheelers and dugouts. Given the age of the rest of the world, this one's so new.

Her mother's house is around the corner and over a block, a hundred years away. If she knew about the baby, she'd knit bunting bags with cheap yarn and preserve puréed beets. And weep with joy or regret, her own losses now stressed by Arden's gains. 'Families don't have to love each other,' Arden has learned. 'Sisters don't have to be friends.' Just as well. A bus moans beside her up the hill. The driver is all lit up behind the clack of windshield wipers and ducks his head at her. 'I'm okay,' she says out loud and waves merrily to prove it. The driver pretends to wear a hat he tips.

In the first month of their courtship, in the Railway Club bar under the viaduct, after a set of Merle Haggard toil-and-trouble tunes, she plugged the jukebox back in and sat down with Nichol, new boyfriend. He bent forward across the beer-stink red terrycloth and told her, 'That was great.' The ceiling was low and her sound was stingy and muffled. There was no snap to the drum machine's snare, and lyrics had to swim through mud like the intercom of a jammed airport. The wide room was cedar-panelled, and that should have given the sound some brightness, and large glass-covered photos – a half dozen track-walkers knee-deep in snow; team photos of the lanky tough lacrosse boys who've won for the Salmonbellies – could bounce some treble, but the curtains behind the dart boards were red velvet. And everywhere, the indoor-outdoor carpet climbed the walls to where chair backs hit and rub and swallowed the rest of Arden's crunch. 'You're good with working-class people,' he added.

In this bar? Prickly pensioners sustained by puppy chow and cheap draft. Or menacemen: black leather vest over thinned black cotton T-shirt tucked into tight black and shining jeans that skim black blakeys, the pogey check gone to touch up the trim on the black Cougar he's had since he was fifteen and to buy his similarly clad patho-chick her customary half-dozen double spicy Caesars (no celery). 'Buy me a Scotch,' she said.

'I think you're a very honest person, and people who've worked hard for little reward recognize and respect that.'

Bates Rose – the bartenders called him 'Punk' – played with the Salmonbellies as a young man and, at eighty-two, he was old enough to have won both the Minto Cup and the Mann Cup. His body curved over in a permanent ready-with-stick pose and leaned on every table to get to Arden's. 'Got a story for you, lady singer,' he slurred, and John the bartender pulled up a chair, handed him a draft – 'On the house, Punk' – and put a second one on the table. When Bates brought a glass to his mouth, it was a seismic event. Nichol watched the old-timer like it was a documentary. Arden had heard it before. She wanted another Scotch but John ignored her.

'My grandfather was the chief, you see. Dunstan Rose, chief of the Hyacks.'

'Where was his tribe from originally, sir,' Nichol said.

His flow interrupted, Bates took a while to pull a second time at his draft, to empty it, clutch the second glass and drink it halfway down. He took fifty cents from Nichol's pile of change and shoved it way down into the breast pocket of his pearl-button satin special, and then wiped the offending hand across his whole face.

'Come the dry years, they used to have to take the water from outta the river. He ran the Fire King, bought it in San

Francisco for two grand. Then one time the waterfront was on fire, and that engine got away from him going down the hill, and it landed up in the river. Took Joseph Wintemute six hours to raise it with some kind of derrick he'd put together. But Dunstan Rose was perfectly okay.'

'This is your grandfather? A firefighter?' Nichol signalled the bartender heroically for another round while Bates scoffed another dollar and filled his jingly pocket. Arden worried she'd get shit for taking a long break, but you can't walk out on Bates.

'That was my grandfather, that was Dunstan Rose. On the Queen Victoria's birthday, 13 November 1861, my grandfather was bartender in the Blizzard Saloon. He was supposed to fire a signal salute, but when he rammed the charge, you see, the whole thing went off, and he was blown into the river and drowned.' Bates looked deep and long into the bottom of his glass.

'Gotta get back to work, Bates.'

'You sound too high,' he bellowed at her, suddenly cranky. 'You sound like a stupid little car in a big garage. Turn it down, or I'm going home.' He was so loud and the bar suddenly quiet. Arden looked over to John, and his right hand turned an invisible knob in the air, the boss, alert to his regulars, his old-timers.

She started off low and slow and in thirty minutes had climbed the hill to Chuck Berry chunkachunk and into the red. Bates was bent over and asleep at the bar. Ice-eyed and balloon-waisted Stella – twenty years retired from Woodward's candy counter – twirled her make-believe tassels alone on the dance floor to 'C'est la Vie.' Bates woke when people clapped and cupped his huge and stick-slashed hands over his ears, tortured.

'People talk to you, Arden,' Nichol said at the end of the night, standing at the edge of her stage. Brazen house lights turned up, he looked pale and artificial. He was drunk and kept smoothing back his hair from off his face to pretend he wasn't. Arden put a beach towel over her amp, her beat box, the little clock she used to keep track, and clicked shut the snaps on the guitar case. She moved the mike stand to the back of the stage and hid the microphone under the towel, watching to see menacemen see her do it. 'You are in touch with some important people here.'

'I have brandy at home. No, drop it. I carry my own guitar.' Nichol held her elbow to the exit, held the door with one hand and placed the other in the small of her back as she passed through.

* * *

At the top of the hill, she turns around and the river is behind her. Mrs Kriegie barks once, slow and shrill, more question than threat as Arden comes around the laurel hedge. Each hand cups a heavy breast to clear some space for air. Winded, yes, but also clear. 'It's me, Kriegie. It's just me, you dirty little wiener dog.' Porch light, bedroom light upstairs: no mattress on the floor this time, she resolves, it's me. She leans hard on the cold metal railing and takes the front steps one by one, a matinee fist pushed into her lower back.

In bed, Nichol's hand is firm from the wine and the attention he got for his gypsy story; he has status as elder, as prophet. She takes his hand from her ribcage to stop the pressure and says, 'You seemed happy tonight.'

He turns off his light, and they are in such darkness for a moment she believes the power has gone out, as if gale force winds have come up from the Fraser River and dropped a branch onto a breaker. 'Happy is a banal word.' Adjust, she tells herself, and waits for the power to come back on.

He wants to find a motif, or a way to be a father who is part superhero, part Rilke. 'I think those gypsies taught me about what you probably call happiness. Despite the filth on their bodies, the scars and holes in their faces, despite the ribs

of their children and the cardboard boxes they lived in –
which wilted, by the way, in the Welsh wet – they laughed.
They sang, danced, drank their own putrid wines, savoured
food and didn't wipe it from their chins. They took pride in
their thievery. The women, too, were always pregnant, their
husbands and brothers always proud. Death was a
celebration. Men cry as a convention.'

* * *

At three the next afternoon, Mrs Kriegie lapped amniotic fluid
like it was beef blood from the fir floors in the front hall as
Arden spoke with Jehovah's Witnesses, two women in rough
grey coats erect at her front door: 'Not now, thanks, I see my
water's broken.'

'We have a car,' they offered. 'We could drive you there,'
and they shuffled down the stairs without her, terrified.

'There's nothing like spine pain,' the midwife, Anya, told
Nichol over chamomile tea and rabbit stew. The two passed
hours ten to thirteen at the kitchen table, waiting for her to
request drugs, a needle, a quick getaway. The books did not
go into spine pain, and Arden writhed under headphones that
shrieked a cocktail of the B-52s and Glen Campbell. Anya and
Nichol waited for her to say 'hospital' and aligned themselves,
superior in their well-being and well-cut clothes, with the
collective medical knowledge of hundreds of home births and
a few bicycle mishaps, but Arden climbed in under the covers
of melody – *I am a lineman for the county* – and would not
speak. They flirted to fill the space between her pain and their
impatience and thought she didn't notice. 'When the baby's
ready,' Anya repeated but was thinking, 'What's the hold-up,
sister?' Arden picked up the complicit undermining of
support; she caught each twinkle. More alert than schooling
fish, she saw them be intrigued by each other. Saw it.

'Contractions are volcanoes,' Anya lifted one tiny speaker
as Arden stomped past with arms flying and Mrs Kriegie

bouncing off her ankles, and told her, 'Think of the lava and its great warmth and how it comes in spectacular orange waves that burn away the old and leave a clear and clean place for the new.' If you're going to show off, Arden quibbles, pick a good image, think it through, work out the implications of the so-called objective correlative. Talk to the dog of Pompeii. Woman's in labour and everybody's Rod fucking McKuen. Drunk-dead Hank Williams comforts via the world's real poetry, *Tonight, down here in the valley.*

'Hospital, you assholes,' she said.

In a 4 a.m. downpour, she tried to make it out to Anya's little station wagon but got as far as Nichol's bicycle, Hiawatha, leaning against the steps. Contraction is such a banal word. Arden draped her arms across the handlebars' rough, creeping rust, the leather seat smelling of rain, old man's leather, and heart attacks. Nichol held the bike so it wouldn't start down the slick driveway carrying his unborn. Rain stubbed itself out on her flaming face. She thought of the Saturday morning she clipped her mother's best bridge cards – the ones with initials embossed in shiny gold – onto the spokes of her first two-wheeler with wooden clothespegs to make it clatter like a train riding the rails. 'How do you think you should be punished for doing something you know better than to do?' her mother had said in a characteristic full-sentence chew-out. Apparently, the answer is back labour.

3. Why Do We Get Out of Breath When We Run?

When we run we use up a lot of air, as an engine-driver uses much air in his furnace if he makes his train go quickly. Running makes the blood rush very quickly through our lungs, where it helps itself to the oxygen in the air which we breathe. The heart beats more quickly, and at last it sends a message to the brain and makes us out of breath, as a warning. If we are wise, we take the warning and slow down or stop altogether.

The Book of Wonder, Vol. xii (1932)

Between Okanagan Falls and Oliver, there is a queer stretch of Highway 97 that skirts marshy Vaseaux Lake. The terrain is rough and high desert, incongruous with rain forest just a morning's drive away. Haunch-heavy bighorn sheep ride the high banks like June Taylor Dancers, like Rockettes, point and step – point and step. At the north end of the lake, the road sweeps up, trumpeter swans detect sanctuary and float safely below, and this is the stage, southbound, for her suicide if she needs it, should it come to that.

Sunday mornings before the baby, she would drive the Valiant home from wherever she had travelled to pitch systems. She was usually up and checked out at six. In rain, she listened to old British folk rock, Marianne Faithfull maybe; in sun, she left the music off and opened the window. The road concedes too much freedom. She thinks too much. She is powerful when she drives this car and yet smaller inside, less sure of trajectory: when will the gas run out and where will that leave me? Should I pack a crowbar for roadside encounters? How smooth is a bald tire?

Now, most Sundays – sales or no sales – she longs to get back to the baby, to see Nichol and eat his roast chicken lunch, drink the cold French wine. She longs to take over, to be greedy. They rent this tucked-in Sapperton house on the ancient outskirts of Vancouver, and the highway leads her close. Their neighbours have ultra-black wrought iron, concrete lions, perpetual terriers scrambling to meet cars, deter the mailman. Gaudy annuals tumble over their wide sidewalks, it seems, year round. Arden parks out front and loves her pretty British gate – its baroque loops and time-bulged wire – and loves the way it opens and shuts so near another generation's climbing rose. Nichol is on the wooden steps, baby perched and bumping on his knees. Mrs Kriegie is thrilled and yaps, cleans the baby's face between trips up Arden's legs. Nichol's hair is not combed and the hem has fallen on one leg of his shorts. An empty coffee mug. Baby Roy gets sturdy when he sees her approach, and then they are together – hug the baby, everybody – and Nichol has gone back inside. While she was away this time, he painted the windows' trim and the front door: deeper than pumpkin.

Roy and Arden nap through the afternoon while Nichol composes the debauched post-lunch table. They stretch out on the big bed in the cool back guest room, and Roy lies along her length, atop her chest, down her stomach, his hot head under her chin and she sleeps too, their hearts beating each other, rivals for air. Before he topples down into sleep, Roy resembles an early John Fogerty, an old man already, holding conversations with other members of the band, his brother, debating the relative sustain and resonance of the snare drum. His nap is customary, hers is to slough off road fatigue and the excess alcohol consumed because she has been out of town, in a hotel, alone with many small and intensely felt regrets.

Regrets? The abortion, not that she did it, how she didn't tell Nichol she was going to; Margaret's death and how they didn't grow closer sooner; sorry that Nichol is more like his father than his mother and that Arden didn't see it; that she didn't finish her degree; her history of booze and poor behaviour and moral fluctuations; didn't learn piano; she led the group of grade-sevens that taunted Sylvia MacDermid when Sylvia's parents got divorced and her brother started wearing lipstick to rugby practice; she left her little sister at home with their mother and then cut them off. Okay, yes, she regrets Roy's birth, how it has already erased her interesting parts. She is not equal to the challenge of servitude. When she eats an apple he gets a rash, when she takes a B vitamin his diaper appears toxic with fluorescent stains.

Arden rolls her baby off and tucks pillows to prop his heavy body. Wet where he has been, she smells like compost, rotting livestock-pissed-on sawdust. He will sleep for two hours exactly and wake with a laugh. Nichol sits at the kitchen table. He scratches his disgust for her, Arden supposes, into his black journal and makes a poem out of her flaws and how it feels good and bad when she comes home. The rain is hard out in her lovely garden; the unstaked bend. Daylight moved farther away while she slept.

Her husband's hands pulling back her hair, her husband's forehead pressed hard into hers to test their strongest bones against each other, the crucial sex, the constant prospect and linger of it. The evening in the yard her husband removed a leaf from her hair, brushed it away with the back of his index finger; the scent of his fucking wrist. Reproduction robs us of these urges: kindness, heat, adhesion. She is now a mother and outside the boundaries of his imagination. There was an all-hours self-improvement channel in this last hotel room, and a stetsoned former Dallas Cheerleader/model told her that intimacy never evaporates; it simply retreats when we are too lazy to bother. An effort must be made.

She pours strong, cold tea and asks, 'What are your regrets, Nichol? What are you sorry about so far?' She touches her husband's neck, which is something.

Nichol closes his book and caps the pen. Big click. Even

today, she has encroached. 'On Sunday mornings, I clean the house – vacuum, dust, wash the floors – because I want to set a standard for the week. You have not yet got the message, but I hope soon you'll prefer to live in a clean home and take pleasure in cleaning this one. I dress a roast chicken bought at the Saturday market the day before with dressing I fixed the night before. Usually, I marinate a fresh vegetable salad, cilantro, tomato. I drive to the newsstand uptown and buy last week's discount Seattle *Sunday Times*.

'Choices are appropriate, none good or bad. I regret, though, that I didn't understand your complexity when I married you. I am sorry you can't build happiness here with us and now want back into the lifestyle that was destroying you when we first met. I thought I could rescue you from the booze and the crappy music. Mostly, I regret the way I misread your bad moods. See: you were sad, not sexy, but I got those switched. And so, the abortion, without my advice or consultation, is my regret. Is that what you wanted to know, Arden? I must be tired.'

4. What Is the Cause of Quicksand?

Quick is an old word which means living, or moving. These words, living and moving, meant practically the same thing long ago.
   The Book of Wonder, Vol. ix (1932)

Arden zippers into a long black lace, strapless bra. It pinches the cleave beneath her shoulders, changes the details and enhances the effect, rubs the wrong way. Her breasts point left when her chin goes right. Ersatz Cleopatra, Liz Taylor without so much bounty. It is a slut's bra, but won't show. She is thirty-eight and too old for this getup.

Hose manufacturers have made panties redundant: control top, ass lift, crotch gusset, reinforced toe. Even the darkened cyst that rides her ankle – floats in a pool of her – is hidden by the neutral-tone gloss-tight weave, the sheen. When did they okay these specs? Has a year changed everything?

The baby sleeps in the closet-room. The upstairs is quiet. Evening last light hits the mirror in the wide hall. Catch the angles through the bedroom door: the bed is smooth, the sheets washed and pillowcases ironed. There will be the feel of steamed cotton on her face at the end of tonight, the feel of that steamed cotton beneath her ass at the end of tonight when Nichol places it, lifts her, acknowledges her depth, his desire to reach the ends of her. He has put on Chopin nocturnes downstairs as he constructs the dinner, lights many candles, high and low.

For tonight, her dressing is an art gallery, and Arden is hot with her own aesthetic, her underpainting, the egg-white hills of tempera, the wash of ultramarine, gouache, the red dots – she is certain of them – on gilt frames and the launch of a promising career.

Margaret made the dress for 1945, the Welcome Home dance

at the CPR train station in Vancouver, waterfront, foot of Burrard Street. The boys returned from overseas, their broad and newly shined faces thrust out the train windows, searching for brides-to-be, and a big band in the station began its Glenn Miller, himself a lost tribe over the English Channel, his music both celebration and elegy. 'In the Mood', they danced, thighs touching at last. That was Margaret's chance for glamour, to set the polished hook in a man gone pale from German turnips and potato screech: it is the truest green, a fabric that's back in fashion for its drape and shadows. A pantyhose of a dress: it covers and holds and announces connotations. The dress tucks in and tightens a thin tide line of piping at the waist, enough gather to flatter a stomach and hide the betrayal of childbirth. The bodice smooths up and over high and full post-birth breasts, tidy-stitched darts point: no leaks. Again, the optimism. Arden has a short waist and so did Margaret; the fine couture adjusts and creates diversions. For example, the necklines. They go low and wide, more so at the back (her hair will cover the other cyst floating back there). Tiny loops of pale ribbon fixed with delicate snaps would cling to bra straps on one more decorous. Without them the gathered shoulders will slip from her collarbones throughout the evening and reveal more back, the lovely muscles from lifting Roy the Boy, from pushing the swing, from picking up bits of toast before Mrs Kriegie grows fat on them. She is taut despite him, that's something. In 1945, dancing to the big band – its now loaded and mythologized sounds, Ronstadt's ilk pushing the swing – Margaret was a peacetime river, chartered, a clean world minus blasts and blight. Arden must breathe deeply, hold herself in, to fit this dress. A *Days of Wine and Roses* dress; she is Kirsten after the baby and before the flower pots of booze, before 'I can't get over how ugly it all looks.' Jack Lemmon still loves her, more in fact, now that her body has given life. Her hair combed silken into waves.

* * *

Musicians come for dinner. Nichol had met them before, but not this way: sober and tidy, upright at intervals around his table. Rocky and Rick are nervous and pretend not to have fucked her in hotel rooms, the glamour of a set table not really their realm. Scooter brought a half-dozen carnations – once white, but now soaked to aquamarine – for the table. Mary-Beth befriends the dog, who tracks like a long-snouted meat hound the mysterious scents in her deep cleavage. Who'd predict a red lace Merry Widow under ass-torn and faded Levi's? Arden takes part in otherworldly reminiscences – song genealogy, gig-rating – which Nichol resents. He cooks and serves and clears while she banters and drinks and takes much and many for granted. At play in the background: Dave Edmonds and Nick Lowe, their boozy boy-raunch, their Fender strut, their shared back-up singers, so-called wives who put the cunt in country music. These, too, not Nichol's style.

ROCKY: You get the gig because they want country. Then you show up and it's pool tables next to the stage and waitresses out of ZZ Top videos and Harleys lined up by the back door –

RICK: So you know it ain't country.

SCOOTER: And you mention it to the pencil-neck behind the bar. He says how they're trying to change the clientele. They want a better crowd, he says.

ARDEN: And you play country and the guys on the tables scream rock titles you could play but you're not supposed to.

RICK: They get drunker and madder.

MARY-BETH: Waitresses won't serve you.

Rick and Rocky light simultaneous Player's to calm down. No filter.

Nichol wanders upstairs to check the baby, comes down in time to refill wineglasses; he pays attention to the format of items on the table, the placement of cutlery. She sees his eyes go to the kitchen sink, to the laurel hedge out the window, a stain on the edge of his chair. He smiles and drinks whenever Mary-Beth laughs: red wine causes her to resonate. Nichol likes her because she quit the bars to be a receptionist for a company that disposes of nuclear waste.

SCOOTER: And so you clear the bar. End of the week, it's your fault business sucked and pencil-neck won't book you back.

ROCKY: You can't hold a crowd, they figure.

RICK: They give you a job and hate you for doing it.

'Did you ever all play together in a band?' Nichol asks as he sits down finally. Everyone does something with their remaining food; back to earth. Scooter passes Mary-Beth the dish of pickled beets; she cackles like a young Joplin, coarse and lewd.

'We're all guitar players, Nichol,' Arden sneers and refuses to draw his conclusions or cover for him, deliberately careless.

Three years ago, Arden was doing a single at a red-on-red Kingsway dive and met Scooter for the first time when he bought her a liqueur the colour of soaked carnations and expected her to join him at his table. 'I really admire what you're doing with your voice,' he said, looking at her directly, leaning into it, some procured substance about to combust in the whites of his eyes. 'With every tune, you're taking your body to some very, very distant shores.' Who would bring a metaphor into this kind of bar? As distinct from the usual anti-hyperbolic, 'You're pretty good. Do you think you're pretty good?'

Scooter wanted to 'date' her but was in the process – at 2 a.m.? at forty years old? – of moving out of his girlfriend's place. 'It never got dark enough there anyway,' he said and scratched a spot behind his ear for the tenth time in five minutes. 'At least at my folks' place I have blackout shades in my bedroom. I can sleep. I like dark.'

Scooter was never a regular; he rarely showed up on time, considered this part of his charm and allure. For their first scheduled date he phoned an hour after his estimated arrival:

'I'm very sorry I'm not there, but there's kind of a family dinner going on here and I'm talking to my grandfather, who I realize now I've never held a conversation with. Ever. I'm forty, I realize, and I don't even know this man. It seems to me I should stay for this and ride the river I'm on for the night. He actually remembers when Woodward's was built! And the war; I'm not sure which one yet, but I'm going to ask. And he remembers when they built the Bennett Dam. And Kitimat. The birth of a whole town and he remembers it!'

'I remember when they did that,' she said.

'How old are you?' An abused narcotic prevented the stress of any one syllable.

'I'm nobody's grandfather,' she said. And so Scooter's credibility began its slimy decline, while his entertainment value rose on some perverse and dirty scale. Both hit the limits of the Scooter continuum with a trip to Prince Rupert.

He called Arden often from up there, from the condemned hotel across from the firetrap cabaret that billed his top-forty show band as the unpronounceable, 'Thuderboldt.' 'Fly up,' he said. 'I'll pay half when we get paid for this gig.' She'd already sent him fifty bucks so the band would stop ripping off the food bank, but she borrowed fifty more from a drummer friend so she could go to Prince Rupert to share a room for two nights with five skinny guys and their dozen obnoxious habits. The girl singer got her own room.

The first afternoon, in bed together finally, while other band members watched music videos and ate non-stop bowls of dry popcorn in the other room, Arden detected a peculiar roughness across one of Scooter's thin shoulders. 'Don't touch me there.' He sat up dramatically, propelled by forced anger and yet another failed ejaculation. The sheets were held over from last week's band. With Arden's fifty dollars, he had hired a woman he met in the bar offering reasonable rates for in-home electrolysis. He'd always been stigmatized by hair on his back, he said. And now four square inches of one shoulder was a mass of number-thirty sandpaper scabs; the other side was still a pillow of soft black fur. 'You did this with my money?' No memory of the last time she felt outraged by anything.

'Sort of for you.'

Arden never got the fifty bucks; he has not returned her classic Roseanne Cash *Seven Year Ache* album. Though she has never seen Scooter naked since, does not know the outcome of the contractual ravaging of his back and any pleasant resemblance to wildlife he once had, still he sits welcome at her table. These are the foundations of musicians' friendships.

After second helpings of Zucchini Tian with gruyère, the bitter mesclun and escarole, and remembering Nichol's aspirations, Scooter asks how the 'climb up creativity's mountain' is 'coming along'. Too obvious, too patronizing; Nichol retreats into observation of detail. Rick and Rocky smoke further and relocate their limp greens to other sites on the plate.

And after dinner, more wine, Nichol brings the weeping and awake baby Roy for feeding. The musicians don't care much for babies and don't say all the right things. They did not come with gifts. They have had many weeks to send cards. 'Hey! He looks like John Fogerty,' Scooter observes. 'Phil Everly,' says Mary-Beth, for she has always had a crush, a thing for close harmony. Roy observes them via his trademark sideways look, without moving his head. Nichol hands her a warm baby, says, 'You're in the wrong dress for this,' and Roy bounces both feet in time with another decade's aphonic rhythms. 'See?' Scooter presses his point, 'He's doing "Down on the Corner", the bass riff.' The shoulder of her dress slips to bicep, and the room stirs with nostalgia for her breasts. Scooter goes pious: 'I don't think I was breastfed as a baby, hence my lifelong promiscuity.'

Mary-Beth goes to the kitchen to watch Nichol grind and brew and dollop whipped cream on cranberry tarts.

'Cranberry,' she says, 'That's the town next to Powell River.' And then, loud enough for all but aimed at Nichol, 'I played with a top-forty band in Powell River a few years ago, and we partied with a country band from another bar. They got a house to stay in, but you can imagine the condition of the house, the smell of it. I'd just had my second, no, make that third abortion in Vancouver, and I was still hormonal and maybe depressed, too. I was in love with the drummer again. Why do I do it? So. I was off in the corner, on the floor, smoking dope and drinking Cointreau from the bottle. A kitten stumbled out of a bedroom, yowled, obviously starved. So young the legs still wobbled. Band cat, hey? He balanced four paws on my foot and teetered up my leg and over my stomach and made a huge mewling sound for such a little animal and then up my stomach and he started to root at my breast, pushed it with his head and nose. Sure, I was drunk; the guys were all TV and smoke, and I felt alone and the liquor made me sexy, too, so I unbuttoned my dress and slipped it off my shoulder and the kitten took my breast.' Scooter looked at Arden across the table, a gracious look. He winked. Meaning? 'His paws went on either side and pushed and pushed for milk. But I don't think he got anything. Interestingly enough? The guys from the country band wanted to watch, but my own band, even the drummer I loved, took a look and went back to videotaped hockey classics – the Summit Series, I think – on cable. He purred. The teeth pinched my nipple and the paws poked. I felt so calm.'

Nichol has already opened the bottle of Cointreau he keeps at the back of the high cupboard beyond Arden's reach. He hands Mary-Beth a brandy snifter he'd warmed with the water for Arden's tea. 'Women,' he says, 'speak in the language of images.' Meaning?

'Canada's first steam-driven railway train was known as the "Kitten",' says Scooter.

Roy flops into sleep, and Arden holds him across herself, needing a reason to be past her prime. She tells them all, 'I've had it with sales, I'm on the road anyway, might as well get something out of it. I found a small PA, the same size as the one I used to have, but with more guts, better reverb, digital drums. If I do it again,' she says, 'I want top quality gear. No more making do with shit.' The dress and its bra feel loose, now, around her emptied breasts.

The musicians leave at midnight. Scooter bounces a fist off Nichol's shoulder. Mary-Beth: hug, kiss, hug again. Okay, one last kiss lingers by Nichol's ear.

Arden rides their contrail and glides the baby upstairs, performs the requisite change, tuck in, smooch and sigh: a lovely old man, this baby, even in sleep. His little cupboard smells of dog feet and urine, of used milk and its by-products. She remembers her sister's birth and the constant smell of her in their lives. Arden was expected to take part, to help her mother who'd gone maudlin and weak and whose milk had dried up with grief. The ugly feelings, the lost voice, the rules and their breakage. Arden feels different with her own. With her sister, the diapers waited too long because she could not, at ten, measure consequences. Her sister was an animal found abandoned in the woods, her sister was an intruder, a refugee, a dirty squatter. Princess Louisa, their father christened her, and then abandoned ship.

Arden had hoped the bedside light would still be on, that Nichol would want to see just what kind of ultra-sexual desire could hold her up under the slink of that dress. She had hoped to spill out the top of it, into his mouth, his soft and pumping hands, to slut her way into his good graces, nostalgia firing her libido, the pantyhose torn away, the no panties further arousal, almost beyond his dreams, her nipples now sore from the hard lace, but a good colour. Why not forget everything and go primal? This acts like the last chance.

'Are you awake, Nichol?'

'No,' he says.

'Do you think you could be, given the right motivation?' She is on her pretty knees beside him on the bed, leaning forward, the retro neckline wide and low. He should look at her this way, see the possibilities.

'Not unless you brought a cat. Did you believe that story? How many abortions did she say?' He has retreated to his corner, the towel thrown in, unable to return to the ring, the sheets over his head as if once a contender but those days are over thanks to the many well-placed punches, the extra rounds.

'What is so dubious about phone systems? A little travel, income – that's what you missed. Just my opinion; you do what's required. But let's go over all the angles.' Nichol presumed she would look for gender-enhancing engagements around town; two nights a week in a corny cocktail lounge would still qualify her as good mother and wouldn't make him crazy from baby duty. A pizza joint, maybe, a neon 'FAMILY' on its sign. Sure, he agreed to the idea of it. Still, he has suspicions and paranoia. 'What about your breast milk? Will this upset the baby?' Nichol looking for doctored reasons to chicken out.

Arden is trying to get through the pattern. Not so simple after all, the lace stitch is cockleshells and requires full attention. The yarn is fine and her tension is often too tight to perform the gymnastics required.

'If I have to be gone long, I'll express more and stick it in the freezer. You can feed him. I'll rent a pump and leave more milk.'

(ROW 4: * K 1, (k1, p1) into 'made' stitch, k 15 (P1, (m 1 dbl, p 2 tog. tbl) twice, m 1 dbl, k1*.)

'What kind of word is that, "express"? Like "fast food"? Doesn't freezing do bad things to the molecular structure?' Nichol doubts the wisdom.

ROWS 5 and 6: K.

'What does Anya say about this – what are the politics of it, I mean. Is there trauma. Or physical; what'll this do to his digestion. Will he resent you? Do we even have enough bottles? Or me?'

ROW 7: * K1 (m1 dbl, p 2 tog. tbl) twice, k 11 (p2 tog., m 1 dbl) twice, k 1*.

'And how much will this pump cost compared to what you'll make? Some of those gigs pay shit. Are they safe.'

'Do you have any concerns?' Dry wit never works. (ROW 9: K.)

'Could you look at me for one minute? I just want to be sure we weigh your need – let's call it "desire" because that's really what it is – against his health. And I mean every aspect of his health.'

(ROW 10: repeat, repeat, repeat....)

'Maybe I'm old-fashioned – as if traditional is now a dirty word – but I consider it your responsibility. What is that? That's not the colour babies wear. You knit?'

Nichol had asked her into the kitchen. Dinner was in the process of. Each stove element was at the perfect temperature to ensure this conversation had a beginning and an end; slow boil. Tomato sauce smell worked its way over to them and softened blows. Bloop, bloop. They sit across from each other at the maple table; Nichol strokes his glass of wine, Arden comes to ROW 11 where she needs to purl all fifteen stitches together on those tiny needles but her stitches are too tight to draw up even three; perhaps this is not the time. 'It's a bed jacket. For me.'

'You're going Victorian?' He laughs in a nasty way and watches her knitting slink back into the velvet bag Margaret made her. Renaissance now a dirty word.

When Arden phoned to tell her 'pregnant', Margaret said, 'Well. Fine,' and then predicted she wouldn't last until the arrival, apologized. And, later, during chemotherapy, a short note to Arden in poisoned, bouncy scrawl:

I think that under a veneer of slight indifference to the actual maternity and birth rites plus a social inclination to joke about many aspects of domesticity, the husbands held in their hearts the same reverence and awe that is in Nichol's. However, at that time, the young wife learned to laugh at herself or sink into a bog of self-pity. In retrospect, I was one of the more fortunate ones.

'My well-being,' Arden says, scratching at a circle of marmalade on the table, 'is more important. I was here first. Call Anya if you need to know what you could just as easily look up in any one of those books you never did read beside the bed.' He had wanted to be the one, but she walks away first.

Her agent calls after Nichol goes off for his cycle club gang-pedal. He wants Arden to take over for some Stratocaster shuffler in a backwoods bar. 'I won't badmouth this character,' Saul says, 'but the bar's booked him before and he's been doing the same tunes so long they got age spots. I'm told the last song he learned was "The Gambler". I can sympathize with management. Go up there and smooth it over, kiddo. They say he's gotta go, either way.'

Roy the Boy reclines in his car seat, safe on the shiny kitchen table. She's pinned a dishtowel over the window – bright sun makes him sneeze and panic. Each time she turns to look at him – phone under chin and her two hands tearing labels from tin cans – he beams. That's her dry milk polish on his cheek. 'What can you get me for the week after? And I don't want the Star of David tour. I want towns close together. Preferably linked by a single highway.' The baby burbles at her tone, startled by such rough music. 'If I'm going that far, I need more weeks.'

By the end of the conversation, Blackpool Entertainment has promised two weeks in the lounge of the only country bar in Kitimat and a weekend in the Burns Lake Hotel beer parlour after daylong strippers. And more to come if she does all right. 'We haven't booked you in years,' says Saul. 'We'll go easy to start. You can sympathize.'

If Arden leaves now, she can make it in time to set up and play tomorrow night. The roads are good this time of year and mid-week means less slowdown. She's hounded agents, learned forty songs from five eras, relearned tempos, feels, lyrics, punching the particulars into digital drums, a synth bass. Getting in touch with the inner voice – ha. Mrs Kriegie will stay with Nichol, that's one bad thing.

Nichol rides Hiawatha. This morning she watched his shaky morning knees slow pedal down the driveway and curve musically onto his route. Nichol bought the bicycle at a yard sale from a widow sloughing off her husband's hasbeens. 'My husband rode it every day after the first attack. He loved his bicycle. Only three speeds but it's been looked after.' Nichol got her down from fifteen to ten, bartered with a dead guy's wife. The bike rides okay but even at ten it wasn't a bargain. The helmet that Nichol insisted should be new and streamlined and rigged-out with a tiny rear-view mirror put the total up, as did the water flask and green fluorescent Velcro pant straps he bought from some high-class cycle shop. He wears a Canadian Navy sweater that covers his thighs. He appears European and imagines the downtown women – sneakers and trenchcoats frisking to work – admire his rear end's bob as it maintains elevation at red lights, propped up at stop signs. He imagines.

Arden convinced Nichol that she requires big transportation at least one day a week, so they bought the poet's Econoline. She is not the kind of person who can stay put with a new baby and a flaccid belly. Instant homemaker and she wasn't even tidy before this. The poet and his wife were ready to part with it: 'We are no longer willing to endorse a society that desecrates the planet, rapes it for fossil fuel. We'll ride bikes, we'll walk. Plus, we couldn't afford insurance.' Nichol didn't suspect she'd make off with the van, all the country tapes, the muffins from the basement deepfreeze, and his firstborn child.

* * *

She wants:
to know how to change her oil, gap points, grind cylinders. She wishes she'd gone to a technical school to learn mechanics. Some high schools have rooms where eager teens get credit for learning to tune up donated clunkers; they do body work, conceal primed rust. She wishes that was her, the kids and the car. Heart like a wheel.

She wants:
to read *Anne of Green Gables* while she drives.

She wants:
her breasts to quit all this swelling and weeping and go back to humble.

She wears black linen pants and a black cotton T-shirt. The pants are wide and floppy and make her feel sophisticated. Her glasses, which she wears for distance and to drive, are horn-rimmed and smart. This is how Arden drives. With loose clothes and bare arms. She does not wear a bra to drive, she sweats and since she's still what's called perky-breasted, she wears a champagne silk camisole that came from a drawerful of her mother's sale silks from the shop she worked in, on Columbia Street in New Westminster. A few the moths got, but this one is smooth and thin. The linen wrinkles when Arden drives, but linen is supposed to. She tried wearing these glasses the last time she played a bar but a) she didn't want to get a good look at the clientele (Haney Hotel) and b) nobody bought her drinks.

She stops for gas and a stale road sandwich in the middle of, or just north of, nowhere. Where would a gas station out here get alfalfa sprouts? She left the baby sleeping in his car seat; the government sticker has shouted DO NOT LEAVE CHILD UNATTENDED a million times. When she comes back, spinny from washroom fumes, a woman with fragile white hair and a matching purse is at the baby's window, tapping with the corner of a lottery ticket.

'When I was a young mum we didn't have anything to carry them in so we just laid 'em down on the back seat and drove slow and hoped for the best or more likely just stayed home.

'Look at 'er.

'My car's in the shop. Man's foot slipped while he was backing up. Now he feels like a fool. My radiator needs work.

'Look at 'er.

'His foot slipped. You miss your car for shopping. Our Government gave me cab fare, so that's nice. Still, I'd rather have my own vehicle. I'd 've had caesarean sections with both my girls if I didn't go to a chiropractor. Still go.'

She doesn't stop until Arden is in the van and plunged into reverse. She limps and holds her purse with both arms and starts down the highway towards out of town. Arden is tempted to say she cradles the purse. She doesn't seem crazy or lonely or mixed up about time. A little self-absorbed, maybe.

The car seat is third- or fourth-hand and definitely below standards of safety and aesthetics. Still, it matches the van:

grey on grey. Roy is strapped and shackled backwards into
the passenger side of the Ford Econoline. No tapedeck, and
radio waves don't lap up this far north. They have their
breaths.

The season has changed and now we are in winter
regardless of month. In the back – bumping and rattling,
raring to go – is her gear. The speakers hold on and stay
upright but the two parts of the microphone stand have come
loose at the join and there is heavy metal clatter over
hardpacked snow. Trucks with chains have made divots, but
the baby doesn't mind. Two parts of his body have come
loose, too, and his head bobs to mike stand clatter. Groovin'.
Arden is tempted to breastfeed and drive, the baby a warm
seatbelt across her belly. They stop to nurse and dispose of the
disposable, and that's it. They'll make good time. Singing to
him would be work.

Some make-it-happen multinational dropped a whole tribe of
people to smelt aluminum and paint the town. They used to
be islanders, defined by a landscape defined by beach. The
corporate world knows psychology – has whole floors for it –
so they built this town from scratch, in the shape of a ring;
one road is circumference and the community centre is the
hub.

The exit to the highway out of town isn't where it was the
last time the unwary tried to leave, and they miss it and end
up circling into the town again. They spiral inward for no
good scientific reason, trapped in a nautilus, and wind up out
front of the centre just a few minutes later. Exhausted by
centripetal force, they decide it's wise to stay another day, try
again tomorrow. An island, a little fib of a place. Its citizens
stay because they buy illusion and because there are no
sailings on which to cross.

The sky is off-white with late tonight's dump of snow;
giant fir trees wear last night's and shift the load, lighten

limbs and bounce with rhythm all their own. The Portuguese must grow restless without perpetual gardens, without the glint of aubergines. The locals putter in sheets of air, drifts of iced snow; they pace sanded shores of curbside. Winter is cold and quiet without a centreline to go by. What could make a temperate climate act this way?

She'll check the oil tomorrow. Is Sunday. No, do it now. She has propped a pillow between Roy's ear and the car seat: he leans skyward to sleep and she's worried his cheek will freeze to the hard plastic, popsicle on tongue. The heater does nothing to melt this town.

The engine has turned on sludge for many klicks. A perpetually denuded dipstick proves her character flaws – lazybones, procrastinator. Arden is drawn again to this stupid edge. Chimneys, same thing. House insurance. Many years ago, her sister Louise couldn't live with the question, the mystery, and drove her blessed baby-blue '64 Mustang and drove and drove and tried – made an effort – to challenge the dipstick, not just run low on oil, but to run out, no top-ups, just to see how long it would take till she knew she was close. Suspicious of gauges, Louise believed she would sense – a whiff of burn, a click – when the engine could no longer sustain the revs. One night she was going home from the bar to her crooked riverside fifth wheel, and in the wake of a half-dozen pints and one Benedictine for the road the block cracked and she was stranded and bereft. She blamed impairment for why she missed the warning signs. All those details in a drunken unsigned letter sent to Arden about nothing else. She won't drive in this condition.

Blanket, bottle, and lock all doors. If the baby can sleep through stereophonic air brakes and demon Harleys in this hotel's parking lot – the management will give them that room, right up there – Arden can make it to the truck stop and back before he suspects. No one in this town could warm to outrage at a child abandoned in a hood-up Ford Econoline. 'Some people's parents,' they'd say and suck frost-heaved lips back into their ugly scarves.

Crunch, crunch, crunch.

'Balloons?' she asks. A tiny jar of decaf, 10-w-40, and –

'What?' the clerk says. Two buttons jiggle on her huge chest, one identifies her as 'BEA' the other: HAPPINESS IS YELLING *BINGO.*

'I'm looking for balloons,' which she assumes are not seasonal, urban, or contraband but now wonders. 'Doesn't everybody sell balloons?' After all.

'You come up with a balloon in this town, sweetie pie, maybe call the papers, let 'em know the scoop.' That's an awfully long sentence for a scarred-up, two-hundred-pound, greasy-haired, indigenous woman in a chartreuse Sayelle cardigan to just throw around into the ice block of air between them. Arden pays for the oil (wrong weight?) and coffee. She hesitates to admire BEA's spirit, wonders if there is a daughter old enough to babysit for four hours every night this week.

A whiff of burn, a click.

5. Why Do We Forget What Happened When We Were Babies?

The things happening to us when we are babies are all of much the same degree of importance to us. We do not then understand what are the big things in our life and what are not. Memory depends largely upon the impression made at the time of the incident; and it is only when the mind is sufficiently developed to judge the importance of things that memory becomes a well-marked faculty.

The Book of Wonder, Vol. x (1932)

In every daydream she is heroic. She tackles the deranged gunman, spots the sniper, talks down the teen suicide, deploys the killer insult against the fascist drunk. But there is always a moment − seconds or a split second? − during the first line of her first song of the night, when Arden feels like the budgie at the end of his iridescence, just before he dropped dead last January. Arden suspected the cage. It was old and coppery and had sat in Nichol's Aunt Cassie's woodshed since the fifties. Virge the Birge, within hours of entering the cage, began to pace. He bobbed his head, never took a break for seed or water or to ruffle his feathers. Back, forth. It was rush hour, day's end, and he had a bus to catch, a deal to make, news to pass on, the bus was late. And then a couple of days later, Nichol called her hotel to say he'd come downstairs to find a dead budgie. Chemicals off the colour TV is what he theorized, looking for a poem in it, a meaning other than its own. More likely the cage. Every night she starts to sing and knows how that bird felt right at the end: the lights are out, the TV's off, breaths stutter and cramp. Alone.

The draft beer kicks in, and she's one hell of a little entertainer.

She is a single mother in a dive hotel. Forty songs a night,

booze on the house: she loses the feel of the room when she
leaves on breaks to feed Roy in their end-of-hall, end-of-
world but gratis room. Twenty minutes later – her breasts
slack and eyelids hormone heavy – she reconvenes with
strangers who resent her leaving. 'Who the hell she think she
is. Big City Girl,' and the hackneyed etc. Truckers and miners
and smelters prefer a singer to flirt, to slur, to sit at their table
and pay attention, take an interest, dedicate a song: 'I'm
sending this out to Dusty over there and he knows why.' She
sets the Telecaster's knobs at sex, dampens the strings with
the hardening heel of her hand, and thuds a crunchy rhythm.
She coats her voice with fossil fuels:

> *Working in a coal mine*
> *going down down down*

Three breaks a night. Maybe she should mingle for one of
them. Give the babysitter a bottle, make her work.

Arden has messed with Roy's schedule and now he sleeps
all day and wakes when she comes up from the bar. He's
anxious for the breast, the reek of cigarettes and stale beer,
the fade and happy swell of country swing and major chords.
Therefore, the young woman she pays to babysit is paid for
nothing but presence. Every night Arden visits them on her
breaks and every time the sitter – Lily – is engrossed in a
different hardcore scene on pay-TV. She smiles at Arden with
beauty and oriental care, says, 'Baby's sleeping now; this is
such a good baby. Lucky you for such a good baby,' while a
hugely dangling black man on TV applies a branding iron to
the ass of a naked blonde hogtied to his bedroom doorway.
Lily came highly recommended by the addict sister of the
bartender's girlfriend. You can't fire somebody for watching
sex on TV.

By the time Lily is paid and thanked and rebooked and
gone, it is 2 a.m. The room is the size of a birdcage. Arden

pinballs off porn channels – tempted but troubled – and finds a quiet documentary about shorebirds and their diminishing habitat. The beers – how many? – kick into their second stage: sadness and the bloat of fatigue. She dresses down from the tight jeans, heeled suede boots and shimmering black blouse into a white cotton t-shirt, one of six she scored from the ironed stack – his obsession, not hers – in Nichol's top drawer. He has had 'Poetry on a Stick' screened onto the front in brown letters that look academic and clever, but she turns his inside joke inside out. The steam iron took any lingering scent of him.

When Arden was nine, her other, older sister died at last. It had been six years of chemical intervention, the elevator to the tenth floor, radiation, the caustic stink of post-treatment vomiting, the swell of once lovely ankles, the support hose and the new smells of her decomposing body, its off colours. There is more to this story, and it is the bass line of every song she picks at the right moment in a strong set. But she can only summarize. Missing: six years of context, a mother who loved only the one fading; six years of no dentist for Arden, no tolerance for complaints, music too loud or maudlin. Why the throwback tonight? Arden's mother – was this torture? ready-to-wear elegy? – kept all the sister's kilts, the lambswool sweater sets, the mauve acrylic blouses and their faint stains, the suede mini-skirt, and ordered them worn by Arden who became her mother's mannequin, a model for the memory. She stood as proof that someone was gone and that someone was alive, a flawed reproduction, a shame. The smell of another's clothes and the habit of wearing them. Arden masquerades as the dead and dying. They are loved; the survivors are never themselves enough.

She starts a slow kettle in the dryrot bathroom and climbs onto the double bed, baby fussing but relieved. Arden has asked the chambermaid for extra pillows for this, but she doesn't understand, and Arden makes do with two plus a stiff neck. Once Roy's latched on, she sucks the swollen fingers of her left hand like a bewildered child. It will only make the skin soft for tomorrow night's flat-out barre chords. Uptempo will hurt, her calluses yet to harden.

It's noon and the baby sleeps, deep in the car seat on the coffee-shop table. Arden is back to beers at lunch. She drinks everything alcoholic; she drinks strong coffee. She believes these drugs alone rollercoaster her body gently, sufficiently. She has never used hard drugs and maybe that is what's wrong with the music. She lacks the possibility of psychedelic; she has not seen those colours. (Is that a regret?) She did not start to drink until her twenties. It was only then that she grew brave enough to reject her mother's distaste: 'Your poor sister needed drugs to live. Why would anyone take them otherwise?' To be honest, she has not had a whole authentically sober day since, but an addiction to alcohol does not have the cachet it once did. Days of wine and roses are upstaged by more rigorous tastes that suggest not only courage, recklessness, but also a self-absorption she lacks. She lived with a greying and scruffy guitar player for a while who was a daylong dope-smoker. This cured her of any desire to smoke it, since when she did, she wanted tawdry sex and he wanted sleep. And his idea of a perfect evening was to smoke, drink cheap wine (made just south of Vaseaux Lake) and watch nonstop nature shows. When Arden smoked she could not understand the plot.

The cheeseburger is embellished with one half of a plastic cheese slice and for this she will be charged an extra dollar twenty. She'd complain to management except that would be grounds for the cold shoulder the rest of the week. Word would spread around the hotel that she had attitude, was not cooperative, thought she knew more about business than those running the business. Arden would not be asked back.

This morning, she walked to the waterfront and discovered a small park – four lodgepole pines, one slide, two swings, a bench – one swing equipped with a system of straps to hold a baby's flop and flounder. It is winter, the swing is cold and has rivets missing, but Roy the Boy is giddy at the back and forth, here and there, cries if she stops. He swings, he is Glenn Miller over the English Channel on his way to perk up the boys in France. He has muscle memory of this sensation and perhaps there is an association with his absent father, nostalgia. For an hour, Arden pushed, trying to call up lyrics of swing tunes – Bob Wills and the Texas Playboys, 'Crazy Arms' – trying to get the vibrato right, the correct formula of cunt and cowpoke. When she found the sultry swagger of 'Walkin' after Midnight' it made Roy so quiet she feared his face had frozen.

There's a nice shot of the parking lot outside the big café window, government chicks out for lunch: they teeter in bargain heels and drag on long smokes, hooked on the prestige of their shoulder bags and day jobs. No nights! No weekends! Look at us!

The young man at the next table smells of diesel and deodorant soap. The soap, in this town, suggests foreignness, and his face lacks local pallor. He shaves. He bathes. He looks up at the nearby stranger in a grubby, low-light coffee shop and smiles at the baby on her table without hesitation or premeditation. He coughs dryly. He smiles. Good teeth and plenty of them; large blue eyes that don't blink much. Arden doesn't usually talk in the daytime. She saves her prefab, customer-satisfaction banter for work and broods during time off. In some hotels, she has been asked to either act pleasant or find other work. 'You're in the wrong business, doll-face,' it has been suggested.

For this man, though, she makes an exception. She has spoken to no one here apart from the ESL babysitter and pre-verbal child. And although he is staying in this hotel – no overcoat, room key displayed – she hasn't seen him in the bar. Could be different. 'I'm a pilot,' he tells her when she asks, and he coughs again, a magician's cough, dry and fake, fist to mouth and she expects a flurry of white feathers to explode from his clean face.

He is waiting for a flight out. Stiff uniform, crisp and firm wife, multi-kids, many-storeyed house he never sees, constant stewardess action, their lips regulation full, slippery and tinted. No harboured taste for a chick singer on the lam from who knows what.

'Nope,' he says quietly, 'not that kind of pilot.' He means a pilot boat, and, making a map out of his table, he escorts ships with his long and pruned index finger from the junction of Douglas and Devastation Channels, through the snags and roots of Kitimat Arm, into the dredged channel of the western shore to dock at the green light of Terminal Wharf No. 1. He is waiting through snow storms and ice curtains for a flight to Vancouver, where he will provide safe passage to a bigger ship into a smaller channel.

The waitress calls him 'Cappy' and Arden asks if she's supposed to call him that, if she has to. 'Why don't you call me Rex,' he says. 'You got a warm bag or something for that baby? Let's walk somewhere. I'll show you the boat. Let's just walk. Let's go. Bring that baby.'

'You shouldn't be drinking beer when you have a baby,' he says when they reconvene in the lobby. He is nautical. A navy pea jacket, a handknit lambswool scarf, a black watchcap that seems cashmere. Something about his income allows style even under these circumstances. Or maybe Rex is married. 'Are you married?' She is huffing from the baggage of Roy across her chest. At three months, he is off the Penelope Leach weight chart. Must be the beer in the breast milk; Penelope would freak, but Penelope wouldn't work this bar, either. Rex coughs. 'Asthma. Not yet,' he smiles in a way she takes to be meaningful. He's what, thirty years old? She is walking with a younger man who travels, who wears good clothes, who takes an interest in her and her child, not because she knows all the verses of 'Lyin' Eyes', but because she had a baby on the table. His gloves are rust suede; she's always wanted rust suede gloves.

The walk takes half an hour. He is much taller, but the pace seems right. They reach the sad little park, now grey with afternoon sun and slush, and her legs have done as much as they are capable of, constantly tensed against black ice, risks. They rest on the bench, their thighs sometimes close enough to touch, the baby snoring, and she does all the talking:

'I was born in New Westminster. My parents owned a small stucco house on Princess Street, a good neighbourhood. New Westminster is old, blowzy gardens and quaint houses. The CPR tracks marked the wrong side of town; downtown there are still tracks from the streetcars. I loved downtown, standing outside the bars, listening to the jamborees on Saturday coming out of the old hotels, the King Eddie – every town has a King Eddie, right? I didn't know then it was smoke and beer I smelled; I thought it was amplifiers, the smell of music, of four chords and a snare drum. From the end of my street, up above Fraser View Cemetery, you can see the river, the muddy Fraser, still jumping with log booms and barges.

'My father worked a towboat, hauling logs on the Fraser. He owned the smallest firm on the river – just two boats – and he couldn't keep up when the big boys moved in, Seaspan, Rivtow. He sold his boats and bought himself a little log salvager. And then disappeared in Juan de Fuca Strait. He told my mother he was going to the Island because no one was salvaging over there. No boat, no body. That's when she went to work – no pension, either – in a lingerie shop on Columbia, just down from the King Eddie.'

There is no mention of her sisters, the cause and effect of the sister's death, the other sister's birth and the father's last trip. Arden relates her circumstances, the reasons she's here, the drawbacks, perks, heartaches and possibilities on the road, away from Nichol and his expectations and withholding, his belief that mothers are not for fucking. Rex asks one question: 'Are you wanted?' but it will take a couple of days before she realizes he means in the legal sense. Today, excited and verbal from the sub-sub-zero and the windchill and the shape of this young man's eyes, his hands, she answers, 'Exactly the problem. He wants only certain parts of me, the parts he defines as essential: compliant, knee-length suits, puréed veggies from the garden for the baby while still breastfeeding, and idle chat with like-minded mothers at some purgatory of a playground so I don't need to bring baby psycho-shit to him in the evenings. He admires the part of me that has a thing for Perry Como. As a whole I'm not that pure. The most interesting stories I have are pain, sex, violence, hard times. I'm reluctant to edit. So, wanted? No, I am not wanted.'

They can either continue the walk, or freeze to the bench bolts. At the wharf, Roy begins to shriek – hear the Fogerty? – and Arden asks to go aboard to feed him. She is unbalanced and nervous of deck ice; Rex supports her elbow, back, asks to hold the baby, but she declines; she can manage with small steps. Trawlers, ghost boats, dip and bob and ropes creak with their dance down the gangway. The dock is a shambles: crab pots tangled with frayed line and fluorescent floats, gull-dropped and ransacked mussel shells, middens of beer bottles stuffed into torn and frozen cases. Rex's boat glints white with new green trim. It is like a sleek fish caught up in the wrong school. The first thing Arden sees inside is a hand-lettered sign – a sea poem – nailed onto the wall of the boat's white-washed cabin:

'That,' she says, 'is good advice. If only I'd given wide berth to
a couple of rocky shores. For example, guys who date *au pairs*
on a regular basis.' The baby's voice is full and as she struggles
to nonchalantly expose and not expose her right breast, Rex
does a Gandhi crouch before her, so close she feels damp
breath on her hand at the baby's back. They are all rocking.

'I've never seen this before,' he says, as if Arden is a classic
movie. 'Did you tell me his name?' He pulls his toque back
and forth on his head.

'Roy.'

'Rogers or Orbison?'

He may be thirty, but he knows his legends. 'Both: the
smile, the voice, the drama, the ideal man.'

'Should I be quiet?' he whispers and coughs.

'Not unless you want to put me to sleep. Tell us a story,
Rex. Give me details I've never heard. Go sit over there.
Gargle at night with salt and mint tea for that cough.'

'Asthma.' His eyes large and blue, a little boy's struggling
eyes: I can't breathe. He takes to his pilot's chair, measuring
the distance between them with long legs, holding a nautical
instrument in his long hands. A compass, or something. It's a
shame to make him get up.

'Could you take my toque off?' She's overheated already,
the flush of the first suck, both hands still required to achieve
Roy's obstinate latch-on. 'And fix my hair.' He pushes her flat
bangs back too gently to make a difference, his fingers are
shaking, his tongue trapped between his lips. 'Okay, start the
story,' Arden says, slurring. There is a foghorn somewhere
and the hygienic smell of cedar. Or is that creosote.

He looks long at the baby, coughs with one whole hand
over nose and mouth, then stares up through a window the

size and shape of a snare drum at the grey air, white trees, the dark line of sky on water. He goes back to his chair, its creak and tilt, and says, 'My family legend goes like this: I was conceived in the lifeboat of a steamer. Every weekend, all summer long, my mother and her charges, children from the True Blue Orphanage – adopted for the day by the Loyal Order of the Moose, of which her alcoholic uncle was one – would board the lovely SS *Lady Alex* in Vancouver and cross to Bowen Island. Excursions, they were called then. A day trip return was ninety cents. A party was meant to take place on the picnic grounds of the estate, a huge parcel of prime treed land, waterfront – Shetland ponies for the kids, a saltwater swimming pool – owned by the steamship company and operated as a resort. But it was the boat, the crew and the captain that people still remember. My mother is firm: she had not been drinking, she was in charge of children, of orphans. However, on each excursion, she had come to anticipate the purser's hand. She admits this. The uniform, maybe. A man with a job, a look, a boat. Tickets.

'She wasn't the only one. The island itself was debauched. As the boat pulled out of Snug Cove each Sunday night, Barney Potts and His Swing Band played for dancers on board while those left on shore sang "Goodnight Ladies" and dangled and splashed their bare legs from the dock. Rows of lamps along the sea wall. Children asleep in coiled manilla. Skirts wet to the waist. The lifeguard would appear suddenly on the ship's high bridge, stripped to his skin, drunk and brown and laughing, and dive and swim the cold chop to the dock where his nakedness was ignored, or preferred. And that would end it all for another week.

'And one evening as they puffed and chortled back into moonlit Howe Sound, reclined in the canvas and hemp and curve of a lifeboat, my mother and the purser found it inside themselves to find me inside themselves. The relationship ended. And then the summer.

'My father, at the time just a sweetheart who worked weekends stocking shelves at Woodward's in New Westminster – Yes, Arden, I know your home town – was never told this story. I can't believe he never knew, that some vengeful or scorned young woman didn't tell on my mother, longing to comfort my handsome and shy father in his needful hour. My mother confessed to me shortly after his death, I think to explain my life to herself. And to grieve the passing of her longest lie. My father was a surgeon; she was a seamstress. No one on either side of our family had so much as owned a rowboat and here was me, at sea from eighteen, unable to stomach solid ground. She believed origin explained everything, excused everything. My absence, my presence.

'Her shady heart.

'I think it explains my mother, maybe says something about Dad, about our chill. But I can't be summed up in a single act of passion on a fading Sunday evening aboard the *Lady Alex* under the moon and lifeboat covers. That's too close to saying I'm attracted only to dark-haired women because my mother was a brunette.

'Christ, he wasn't a seaman, he was a purser. Maybe she went to the island that summer because the pull was in *her* nature. It wasn't the island, but the voyage; not the purser, but his boat.

'Anyway. In the company of True Blue Orphans, I was conceived.'

Arden is uncomfortable. 'Could you hold the baby – he won't wake up – I need to pee. That's what that door is, right? A head, or whatever you call it? How old are you, anyway?' Men's hands grow huge when they reach for an infant. Even with Roy's relative mass, Rex is Paul Bunyan and Roy disappears into his chest. 'Sit down with him if you want. Don't worry, he's really big.'

Years ago in this town – this is way before Nichol – Arden began dating a lounge regular. Richard, she thinks. He sipped white wine with a nondescript buddy and only came into the bar on Fridays and Saturdays. So a serious working type, with things to do during the day, forgoing beer to detour the morning's get-back. And he was handsome. Clean shirt and Levi's bright blue from washing, shoes worn but not wrecked. The white wine is unusual in a town like this. They talked on her breaks. He requested good songs she happened to know – Gram Parsons, Emmylou and an uptempo version of 'Wheels' – they flirted because of that. By the Saturday night, his friend did not come with him, and she went back to Richard's house at the end of the night. Oh, the freedom without a baby. Things were nice. His house was small, orderly, matching plates in the cupboard, towels in the bathroom and no stink of mildew. The bed was made, two fat pillows. That Georgia O'Keeffe print, the one of the buffalo skull, hung over his bed, and a magnet held a poster to the fridge door: LISTEN BEFORE YOU SPEAK.

He drove her back to the hotel the next morning, a kind kiss, no plans. He did not show up the following Friday, and by Saturday afternoon, she had finished a bottle of wine with dinner, and was into her second beer midway through the first set. He came in during the night's last song – *We're not afraid to ride, we're not afraid to die* – took his carafe of wine with two glasses to a back table and stretched his legs out to listen. As Arden walked off the little stage, he poured her a glass. It was clear from his eyes, his posture, that he'd started the evening somewhere else. She does not remember one thing they said to each other for those two weekends, except when later that night, she threw up good Scotch on his bathroom floor, pissed on those lovely deep blue tiles, and he came in and found her lying on the bathroom floor, her face resting against the lovely deep blue cool tiles, he said, 'Jesus fucking Christ.'

The flush of the head startles her out of this charming reverie. She is humiliated retroactively, washed in disgrace, and has a hard time facing Rex when she comes out. Roy is still asleep and knows nothing, yet, of his mother's trespasses. Is she wanted?

'So you might be leaving soon to go back to the city?' She likes the look of his hands with gloves, without. He keeps his nose pressed to the top of Roy's head. Rex has dark hair, Roy does not. She wants to sing to him, show herself, give him books to read. There is the pathos of herself: he is so young; she is bent with the weight of what kind of life to build from what little she has.

'It won't be tonight,' he says. 'Maybe tomorrow, according to the forecast.' He looks up and into her eyes. The light is low but this feels worthy of interpretation. They have told their stories and now, aftermath. His mother and her lust is the part meant for her.

'Come hear my last set then. Listen to me play and then have tea with us, me and Roy, in my room.' She wants the resonance of a public act. She stands beside him, presses her knee against his thigh. It's hard to remember flirting, but this seems subtle yet direct, sophisticated yet unthreatening: the definition of crush.

He coughs: dry, vulnerable. 'I don't think so,' he says and pulls himself together and hands Roy to the mother. The gloves are back on and he's ready to go. He checks some gauge or other and battens a hatch that doesn't need battening.

There may be a way to start over, to regain the advantage she had before she got direct. 'Did I screw this up? Did I speed?'

'Not at all,' he says, sounding like a uniform. Arden wants to slap his back to make him look at her.

'Could you look at me?' She tries not to whine but anger is not her best performance. 'I'm sorry if you don't find me attractive. I thought you did. I thought you were. What's the problem, Cappy? Lactation fucks your libido?' There's last night's booze making her cut corners and damage an otherwise lovely drive in pleasant company. 'Mothers aren't for fucking? Is that it?'

In a gesture that is part gallant, part he-man, he takes Roy from her and cradles him in the madonna and child pose. 'Listen. My girlfriend – Mitsuko – is going to have one of these. Due date's today, but no signs yet, not as of this morning when I called. She sounds worried and lonely. It's almost a joke, isn't it? Stuck here because of bad weather, might miss my first kid's birth. My mother will stand in, make meals and so on. Mitsuko trusts her. I have a good friend in the RCMP who went over as a peacekeeper during the Gulf War. He missed the kid's birth, missed the kid's death, and now he blames his wife for everything. Crib death. He blames Elaine for everything, including the war. Called her Saddam for a while, trying to joke, to make things better. Mitsuko will breastfeed the first one for four years, she says, and then have a second child. Elaine sees a grief counsellor bi-weekly.' Roy is watching those blue eyes.

She takes Roy and stuffs him into the bag, zip and tuck. He objects and grumbles but falls back into sleep. Rex doesn't know what to do with his hands; he is bereft. He consults the compass, checking. 'I thought being with you here would make me feel like fatherhood. I thought I'd learn something, since you seemed so good at everything. But being with you here made me feel like –' His sentence is finished with a fluster of fingers through his dark hair. He coughs.

What she wanted is the touch – pre-planned – of his hand and her hands, their thin skin and riverine veins. Her hands feel nettle-stung without him. Arden interrupts him and tries to stifle the fired moment with a blanket of good will. She says, 'I have two more nights here, and then drive two days to the top of the Island, for a one-week gig at another dive hotel. There will be no snow, no Portuguese waitresses, no one I know. Turn-of-the-century missionaries made gifts of sewing machines to the local Indians, trying to convert them to a domestic God.' Is it racist if she thinks his girlfriend's name sounds like a compact car? 'This was a practical solution to the naked children who roamed the island's perimeter, filthy dogs humping their ankles, ravens giggling. The missionaries – Methodists – took their time and showed matriarchs how to thread the machines, to stitch by pumping both feet, pin right sides together, and then they returned to the city for the winter.' Arden and Roy and Rex walk back the way they came. The light is lower and she feels the stain of tension begin in her stomach, the budgie flutter against the night's doom, and anticipates already the red wine with dinner, the quiet bed at the end of the night. 'The following June, the missionaries pulled back into the bay aboard the SS *Thomas Crosby*, expecting calico and flounce or, at the least, less skin. Influenza had ravaged the tribe through the winter, and cedar boxes holding the dead hung from the conifers along the mile and a half of beach. The boxes held not only the bodies of the months dead, but their most prized possessions, their valuables, remnants. In several trees, sewing machines.

'Sometimes I drive strippers back to Vancouver. I'd be happy to take you part way if you need to get home.'

While the baby slept in their room, Arden ran – slip, recover – to the one-storey, one-style over-permed department store across the street and down the hill. Fifteen minutes before closing, she bought a rose-red, figure-hugging sweater – slight sheen, low neck – with the last twenty bucks from last week's gig. She will run a tab till payday tomorrow night or she will beg management for yet another draw. It is a teenager's sweater, but maybe Rex will reconsider, show up, and see her differently. The skirt is too short, too tight, but this is show business.

Today, she thought he was interested, but every small clue to his desire could just as well have been Christian fundamentalism: polite, caring, passionate. The hug he left her with was perhaps a noncommittal shrug, required by the rule book to comfort penitents. Ten thousand metaphors.

The sweater feels sly against her stomach, beneath the Telecaster. Different guitar, fuller redder hair and she'd be Bonnie Raitt: greying, authentic, on fire. First set: Merle Haggard. Arden whines and cracks and grovels in the bass note dirt with country music's most legitimate ex-con:

> *Now I'm a hunted fugitive with just two ways:*
> *Outrun the law or spend my life in jail.*

Arden does not bother to look past the microphone stand, she is enclosed in irony and a tune – all its ups and downs – she loves. Even the bartender, her back to Arden but probably discussing her with the manager's wife over the phone, is inconsequential. There is no point in wasting top-forty crowd-pleasers on two guys in suits – fiscal managers, no doubt – who have barricaded high-end briefcases on their table: anti-wall of sound, Phil Spector's accountants. Where are the cowboys who roll stagy cigarettes? *I'm on the run, the highway is my home.*

Or the other suited guy. 'What kind of throat spray do you use?' He has his arms flat out on the bar to mark which part's his. The ashtray he believes belongs to him bisects the triangle formed by his arms and the two beers at the top. Very tidy. His bills are carefully perpendicular to him. He tossed gallant coins at his bartender with every round. 'You must use something to sound that pure.'

With no one else paying attention, Arden has kept an eye on him through the set. Occasionally as she sang, he would pat his little paunch to the beat of her electric drummer. Then he would turn around to her on his stool and make a gesture as if lifting his left breast, as if describing the virtues of a good underwire bra. He was trying to tell her to lift her diaphragm, to sing, in short, correctly.

'I don't use throat spray, I've never needed to.'

'Oh come on. You must use something. You can't possibly sing every night and not protect those vocal cords.'

He lights a Turkish cigarette from a nifty tin box and pays no attention to where the high-test smoke scatters. This time Arden pretends to be unaffected. Other times she makes a big deal about it. Just depends.

'Okay. WD-40, then,' she says calmly. Arden turns to walk back to her little nothing stage.

'What?'

'Always on sale.'

By the time she's up on stage and ready to start the next set, he's got his back squarely turned to her and he's yakking a mile a minute to the bartender who, she can tell, takes his side. She's guilty. You bet she is one frigid bitch.

The things she wanted to say to Rex if he came to her room for tea:

Describe your temperament.

You make me so nervous.

Is it up to me? To me?

Put your hand out on the table (she places hers alongside his, side to side, edge to edge): look at me while you do this.

With your index finger, clear a path through the dust on me.

There is a note under her door when she goes up to feed Roy on her first break:

'Good tide, good sky, good bye! p.s. Good food = good food (baby). There is no truth but in transit.'

She puts it in the pouch at the back of her suitcase, next to the latest letter delivered that afternoon, when she was off floating with Rex, from Nichol.

Dear Arden,

The dog had been moping since you took the baby, and when I found a small lump on her teat, I had Dr Persson put her to sleep.

This morning was bright and clear and cold, but no frost. I dug out the rambling rose ('Seagull'?) you planted for my mother and went much deeper and wide – an hour with the mattock – and placed Kriegie in the deepest part, sprinkled a little dolomite lime (some culture's blessing), and a bucket of that goat manure you hoarded behind the garage. I backfilled and replaced the rose. The roots look fine; why won't it bloom? No need to ramble I suppose.

Which explains why you're there, and it's planted on your dead dog.

Nichol

6. Where Does All the Bad Air in the World Go?

This question can teach us about words such as 'good' and 'bad'. In their right places, all things are good. That is certainly true of what we call bad air. We may rightly call such air bad, because it is bad for us; too much in the air any animal is given to breathe, and the animal will die. This gas is of the utmost importance for our lives, even though we rightly call it bad when it is in the wrong place and in the wrong quantity. Without carbon dioxide all the green trees and plants would die of starvation; then all the animals that live on plants would die; then all the animals that eat vegetarian animals would die; and, lastly, when everything else had died, we ourselves would die.

The Book of Wonder, Vol. VIII (1932)

In Vancouver, this would be the bar of choice for stockbrokers. On creosote stilts above high tide, windows and carpets grimy with salt and algae and body fluids; out there the Johnstone Strait, waters that tag along with hopeful currents to Japan, Russia; a fleet of fish boats, aluminum like bridge girders or wooden-hulled, like artifacts. The floating salmon processor loiters offshore, anchored in the deep bay like some kid's Kool-Aid stand. The trawlers belly up; they rumble and the bar's windows shake. Three o'clock in the afternoon is a good time to set up the gear, quiet drunks not yet on edge over the conflict of interest with the dinner hour. Bartenders stand alert and friendly from their first pulls on the Chivas.

They want her against a cedar wall but the sound may be too bright with all this glass and wood. Arden gets shrill in a room this size. Whisky voice preferable to gin and tonic, tamp down the female. She tucks the baby in a corner of the stage.

He is awake, but the car seat closes around him and makes him appear drugged. Four huge Indian men lean down and compare faces: round, shining, infrequent teeth; they delight at little things tucked into corners. 'My name's Norman,' the biggest one slurs, jeans creeping south as he bends close. 'I own this town. Ha ... Ha.' He is speaking to Roy, balancing with soft hands on either side of the car seat. He is so wide Arden has lost sight of her baby. 'And if you need anything in my town, you ask me first and I'll make sure you get whatever you need.' He is speaking to her?

'Okay, Norman, I've got your toast here, come on and sit down and let the lady do her job.' A good bartender – John this time, most times – senses risk and insult and intervenes, watches out for girl singers and potential harassment. Arden senses that John is watching out for Norman, not her.

Norman's buddies heave her speakers onto tabletops and in the time it takes to keep toast warm, the Econoline is unloaded. The gear – suitcase, baby bag, toy bag, diaper bag, fold-up crib set aside – is upright and well-handled. Usually, she doesn't let anyone help with her gear, but it's too late to object or to say thanks since they are at their window table, sucking smart beers, their centrepiece an origami mess of crumpled fifty-dollar bills. How festive.

Two white guys with buffalo wool toques (in August?) say they've bought her a beer: 'Bring the baby over.' Roy's grateful for the ocean view, for male voices; he curls his mouth. 'I've got one of those across the street,' says the handsome one, a finger pulled from his beer glass to point at the baby. 'I indulge at naptime,' he grins magically. 'A couple of beers, a suck on a doob, and I'm connected enough to know – to *intuit* really – when he wakes up. I sense it. Right, Marc? I always know. Like you and the whales.' John jabs three poor examples of wieners onto a squeaking rotisserie behind the bar. A bendy fourth, he holds up and catches Arden's eye. 'No, thanks,' she smiles back. There is vanilla yogurt, fresh fruit, good cheese and white wine in the cooler over there by the stage.

'That's right, Jason. I believe we all have this capacity.' Marc is playing scientist for this lifetime. 'The pace of modern time sets up an anti-resonance which conflicts with more natural convergences of tone and miracle. We human beings dwell in a tired realm and soon it will pass beyond this confusion, to a more charitable kingdom. I gotta piss.'

She missed the point. She needs a map. They are weekend whale watchers, marine biologists counting killer whales for the Department of Fisheries. 'Dee Oh Eff,' Jason spells it out. 'A little cash, a nice flight, all expenses paid – big deal, they buy the burgers and beers.'

A shitty bar in daylight. The pool table is too loud, too loaded. 'Who neglects your child when you're off looking at big fish?' Arden asks. Idiot city-girl strategy for the first day, too judgemental. So she flirts with fingertips on his thin brown wrist (you call those working hands?) and giggles. 'Inside joke,' she enunciates.

'My wife,' he says, as if he's turning in a bad guy to the cops. 'Unless she can find a babysitter.' What's keeping Marc?

'What does your wife do in a town like this?'

'Schoolteacher. Grocery clerk. I forget which.' Arden has caused him to hate retroactively every woman who ever shit on his bullshit.

Norman's gang are regulars, meaning they inhabit this bar any time they near consciousness. Deep hulls nose into the window's frame and the six men christen the vessels returning to port, excited, calling out the owners' names like announcing tonight's first shift hockey lineup: Matilpi's! Hippie's! Speck's old lady's! Stinkin' hippie's! Hippie school teacher's! Cook's! Diane's kid's – uh-oh, too bad, too high in the water. Their own boats are confiscated or sold or lost to naive white guys; Norman's group treated fishing quotas the way rum runners treated Prohibition: invitation, prospect, permission to overdo. Dee Oh Eff stepped in. Of course, now Norman owns the town. 'The nation's mine, too,' he adds one night, to clarify.

Tonight, they clapped once in her second set as the last of the light smoothed off into Johnstone Strait and left the bar moody: Hank Williams, 'Cheatin' Heart'. Shaved off every round they order, a draft beer goes to Arden, but they do not otherwise acknowledge her. The beers keep her owned. At the end of each set, they wave her over to listen to the long pauses between their chatter. She can stand at the bar, flirt with John for a few moments, but if laughter or carefree good times ensue, they will hail him for another round. Then John hands her the draft and escorts her to the chair they have pulled out. Arden has initialled this contract by drinking. Younger, she signed with good Scotch and Grand Marnier, but there was trouble behind those, expectations, a nasty hand around her upper arm, a deep bruise souvenir. A veteran would know if trouble was behind Norman; it isn't. Norman owns everything because there's nothing.

Roy the Boy stays in her birdcage upstairs. Norman's seventeen-year-old dropout daughter, Emma, watches him all night until Arden starts her last set. Then Emma takes a cab home. Her last set is half an hour, six tunes – and Emma's mother demands bed before midnight. Arden slides through the songs, finishes ironically with Asleep at the Wheel, 'The End Is Not in Sight,' and thanks everybody for whatever they've done, packs her guitar, slips a stained white damask tablecloth she got from her mother one Christmas over the amp, the beat box, the set lists, and climbs the sunless, moonless, starless stairs, guitar case hitting every other step and often the wall. Five nights, Roy has been awake when she comes in, slick with tears, frazzled by the thump of her drum box downstairs below his crib and then wondering what happened to that lovely big heartbeat when it stops. Saturday night, he is shaking and kicking, wet with anger and the diaper Emma did not change. He refuses to look at Arden, refuses the breast for the first time, his little fists irate and rude. She makes chamomile tea and pours some – half tea, half formula – into his bottle. He's cutting a tooth – at seven months? – and this will soothe his stubborn gums.

She is not sentimentally attached to breastfeeding. It has been good but also: a branding iron, an inconvenience, a profiteer, a superstition, an eye for an eye, an ounce of cure, a ghost.

She leaves the television off for as long as she can, tries out the quiet, the waves meeting shore down there, her ears awash and hissing with the Telecaster's chop. The bar lights go out, John locks the front door, she knows, with a paper-bagged bottle of Chivas under one smooth, toned arm, and Arden holds Roy to the bottle. He breathes two staccato sighs, wiggles his head no, takes it anyway and closes his eyes. They meet again.

She is the only girl singer to last a week in this bar, and John says the white man who owns it wants her for another month 'then we'll see after that.' The agent will have to cancel Port Hardy and Duncan. This guy won't pay more money – *I get paid weekly. Very weakly* – but Arden won't have to drive on her day off. John says, 'My ex-wife's got a house on the south point – that's the white end – you can have it for the month. Go see Diane at the Shipyards, she'll get you stacked up.'

The house is next to last on the rocky point, coastal and unpretentious. It was used historically only in summer, for nomads, gypsy fishing families. Each small and square room marks the annual addition of a child, an artless tangle of parts tacked together. Each rotten window hangs poetic with cracked glass and crumbling caulk. The brick fireplace – whitewashed – vents into three rooms, which seems a tall order for wood heat on open coast. An oil stove – no fan – will give her hot water but not enough for a full bath if the stove's not high and hot. Outside, the soil is too far north for pH. The garden consists of a seedy shrub-like parsley at the front door and a clump of burgundy chrysanthemums along the bright side of the driveway. Someone brought round stones up from the beach and lined them along the driveway, painted them white like a welcome at a slip-strap motel.

But there is a pantry by the back door, thick with the promise of Mason jars and jam pots. And a glassed-in front porch. These – the way in and the way out – are possibility. She could grow cuttings and send for seeds in spring, bulbs in late summer. Compost kelp and pulverized oyster shells and build soil. She could have a berry patch – logan, tay, goose – and fill the shelves with identical archaic pint jars, and start purple sage from seed and put up sage jelly, tie ribboned calico bonnets on them, meticulously letter labels with a flowery hand and bestow them on members of the community and new friends at Christmas and baby showers. Salmonberries sound edible.

She has a month and if she watches herself, talks nice, plays the right tunes (Creedence Clearwater with a Hank Williams chaser), drinks the right brands, sucks up to regulars, she could get a house gig in this bar. She knows the slant. She can fit. They could keep her on and she and the baby could live here, the ocean out front, this little island two ferry trips and a four-hour drive from Nichol and what must be by now – she has been gone four months and three weeks – his desire to father a stolen child.

The cottage next to Arden's is encased with a purple clematis vine. The old man who putters ignores her but they might be neighbours, he might keep an eye on her as old men do; his wife will be jealous but proud, and they will be glad for the baby as it grows and brings big feelings back. They get sockeye cheap and will share; he will have a line on seasoned firewood and will fix it so she gets enough cords to heat the house all the long winter long.

She was too drunk to drive. She was too drunk to walk, but did it anyway; there's no law against that yet. They picked her up outside the Shipyards walking toward an early version of sobriety. They dropped her off at home at 2 a.m. and took the sitter – everybody's cousin by declension – away in their fumbling car. At 6 a.m., after homebrew all night, they returned and the morning bloomed blue.

The baby was still asleep. Each man took a limb and dragged her behind her own home, out to the alder saplings and lady-ferns. They were in their element. The Douglas fir and its attendant vegetation – so much peripheral life – camouflaged their crime and of course there was that Christmas smell, along with wet dog and a top-note of nearby rotting bivalves. She had heard on public radio once – National Tree Day? – that members of this tribe – no, all tribes – say a complex prayer to affected flora and fauna whenever they fell a tree. They appease aboriginality. With this hokey bylaw, they acknowledge the dangled self when committing the murder. They did not kill her, though, so no prayer incanted: colonial history provides her torture with context. It's come to this.

Sex has been rough on other occasions and she called it passion and delight, good. She asked for it, all in fun. The men here are soft with generations of bad wine and candlefish. Between their ineffective slaps and feral bites, she kept track of thrusts and no one did better than three, as though they had stored up, constructing the confection of her breasts, anticipating the tightness of her hole(s) while they listened from their table and bought flat draft. She sensed fierce displeasure at the size of her nipples, for example. They bruised the bones of her ass, wishing for more flesh, and then their fluttery spasms came, painless and without velocity, like

the song of a winter wren. Only one – Norman, the owner –
wanted her mouth, trusted it around him. 'Sing something,'
he jerked and hissed, fists in her hair and pulling the reins.
'You heard me, you fucking bitch singer. Sing something I
like.' He stroked his bent cock unkindly and watched her
mouth like television. Bickering ravens above linked with her
voice's sweet needles.

> *Oh give me a home where the buffalo roam*
> *And the deer and the antelope play,*
> *Where seldom is heard a discouraging word*
> *And the skies are not cloudy or gray.*
> *Home –*

He plunged at this point, the shape of her mouth an open
invitation, provocation, an opportunity for artistic control.
The emptiness of white. The corners of her lips lifted tight
and then split, Norman's signature. As always, she wondered
how to breathe. And what they say is true: she slipped away
to another realm, detached from ordeal.

In the Fraser Valley cranberry bog her grandfather farmed,
the day of harvest, the sun is quiet behind Whitney's Hill, and
she lies in the bright red fruit awaiting flood, for the wash of
water to lift the vines and their perfect weight and float their
wholeness for easy picking, for her grandfather to finally relax
and run his gentle beater, the berries corralled with wooden
booms. Heavy crop: in its wake, Santa will permit the shiny
shoes and leave them under the tree. The irrigation begins.
Floating in her family's cranberry bog, she is suspended
above root and vine and berry, swimming laps along the
sandy rows, showing her grandfather she is fast and clean and
does no damage. The first-light linger of chicken manure
confirms she is happy and rich.

Evergreen is just a pretty word to disguise the constant
drop of needles. The taste of Norman was immediate and sour

and he slapped her grimace. She wanted to see what the others were doing while Norman had her face. They seemed far away, as if the procedure was intimate and they knew manners.

They've brought flowers. No.

Each man carried a stalk, ripe green and tall, tiny blossoms tilting. Ribbed stems with fine spines. Stinging nettles from the boggy garden she'd hoped to clear behind the woodshed. She expected resistance from herself but – who's this sitting on her chest? His back broad with flesh and the absence of visible muscle. Once a bright flannel shirt bought with herring roe profits, now skin-thin cotton. She smelled semen from her hair; his own wafted by, mingling with sweet diesel, hotter than Norman's, as the first nettle rubbed hard back and forth across her clitoris. She became all current and sensation. They did the mutant nipples, of course. And they inserted leaves with their fat fingers far into each orifice, which made her wonder if some yet darker and lost tribe uses this method to payback menstruation. Norman chose her tongue. By the end, every available skin cell was exposed to coarsely toothed leaves covered with fine stinging hairs. When they were done – eyelids last – she throbbed electric. Hydro-electric, subaqueous with grief, a power source, and yet so dead she wept for her own passing unable to wait for perspective. Each pissed on her stomach for punctuation, formed a Boy Scout line with Norman as Lord Baden-Powell, clearly the leader, and disappeared into salmonberry thicket.

You knew this was going to happen.

You saw this coming and stayed in its way. There's the regret.

The baby was hotly awake, abandoned. Arden held him for the rest of the morning as the sting returned in waves, her lips swelled and welted and throbbed and she thought of Nichol: further torture. He is, like most men, just under six feet tall, but says he is six feet tall. His hair is shoulder length, straight and thick and the colour of wild rabbits. Occasionally, he wears it in a ponytail to keep it off his face. He likes the look; they disagree on this, too. To her, he appears overly arty and Arden likes to watch his hand's angles when he pushes the hair from his eyes. They are a very bright blue. His skin is pale and freckled, like his mother's, and so he waits for the melanoma and wonders what scalding afternoon at the lagoon will show up, back to haunt, on his own future brain scan. He wears two small but deep scars on his face, where the childhood dog, Digger, grabbed his head to make him drop the bone. His mother watched and couldn't move from the kitchen window. Her little boy reaches for the dog's dropped bone, puts it in his own mouth, pretending to be a dog, wants to share with the other dog, moves close, and as she finally runs and leaves the doorway, all the blood begins.

Married, Arden found his touch too poetic, detailed with corny imagery – 'Feel the earth breathe. Many breaths, in and out. In and then out. You are the island and I am shipwrecked here. I find the dew, lick it.'

'Fuck. Come *on*,' she growled. She wanted it fast, the race from desire to pleasure a sprint that explodes muscle molecules. A whole socio-economic sub-group of leggy women wants men to slow down, to employ Nichol's hippie pyromania, but she remained petulant and unsatisfied. Still, after a morning of many rapes, breast bites, hard slaps and a prolonged body rub, she wanted to soothe her ripped face in the long space between his chin and collarbone. But fuck the romance.

On their second date, as they reclined naked together on his mother's lounge chair in the back garden at 3 a.m., her hair sour with bar smoke, Nichol asked if other men overlooked or just sort of forgot about her breasts. At lunch today, Roy refused the breast for the second time: so it's unanimous.

All day, she cluttered her brain with words to describe the unspeakable subcutaneous vibrations. She rocked the baby in the sun coming off Broughton Strait through the wide window, to the music of what has happened to her and what she's become. She settled on three words: stigma, penalty, spectre. Let him make a poem from those.

Nichol's favourite colour is a kind of cedar red. The colour of brick, but also of tree bark, the skin of the Indians he grew up with, and the bottom of that creek where he grew up.

The *British Columbia Recreational Atlas* depicts this island as a semi-erect penis. This island is fringed with beaches and boulders and shingle which extend nearly a cable offshore in places. At the northern end of the bay, an Indian residential school – THE BOYS' INDUSTRIAL SCHOOL (1894) – of red brick. The ghosts of sewing machines hang along the shore, of women and waist-length hair plaited with copper, in long red skirts, cropdusted with Evening in Paris, and smoking Popeye pipes. At the 5 p.m. ferry line-up, she is behind Norman and his two teenage daughters. The sitter, the lovely Emma, is off to Vancouver where she will study drums at a music college, hooked on the smack of the snare. Those schools, Arden could tell her, will rob her rhythm, her feel, peopled only by bitter and wasted jazz slugs who watch for promise and then wish to fuck the student in whom it occurs. Norman loves his music. He watches Arden in his side mirror, same shirt, leaning on his fat elbow, cigarette tacked to his bottom lip by some ancient viscosity. He wears mirrored sunglasses; she could get a good look at herself if she walked to his car door and told his daughters what their father did to her just this morning.

At four-thirty this afternoon, she packed her gear at the bar; the waitresses and the bartender said nothing. Clientele – the Breakfast Club they call themselves before five – watched the Calgary Stampede highlights on the big-screen, sipped

orange juice with a draft chaser. Somehow the smell of toast.
Arden was careful not to interfere. For the first time since she
arrived, she did not leave the baby unattended. She set him on
the table between her and the door and never turned her back
even when loaded sideways with speakers. John reached her
pay envelope across the bar and turned away before her hand
met it, back to his little shot glass, the bucking and roping.

Take away the Chinese grocer, the Chinese cook, the
burnt-out teachers, time-warp hippies and potters, and you
have a town of taxis, stray dogs, and G-men. Across that
jagged breakwater, the strait, the cedars and Douglas fir, the
mouth of the Nimpkish River, the seiners and their tangled
nets, inadequate catch, the Orcas and their PR name-change
are without resonance, forgeries pretending to mean, to
intersect myth and reality. But a garden is also a garden:
grow, decay, grow. She is turning poetic. Nichol will
understand.

Roy gets cranky at the wait but she can't leave the van.
Norman or Emma will do or say something, and what is left
on her face of what she found in this village will come apart
and scramble. Babies are shiftless and Roy senses her unease,
pierces it with whines and stupid boo-hoos. He makes her cry
and so then he wails. She is tempted to lean on the horn to
make him stop, to scare the shit out of him, she is tempted –
she believes she can say for the first time – to slap his face
and shoulders and shake his fat thighs till he promises to
stop. The wetness of his diaper – when did she change that? –
has crept across his faux-jeans and into his undershirt. She is
appalled. And then they are invited to board the ferry. They
slide on and are placed alongside Norman's rape-mobile, but
at least she is over the bow. The ferry guys kick stoppers in
place in front of her tires to keep her from slipping away.
They do not see the signs on Arden's wet and cracked face
that she is already slipped.

Without his clothes, stretched long on the cool bucket seat, he is lovable again. The feet pump air; the bottle is a comfort. There are bruises on his arms, press points, just above the elbow. There is a broken and leaking blister on his chin, probably impetigo. The rash, the smell of the throbbing rash, suggests he has not been properly bathed for some time. His legs are mounded with hives, a response to a food his system cannot yet decode. There is the bleary suggestion of conjunctivitis in both eyes, red now from crying but crusted, too, with a yellow something more. Arden makes a Mister Yucky-Face and whispers an elongated 'eeeeeew'; he gets the joke, is happy, humoured, repents sins on behalf of us all. She cannot offer a breast while Norman waits nearby, but will book a good room in Campbell River and sort this out.

'Will I be arrested or — whaddaya call it? — *detained* when I get home? Have you been in touch with authorities or something? Am I wanted?'

'Is that Roy crying?'

'That's Roy singing.'

'Are you ill? Is Roy sick? You sound small.'

'I'm in a small town. I appreciate that you aren't being mean to me, Nichol. I expect anger, but you are being nice. You are a nice man.'

'*This* should be over now. *This* has been done now, Arden. I'll be as nice as it takes to get him home. The books say eight months means he can move on from bananas smashed up and rice. Brown or white, I can't find out. But I'll have organic when he gets here.' Nichol has researched his primary source. He knew all along she would not last on the road.

It is the part about the food — the word bananas — that causes his voice to rise, his grief to spill. She is a target and so hangs up.

If she built a house, if she and Nichol moved away from Sapperton's worker houses and histories and built one, it would be in the country, so the land and the house could be the same as voices and harmony. But not a farmhouse, it would have shingles and be small enough to make three people feel close. Nichol would have an office – or a one-room shack down a primrose path in their woods by a slow creek – and she would have a room set up to record songs she's writing and to keep all her wool, and maybe a garden shed for helping plants, exotic ones you have to send away for. The top floor, all of it, with wide and deep windows and wooden floors, would be for Roy. And there would be a porch up there that could be screened so he could sleep on a porch. The garden would be vast and tangly, and brick paths – old brick – would wander through to secret gardens and benches. They'd have sheep so she could learn to spin and dye and build her own wool for knitting, some breed that's good for meat and for wool.

She needs to be on an island, she can't handle being part of this huge thing she's in. Close beaches, woods. She was born in the city, grew up there, but. Nichol calls her a Renaissance woman, but that makes her sound Victorian, as if he's trying to get rid of her. The things that are important to Arden are a logical response to a wild world steeped in bad food, bad air. This house would be on Vancouver Island, right at the bottom. The Pacific Ocean is the greatest producer of oxygen in the world, even greater than the rain forests. With the prevailing winds coming from the west, and no industry out there, the air is the purest on the planet. That's where she wants to be, that's the air she wants in her brain, in Roy's lungs. She wants to be first to breathe it, then let the rest of the world suck on her hand-me-downs. And the house should have dormers, and places to nook and gaze at sheep. Nichol will need a large kitchen.

If Nichol built a house, he would hire his architect friend Damien, put it up in Vancouver, an older neighbourhood, more industrial than pastoral, and it would be modern, ultra chic, tall and narrow, anti-sentimental. Lots of metal, even the shower stall would be hammered copper; the stairs the same. It would be designed so that the rooms do not require walls, absolutely no demon drywall, but are instead divided by the *idea* of division, the suggestion of it by certain functional pieces such as bookcases and a large fireplace, again insulated metal, no hint of the traditional brick or river stone or slate. The kitchen would be bistro style, stainless steel and windows. Concrete floors throughout, a kind of slaughterhouse cleanliness, yet subtly permeated with the colour of cedar. A kind of ironic allusion to the natural world. In fact, he'd want huge neon signs – Las Vegas-style – to hang in the front hallway, one that says IRONY, another maybe HEARTH, and then BEAUTY. They line the hall to the back of the house as if it's Route 66 or the Vegas strip, where the sign is more important than what it marks. There would be no need to have a playroom for Roy, because those distinctions – play versus work – would not exist here or at least would not be emphasized by the space.

He was born on the Island. His parents bought a farmhouse named Primavera, built in 1911 on twelve acres of woods and paddock and marsh by Margaret's Aunt Cassie. Through the trees, the ocean. The house was small, the light from the pantry spilled through to the living room; with the front door open, the hallway and library and even the fireplace danced in light. Tremendous light. The upstairs, one huge room, was his unless Margaret needed to sew and spread out. She made Tom's shirts and her own dresses, and for a while she made Nichol's pants until the elastic waists embarrassed him. A creek ran out back, where their small flock of Dorset sheep drank until July when it dried up. Nichol built boats from scrap wood left around from Tom's weekend projects. He tried to find bits that matched what his encyclopedia said were the proper dimensions for

seaworthiness. Still, it wasn't an ocean boat he most wanted
to build. River steamers should service the creek; they were
important. He'd load them up with supplies for the little
villages along its banks – cedar bark, maple seeds, bracken –
and simulate the sound of a steamer shhhhhhh-shhhhhhhh-
ing downriver. Nichol was shipmaster as far as the
neighbour's barbed-wire fence, what Tom called the stolen
property line. In July, Nichol climbed down the bank to walk
the creek, looking for evidence of the several ships he'd
floated down, but came always to the fence. He looked, too,
into the warm lagoon where the family cooled off in summer
when Tom came home from work, the site of Nichol's first
swimming lessons. Maybe kids found his boats and kept
them.

She wishes for the Valiant but this van is all she has to get her
home. Windows down, she hears the music of the Nimpkish
River, of the logging roads and their massive and precarious
cargo. She hears the chant of the Douglas firs, dropping
needles, acidifying, taking over again. They are the roadside
screen; behind them stand ghost conifers that haunt the new
plain, on this desert we summon another Las Vegas and
prepare for the neon. The land is ruined and that's another
reason to move on.

Music is her temptation to exist, to stay. But it is also:
stigma, penalty, spectre.

Nichol is taking Roy to their doctor, then to clean and sun-
warmed swingsets, to tidy and civil friends, to fun. Arden
watched them sit out in the happy green Valiant for the
longest time this morning, Nichol turned with his arm across
the bench seat like a helpful cabbie, Roy in his car seat in
back, kicking his bare feet and sucking his fingers, offering
them to his handsome dad. She saw Nichol talk and talk and
shake a finger towards the house and lean way over the seat

and kiss each of his little boy's toes and then finally start the engine, cover his face with his hands, push back his hair, and then drive, the gentlest acceleration as they pulled away from the curb.

Nichol knows nothing because she will never speak again. She slept through the daylight and woke curled tight on the loveseat. She pours herself a water glass of brandy. Her mouth feels stiff. And she swallows half. She wanders a house that is now only a frame. It is dusk, and light is intermittent through doorways all lintel, jamb and sill; walls all stud and joist and free of drywall's mask. The risk of slivers: she lifts each foot ballet high and floats from window to window, crosses so many thresholds. These windows − not yet windows, just sash − are wide and round and shape the house's wonder (O!) and she is inside. She is taken with the structure, flirty, circumnavigating from within.

From out there, say if she hid in the flicker of alders across the north end of marshy Vaseaux Lake, from out there she might appear wanton, an erring sister, a siren buoyant in this gulf, her breasts a lure, framed as they are, again and again, by this structure, these facets of the house. You might think − you've read bad books, you've *read* it − that nipples high and hard like these (champagne silk camisole that belonged to her mother) signal complicity, want. From there, these windows echo − O! − delight.

But you are not out there. What burns in her fast and fouled blood is inside here, not outside there, where you are. It is: what could be closed is left open; there is a plan or not; an end or not; a reason or none.

Here is a moment of clarity: it is only hours to Vaseaux Lake and the van will fly with her.

At dawn, the Econoline with its bright stickers and

shuddering clutch strangles Highway 97, follows this dreadful line.

This is the stage, she thinks, it *has* come to this. She goes on.

A red-winged blackbird sings a perfect pitch across a deeper threshold, the big-horned sheep postcard. The cheap speakers arc with Emmylou and 'Hickory Wind' and Gram Parsons burns for her in the Joshua Tree at the north end of Vaseaux Lake, where the road sweeps and the swans float below. 'I am up,' she thinks, 'finally.'

II
Sylvia

7. Why Does a Noise Break a Window?

A wave of air may break a window exactly as a wave in the sea breaks a wall. Plainly, the noise has only to be loud enough – the waves in the air have only to be big enough – to shake the window more than it can stand. Then it breaks.

The Book of Wonder, Vol. xvii (1932)

This was supposed to be the first official night of our trial separation and now I'm sorry I ever asked Nichol to move out.

Here's the reason for my change of heart.

The first time I asked him to go, last month, Nichol wanted to know what was wrong with our set-up, with him and his kid, Roy, upstairs and me downstairs. We shared the kitchen and bathroom on my floor, took meals together, lined up for the shower.

'It's draining me,' I said.

'Draining you in what way?' he said. 'In what way could this possibly be draining for you, Sylvia?' He figured the honour was all mine, since he pitched in for half the rent.

'The erotic way. Emotionally. I lack confidence because you're up there not wanting to come to bed down here. I find this hard to take,' I said. I thought he would be sympathetic, but he folded his arms across his chest. He was wearing the denim shirt I gave him for Christmas. Blue eyes, blue shirt.

'We agreed, Sylvia,' he said. 'No more sex. You thought of it first. You said I made you feel like a poor substitute, a second fiddle.' I was fed up, more like. When we talked last month, I did not mention the little problem he'd developed.

'I know,' I told him, 'but I need for you to at least start looking for another place.' I said, 'Please.'

He moped around the house. He left classified ads folded

up next to the toaster with crummy-sounding basement apartments circled in red. He'd never lived alone before. I knew he was tormented by the idea of living alone. He can cook, so that wasn't it. One night, last week, late, Roy in bed, I found him sitting on the top step of the back porch, drinking Scotch and crying. I'd never seen him cry. The snow was hard on the trees. He poked at the ice cubes in his glass with two fingers. I leaned down and put my warm hand around the back of his neck and told him he could stay. 'I'll do my best,' I said, hoping his tears were a sign some sex might start, that he was done with the brick wall act.

'That's all I ask,' he said, and went past me, inside, upstairs.

This time, though – tonight's version.

We were out at a lousy local bar, listening to a bad local band, with his most recent former girlfriend Darlene and her new nameless boyfriend. Darlene gave Nichol his certified walking papers six months ago. She complained – and I support her in this aspect – that Nichol was not done grieving his first wife, that issues were unresolved, feelings being repressed. Guilt was a factor, she felt, due to the wife's suicide and his moods. Also, his kid can be a burden, especially if you never wanted kids in the first place. I always suspected some unresolved feelings were on top of that, between Nichol and Darlene – the split was not his choice – but he reassured me he had no interest in Darlene, in any way. There was no love, nothing. 'Good luck to the next guy,' he'd say when I pouted and pushed it.

Darlene is a truly physical woman, rounded and curved, and she dresses in flashy colours to stress her size, sprinkly eye make-up to light her face, then pricey sunglasses to cover it. Her legs, the knees especially, are flat-out fat. Most of us look for ways to hide rolls, but Darlene prefers shiny pantyhose and short skirts. Nichol has since mentioned

Darlene and sausage meat in the same sentence, but men fall for that look, the invitation in it. Face it. Every man folds up in a Darlene once in his life. I never believed it was over for Nichol. He called me by her name on occasions when it seemed too loud to be an innocent slip.

Last night at the bar, into our third pitcher of beer, the band on a break, Darlene and Nichol did some reminiscing: disaster camping trips, favourite war movies, the poached salmon and roasted garlic with three bottles of champagne, the Air Show and swimming nude after it. Boyfriend and I played along, a nice audience. Then Darlene told what was supposed to be a humorous anecdote about Nichol getting pulled over for speeding at two in the morning a couple of weeks ago. The cop comes over and Darlene's spread all over the passenger seat of Nichol's Valiant, passed out, nude except for Nichol's leather vest which covers only bits of her, an empty bottle between her fat legs. They only got a warning, the young cop too shy or green or turned on to file anything.

'Woops,' said Darlene, smiling at me. 'I guess that was supposed to stay secret.' The boyfriend seemed young and hurt by the whole thing, kept his sad eyes on the band tuning up.

I remember the night she was talking about. Nichol coming home in a cab, smelling of ginger and baby powder. I'd been up most of the night with his kid's fever shrieks and nightmares. Nichol told me about getting pulled over, hence the cab. But I never got told the part about Darlene or the vest I got him for Valentine's Day so he could look more masculine. As far as I was concerned, it was just him in the car that night. Somebody lied.

We got back from the bar, Nichol walked the sitter home. My imagination fired and wondered what was taking him so long. He came in, put the chain on the front door and started up the stairs to his room without saying goodnight, without anything concerning me at all. Both of us were loaded from last call margaritas (Jimmy Buffett medley). I caught his ankle on the fifth stair and brought him down. I hit his face. I slapped his ears. He didn't fight back, just defended himself when necessary. I wanted him to put me in the hospital. I was screaming, 'Liar, you fucking liar,' or something to that effect, and smacking him and trying to bring my knee up fast and hard between his legs. But I was drunker than him. Finally, he grabbed my shoulders, shoved me against the front door and I fell. I pretended to pass out, too spent to fight any more. My hands hurt. He went up to bed. I could hear his deep voice talking to the more sing-song one of his kid.

Despite the headache, this morning I was listening to early news on TV in the living room and bowling with the boy up and down the hall. He's accurate for three years old. Nichol announced to me he'd found a place. He appeared proud. The boy had been told already and yelled, 'Stee-rike,' loud and long the way I'd taught him.

'Whereabouts?' I asked. Now I was looking at TV news – tarty starlet, unknown cause of death – drinking a glass of cold beer, eating the pumpkin pie he made yesterday (yes, flaky).

'Just a couple blocks from here. We're gonna be neighbours, Sylvia,' he said. Then he reached calmly for my beer and took a long drink, like someone who's just won a lot of money and isn't going to share.

Tonight was night number one in their new apartment. The little family. Tonight was our first try at being neighbours.

About six o'clock, I thought I'd go over there out of curiosity, just to see. I'd bought him a Boston fern and a pot-holder shaped like a crab. I'd got his kid a laminated map from downtown: *Proposed Canadian Pacific Routes in British Columbia, 1879*. The boy loves his trains. So there's my excuse. His phone wasn't hooked up yet, another excuse. I just went over there unannounced. It was cold outside, past freezing. I worried about taking a tropical plant into that kind of weather.

His new building has one of those security intercoms, so I buzzed. He came on with lots of background hiss, and I told him it's me.

'What's this all about?' he said.

'It's a housewarming,' I said, when it was my turn. I could hardly make out what he was saying.

'I don't think you want to come up here, Sylvia,' he said. 'I've got Darlene up here.'

'I think I'd better come up,' I said. I'd had a glass of Southern Comfort after dinner – one of Nichol's chicken pot pies from the freezer – and I could feel it making me rowdy. I wanted the three of us to prove my suspicions, once and for all.

'No, Sylvia,' he said, 'We're having a nice meal. I'll come over later. Just go on home.' Then the intercom went blank. There was to be no further discussion. So I went home, like he told me to.

I knew one day I'd be glad I rented a house with a garage, even though backing out is a nightmare. It's too small, but tonight that seemed a point in its favour. I didn't even go into the house. I went straight to the garage door, off the back yard. The lawn crackled, my feet left marks. I wondered if I was hurting the grass and if yellow footprints would show up in March when everything thawed, tracks of my tears kinda thing.

My kitchen window and a street lamp over on the corner gave off enough light so it wasn't too dark to see what I was doing. It's an old garage, it has windows, though only the one facing the kitchen isn't boarded up. So I could see around in there. I could see my car, the last tenant's garden tools on the walls, the blade of Nichol's chainsaw locked to his bicycle.

The big doors, the ones that open onto the lane are held

shut by a two-by-four, like a barn door in the movies. You see the hero lift it off when the barn's on fire and the horses need to make a run for it. I knew I had to find a way to plug up the spaces at the bottom, the sides, along the top. There was air getting in and out all around those doors. I had to stop it. My car took up most of the space, and there wasn't much room for anything else, but I found a pile of empty plastic bags stuffed into a corner, behind a stack of somebody's bald tires. Steer manure bags. I had spread it on the vegetable patch in September, looking forward to a little salad garden along the fence, maybe some herbs, sage, basil. I like the feathery look of fennel and its liquor smell. Nichol wanted something called cilantro for his recipes.

I had about ten bags to work with. I folded each one lengthwise and tried to place the folds to the outside of the garage so I'd get a seal. This took patience. Of which I have practically none at the best of moments; this was not the best of moments. By the end, I was just stuffing bags any place I could feel icy air coming in.

It had been a couple of days since I'd started up the old tin can, as Nichol called it. Or 'coffin on wheels', he sometimes said. I pumped the gas six times, seven times, held down and turned the key. The battery didn't like it, but the thing started, first try. I turned the heater up full, got out and crunched into the house, trying to hit the stepping stones this time. Lawn care, you could call it.

I can't emphasize enough how cold it was. So the first thing I did was find warmer clothes. I wanted to be comfortable at this time. I wanted good music, the right music, so I dug up some Everly Brothers I'd taped for Nichol, the first time I thought he was moving out, something that would make him think about me, regret the split. The kid used to dance to 'Wake Up, Little Susie', but I was not permitted to observe: 'Don't watch,' he'd whine until I turned away. I got the bottle of sparkling wine I always have at the back of the fridge for celebrations or good moods. I went to the bathroom and swallowed – I think this is where I made a mistake – a whole package of antihistamine pills. Last spring was good for my hay fever, so I had lots left. I thought they'd put me to sleep. I wanted to sleep through the rougher parts.

There's always the question of leaving a note. I wasn't mad, I just wanted to get away. I didn't want Nichol to suffer or feel guilty for the rest of his life. His first wife took care of that trip. The little boy was never fond of me; we'd had our mishaps, our fights, our power struggles. He has taken on, I am told by his father, a few of his mother's better qualities and also most of her flaws. As in, he wants to do what he wants to do and cannot cope with the word no. Hence, I have needed to slap his face; I believe I was justified in this. If they are not disciplined at three years old, by fourteen they are skinning cats and kicking heads. (My brothers, for example.) Once, when I was grouting tiles around the bathtub, I became impatient and understandably frustrated and carried him roughly to his bedroom and closed him in there. After that, he would point at me and say to Nichol, 'in the dark closet,' but I never went that far.

No, the kid would not be traumatized by another gone mother.

Back to me. Furthermore, I had no interest in making Darlene pay for hanging on when letting go would've been right.

I felt tired, that's all. I was worn out by it. I wanted to get away. I was willing to be dead to achieve that goal. So there didn't seem to be any percentage in leaving a note. Just the same, I craved the last word.

But as I put a pencil to the back of an old grocery receipt, there's someone pounding on the back door. I opened it, thinking, him? And there's some short guy pumping his legs, slapping his own shoulders, trying to keep warm.

'Sorry to bother you, but I walked past here a while ago on

my way to the store and I noticed a car running in your garage. Now I walked back and it's still running. I just wanted to make sure something wasn't going on,' he said. He's wearing women's gloves.

I've got my winter coat on and a scarf wrapped around my neck so I know my story's airtight. 'It takes a while for it to warm up,' I say. 'And then the phone rang and I got stuck in a conversation.'

This and my big smile seemed to satisfy him. 'I just didn't want anyone to get to the point where things are that bad. Things are never that bad,' he said, and started down the steps, taking care not to slip. Not very masculine in a lot of ways.

'Thanks anyway,' I said, and closed the door. I bet he went home feeling like a good Samaritan, like a million bucks.

So I put in the note, 'Nichol. I went out. Sylvia.'

The engine in that car never did burn clean. There was blue air hanging in the garage, but I figured that was a good sign. More toxic. I closed the garage door and noticed the light I'd left on in the kitchen coming in under it. I took off my coat and took off one of the sweaters I'd layered myself into. I made it myself, Irish knit, off-white like the classics but I'd used sale Sayelle from Tanner's drugstore. After that, I never bought synthetic again. Cables and bobbles and calculating – all that work – for no heat, heavy pilling, constant squeak. I shoved it under the door with the toe of my boot. I put my coat back on in a hurry.

I got into the car.

The heater was only working so-so; the coat was still necessary, but bulky. You are not supposed to drive in an overcoat; they restrict movement. I put in a tape, unscrewed the wine, adjusted the seat all the way back. I turned the music louder and guzzled, felt fast. The dim light in there was soothing, like a lounge.

What confused me was whether you're supposed to roll the

windows down and breathe what's in the air, or leave them up and breathe what's in the car. I left them up for one side of the tape, and then figured that must not be right. I felt fine. However, the cold came in fresh with them down, and that didn't seem right either.

By this time my lips were numb from the drugs and I was almost drunk. I was impatient, not sleepy yet. I had no idea how long this was going to take. I replayed all the rotten things Nichol has done to me: called me by the wrong name; talked over my head on purpose; criticized my taste in music; believed Roy instead of me; read books in bed; Darlene; made us sit at the table for his perfect meals; I had to set it, cloth napkins and everything, matching salt and pepper, no television. These memories only activated my adrenaline.

So I tried to put myself to sleep with happy thoughts about my childhood on the river in Ontario, the summer we fixed up the dingy and swam nude with the boys, my dead parents and the values they gave me, favourite singers and good songs, flowers I like.

All the time, I'm thinking: 'I'm glad I'm doing this. Do I want to be doing this? I'm glad I'm doing this.' Always that back and forth. Another reason to just try to go to sleep. I wanted to wake up elsewhere. It occurred to me that I bought the car from a close friend. His reaction?

Instead of sleeping, I started to throw up. It must've been the antihistamines because booze never does that to me. I don't even get hangovers. I made it out of the car, hauled the garage door open — finally ruined my cheapo Irish knit — and fell down in the back yard. The hard grass bit my face.

When the throwing up was finished, I was too depressed, defeated, to start all over, but sober enough to be afraid I might try again later. It was getting late by this time, and Nichol's absence did not go unnoticed. He'd promised he would come by tonight.

We all wonder what it would be like to use a so-called crisis line. I picked one out of the phone book, the one listed for my neighbourhood, for my needs. I didn't realize they were that customized. The woman I got didn't put me on hold like they do for a joke on television. She sounded early twenties and kind of sad or bored or immune to everything hard. She lacked energy but she got my name and address, professional. She had no sense of humour, or maybe they're trained not to find things funny. I started to laugh about what I'd done, but she didn't. So then I cried.

I become verbally abusive when mistreated.

'Are you still feeling self-destructive, Sylvia?' she said.

'What's your name?' I said.

'I'm Sue,' she said after a second. 'How are you feeling – now?'

I started with something like, 'What do you know about pain?' and then went on, hollering at Sue and trying to make her cry, too. She wouldn't, they train that out of them. She just kept asking safe questions. I don't think I called her any truly filthy names. 'Cunt' rings a bell. 'I want to go to the hospital,' I said, 'I just want to sleep.'

'Do you want me to send someone?' she smarmed.

'Sure.' I thought she meant an ambulance. I like the idea of being carried on a stretcher, slung between able-bodied caregivers.

I made strong tea and by the time it was cool enough to drink, I was completely straight, except for the headache. I took my mug into the little sitting room at the front of the house. The vacuum cleaner, I noticed, was in the middle of the floor, still plugged in. On the sports channel, country music celebrities played charity golf in Nashville. I dated a guitar player for awhile – Johnny Constabaris – and I'm told he caddies for Reba McEntire. When he's not screwing groupies. I stood at the window and waited for a siren.

When the cop cars flash up I think, 'Just great. They're

gonna run me in for being fed up.' A doorbell seems too sweet for this scenario.

There are three huge young men standing in the doorway of the little room, all of them stretching to get a good look at the woman going nuts. One of them takes charge.

'Somebody here got a bad case of the blues?' he says. What crappy radio station has he been listening to?

'Don't put it that way,' I say.

'You're Sylvia MacDermid?' he says.

'I'm trying not to be, but I'm doing it all wrong,' I say.

The cutesy banter seems to win him over. Men. The other two guys are looking around the room. Keeping track of my hands. Waiting to catch Shania Twain tee up on the tube.

'What's got you feeling so bad it had to come to this, Sylvia?' he says and crouches down like a baseball catcher. He takes off his hat. He's got a gun. 'Why don't you let it all out and see how it feels to just do some straight talking,' he says.

I'm just about throwing up again at all the phony baloney but for some lonely reason, I tell him things. I say I'm unhappy at my job, that I don't feel there's any future in waitressing and I get treated like a fucking servant all the time. I have bad dreams, I say, about too many customers all at once and all the ketchup bottles are sticky. I say I'm unhappy with my personal life, that I'm trying to make some changes but don't think I'm doing it right. That I'm afraid I'm not mother material and never will be. I tell him I love a man whose smart-aleck wife is dead, he is always mad at who knows, no tender kisses, but I love him in a way, his boy, too.

'Why don't you become a police officer, Sylvia?' the one in charge says. 'We're recruiting all the time.'

'I believe I fall short of the height requirement.'

'That's all been changed now. The department is consciously recruiting for more females,' he says. 'It's a good time to be a woman. Think about it,' he says. I expect him to give me a business card, but he doesn't. It feels over.

'I don't think I'm as bad now. I'm going to bed. Thanks for your company, you really got me through.' I say all this as I herd them out the front door. Glen Campbell eagles and the crowd shrieks. They don't make me sign anything, or want to check the garage for evidence. I wonder if I have a record now. Will Mr Fraser across the street ever help me prune the apple tree again?

Nichol said he would come but I know he's gone.

The sheets are cold and blankets heavy across my stomach. I slide my legs, scissor them, across the cotton, under the wool, to warm up the bed. I make small circles on my stomach with my right hand, and twist curls in my hair with the left. My lips are still numb. My face, I know, has gone puffy and white like someone who takes pricey drugs on a regular basis. The house is quiet; cold twigs snap right outside the bedroom window. I think of the friend who sold me the car, how he gave me a deal because of knowing Nichol, and I am grateful, knowing there are men like that in the world. I am glad there are men like that in the world.

III

Elizabeth

8. Does the Smoke of a Train Go the Opposite Way to the Train?

When the smoke leaves the funnel of the engine it is really moving forward, like the engine itself, and at the same rate. The smoke is poured into the ocean of air through which the train is pushing. The air tends to stop the train, as it tends to stop everything that moves through it. But though it retards the heavy train a good deal, it retards the light smoke far more. The smoke does not really go the opposite way to the train; it is actually going in the same direction, but so much more slowly that it seems to be going backward when seen from a fast train passing it.

The Book of Wonder, Vol. VIII (1932)

Elizabeth Dixon was awake at midnight, so there was no panic when the night had its trauma. She was drowning her son's pyjama bottoms in the laundry room tub, fast cold water to soak another set stain. Turn off the tap, and sirens come along Rocky Point Road; they turn in front of Lester Frank's barn and climb the hill at the low end of Bilston Creek Road, past Declan's field of just cut hay rained on that afternoon, louder at the bottom of her driveway and gone past – *Well, it's not me they want* – up and around to the unpaved end of her road. Three: Bickerdike's firetruck straight from the hall; the police cruiser from Quick's Bottom curve, where they lurk on Saturday nights; an ambulance almost six minutes behind, smooth from the new hospital off the highway.

Danny stood in the dimlit kitchen, fresh pyjamas cinched at his rainbarrel waist. He tidied the night air with both hands, shrill sound waves softened by his full fingers catching the rascal bits that flew for the ceiling. 'Somebody's going for trouble,' he said with fatherly articulation and stretched to look out the sink window, still typing the keys of the night. The siren shrieks dimmed, but the sky flickered like a campfire's heart. He pounded off down the dark hallway, stopped outside his mother's bedroom, turned back to look at her in the kitchen, peered again into her room, and proceeded to his own.

Elizabeth Dixon set her mug of tea on the counter and had the bookmark out of her novel, was about to sit for fifteen minutes' transition from duty to dream, when the thump and throaty scrape rose from the low-end hill of Bilston Creek Road. 'Oh boy, now we know,' Danny sirened from his room. She went to check. Not in his bed, not at the window watching tomorrow's news. In behind the door. 'That was my father's train. It's a good train and it was the last of the old cprs. That train's wrecked. It was a good train, it was a darn good service.' Mrs Dixon purred to him, called him sweet names, held his hand to bed. He fell hard to sleep.

So hard he didn't hear the night tangle. Sirens from both sides of town converged down the hill, the sky bright with vehicular panic. Bickerdike, cruiser, highway ambulance backtracked so fast we're in the jerks of a silent movie, slapstick, the tinkly piano trying to keep up. And a night that started good and dark began to tempt neighbours with special effects. Those who wished to look into disaster, or to see if disaster looks back, or maybe watch for good news and a way to wear it, these neighbours emerged from their homes to pilgrim down the hill. Elizabeth Dixon, white robe buttoned high, looked gothic and frail, greyed hair short but tumbling long on top, stood at the deer fence beyond the raspberries, her hair gone girlish in the breeze and summer heat.

'Liz.' So many intrusions that this one did not startle her.

She wears a pumpkin house coat which reveals old knees and the dip of disappeared thigh. 'Mother.' Without slippers, her mother's enormous raptor toenails are plainly visible. Elizabeth said, 'I'm not going all the way down, you go if you want. I don't want to look. You might need something on your feet.' The women stand together, move a few steps forward and stop.

'I heard everything,' her mother said. 'I've been up to the bathroom, and I heard two sets of sirens and what sounded like a car hit a house. There's Mrs Bowen-Roberts off to have a goggle.'

'Go on if you'd like, mother, but I'm tired. Danny's had a night.' Elizabeth Dixon held her mother's elbow and they walked together to the end of the driveway.

'Have a look through these,' and the mother slipped sparkling opera glasses out from her deep pocket, tried to loop the strap over Mrs Dixon's head, but could not reach that high.

'Ambulance chaser,' Mrs Dixon said and pushed the glasses back at her mother, a customary dry tease, no harm. They walked out past the newspaper box, stepped from driveway to road, and the mother had a look through the glasses.

'Mrs Bowen-Roberts has her son with her, grown taller than his own mother. Lester Frank doesn't have a shirt on and his idiot black Lab is in and out of the ditch at a limp. Nichol is balanced on his bicycle seat, as usual; no fancy helmet tonight, no ballet pants or bare ankles, no little boy. The ambulance is backing up, but I can't make out what for. Nobody's talking down there. You have a look.'

Elizabeth Dixon took the tiny glasses and turned away from the road to look, instead, back at Danny's dark window, her bedroom, her mother's runway deck wrapped around that end of the house. She looked to see her realm enlarged and yet at a greater distance. 'Who's that just getting there?' her mother asked, and Mrs Dixon turned back to peer at the cluttered night. The little crowd blurred and softened, moved slowly as if filmed now by deadbeat photographers. That far away, feet make no sound.

'There's the woman Willy married. Sandra Bell. Seems to know Nichol or what else would her hand be doing there.'

'Do you see the Mister anywhere?'

'Just her, and she's got some sort of baby doll pyjamas –'

'Let me look.' Sandra Bell stood beside Nichol's bike as if teaching him to ride a two-wheeler, one hand on the handlebars, the other at the back of the seat, her arms long and smooth in the flash of red lights. 'No sense of occasion, that one.' Sandra leaned close into his shoulder, to keep him safe, motoring. 'Single parent,' said Mrs Dixon's mother with anxious disrespect.

'He is, she's not,' said Mrs Dixon. 'I'm done with this. Don't get cold.'

Nichol imitated his own father, pulling horsetails along the fence line one at a time and stuffing them into a huge plastic bag. The little boy could just be seen down in the low corner of the field where the blackberries part over the water hatch, having a long look at the accident site, the young people, the teenage mourners come and go, the pile of artifacts that grew and toppled into the mangled ditch. 'That's a big job but I appreciate what you're doing there,' Mrs Dixon said as she approached Nichol's work zone. She was in uniform: knee-stained slacks and heather grey cardigan, men's cotton garden gloves. Her last tenants had let the lawn drain and the water collect, had failed to clear the culvert many times, and the horsetail grew thick and spread under her fence to infest the berries and the dahlias. Pleasant green from a distance but not a prayer for crops.

'It won't do much this year, Liz, but maybe a start on next,' he said. 'I've got a guy coming to talk about drainage next week. I'm told he has a machine that turns the soil and plants drainpipe wherever you need it, eighteen inches deep, if you're interested.' He demonstrated the action. He curved and turned his body and arms like a belly dancer. 'Roy wants a horse, but your field's too wet for big hooves.' He accepted the yellow plums she took from her sweater's pockets and ate them both whole before he spit the pits into his plastic bag. He looked over to where the boy powered short legs up the hill, through the mangrove islands of swamp grass the sheep won't touch. 'That was quite a night for around here.' One teenage boy, the driver, had died as he attempted to escort a carload of drunken friends away from the detonated party house, to evade that first set of sirens, and turned over at the bottom of the hill into the deep and wide ditch dug last winter by Declan – her other son – to divert subdivision run-off from his machine shop.

Nichol suggested a 'Hello, Mrs Dixon' from the boy before the list proceeded. Roy looked sternly into the distance and counted off his fingers, started and restarted on his hands:

> 'Six teddy bears,
> soccer ball,
> lacrosse stick,
> track pants,
> electric guitar,
> twenty-eight bunches of flowers,
> someone's nightie,
> a case of beer,
> a dictionary,
> a ship in a bottle,
> a small black-and-white television,
> a stack of record albums,
> a shiny pillow,
> a black leather jacket (like the one I've got that was my mom's),
> a Barbie doll in a wedding dress.

'And they've made a circle of rocks, like in a graveyard, and all the kids are sitting in a circle holding hands with each other and sometimes they sing together, but then the girls cry

and they all stop and hug. Okay, bye, Nichol.' She handed
Roy another plum from her sweater pocket and he said,
'Wow, thank you very much,' his new teeth too big for his soft
little face, and peered at her eyes and spat the pit into his
father's outstretched palm. Roy was not like boys Elizabeth
knew, nothing like her own. Her husband would have had
him on weed detail six hours a day at that age. Her own two
boys were put to work – Danny too – because there was
firewood to cut, drainage ditches to dig, fence wire to pull
tight around the posts, and chickens to harvest, slaughter,
scald and pluck. Had they even known his first name?

'I probably should have got him up to look last night, but
now it's a mystery he wants to solve. He doesn't mean to be
morbid,' Nichol said.

'Seems like every little boy,' she said, but she wondered
about little boys and couldn't remember typical and not.

Nichol and his son arrived at the start of the wettest winter
in memory except for the flood year in 1963. Nichol had
signed the lease, had given her the bundle of cheques, and she
did not see them except once at Christmas when they brought
her a spangled greeting card the boy made. They met Danny
on that good day and so no doubt got the wrong idea about
him: manageable, calm, just somewhat odd. By January,
Danny was back to restless and rough, but Nichol and the boy
had not come again.

Through January and February she watched their
windows: brightly lit until she went to bed at nine-thirty, still
lit when Danny got her up at three a.m. When Roy tramped
off to kindergarten at eight o'clock, the curtains closed till his
return at twelve-thirty. Music played through the morning,
women's recorded voices clear, high and sad, wavered up
from the fields, an intrusion, at first, and then a good sign: he
was there, still there. When the school bus dropped the boy at
the bottom of the hill, Nichol stood in the middle of the field
with his arms above his head waving and the boy ran all the

way, sometimes disappearing behind winter canes of wild
rose, until they came together in a sweep of hug. The one
deep snow in February, miraculous so near the water and last
straw for the church hall's roof, Nichol waded out in the field
in shorts and high gumboots, no shirt or hat, snow whipping
up the hill off the water, and the hug proceeded as always.
Then the little boy unravelled his own long scarf and draped
it over his father's thin shoulders, wrapped it twice around his
father's neck. They disappeared into the house and began the
broken code of windows again. She couldn't get over the
shorts.

She thought perhaps the father drank, or was running
from work, but when spring erupted and he put new lambs
and ewes in the field, borrowed her rototiller to turn the
crusty vegetable patch, started spinach and onions growing in
rows, asked for a rhubarb recipe, she knew something was
over. The wet of winter had finished some torment for him
and now he could neighbour. Nichol dug holes for her new
sequoias, drove sturdy stakes in the right places to support
her Austrian pines – a screen for her mother's deck – against
March winds. He repaired the breaks in her hoses, spliced
ropes, and they shared ginger beer on his lawn when the work
seemed done for the day and the wind was calm. After school,
Roy let tennis balls sail over the fence, fetched them, stopped
a while, and scanned her brown and wrinkled face. They were
friendly to Danny. No, Nichol was not a drinker. He was
ghost-drunk.

By mid-May, revelations and secrets were divulged. Each
afternoon in the pin oak's shade prompted one step further
into clarity. He was waiting for his own property to come
vacant. It was family land, some waterfront, an old house
called Primavera at the southern tip of the Island, exposed on
all sides. He had signed a lease to a family in need – two
years – and would have to wait out his generosity to move in
himself. One mystery solved. Over the years, Mrs Dixon had

thought the property was bought by off-shore Netherlanders, had heard and relayed this rumour herself. And now the real story was coming into view; it felt like a refreshment. So Nichol had been that quiet little boy with Declan at school. His mother had lovely blond hair and would swim the length of the lake twice a week in winter. In summer, she would be down at the beach below Rocky Point Road, oblivious to kelp and cold. His father was a blank, she could not remember him.

'You *knew* my mother?' Nichol said, on a break from staking her peonies. Why should this surprise him, a matter of mathematics and geography?

'I've been here for forty years, Nichol. We didn't all leave when your parents did, you know. And we didn't all show up when you came back. Some of us have been here all along.' She was annoyed by what could be the arrogance of his youth, the assumption that the world follows one human being and all others trail behind to watch the only important version of history unfold. The wind was coming up the hill, a dark rain cloud behind it, and she wanted the bean patch tilled today.

He put a hand on her forearm, their first touch. 'Sorry, Liz. Let me explain. I've had to think of myself. And Roy. Under our circumstances, I forgot others. This place has been far from my mind. Sandra Bell tells me many who grieve go through a period of emotional blindness.'

'Well, I'm not sure about any of that. I was teasing you.'

'Humour, too, in short supply.'

Nichol began to mention his wife, Roy's mother. In all their garden conversations, he never did say she was dead, but Mrs Dixon knew it couldn't be said. Nichol was careful with words, understood their subtleties, and would not use such lean ones as *passed away* or *gone* or *widower* or the more direct but too dark, *died*. He did not avoid admission, just flaccid talk. One morning they trimmed seed heads off

Canada thistles in the lot next to Elizabeth's, Roy the boy searching nearby stumps for renegade chicken eggs. Nichol straightened and said suddenly, 'Arden saw the world in images but lacked the imagination to give herself a happy story.'

Had he come to that conclusion with the shades drawn and the music playing? 'What about your wife's family?' Elizabeth returned. 'Does Roy have another grandma he should be visiting?'

'That, you see, would annoy his mother. Arden left her family for good when she was a teenager, lots of reasons, mostly bad ones, but reasons. She still had a younger sister and mother in New Westminster, but Arden's rule: absolutely no contact. I think it went both ways.'

'That should have been mended, for the boy's sake.'

'Should have been mended for Arden's, too. No one should make themselves that bereft. But she would not be pushed, she would not be shown an easier path.'

'Then none of it was your responsibility, Nichol. She was a difficult weed: prickly, stubborn roots.' He looked at Elizabeth's gloved hands, grew quiet, handed her his clippers, and went looking for Roy in the trees.

Sandra Bell wears hats: red toque, straw Maquinna, purple velvet pillbox and others; they carry and conceal mounds of thick strawberry-blond hair. The hat comes off – that stagy moment – the hair tumbles over her shoulders framing her almost lovely face. The many boots and shoes appear soft and clean. Her filmy skirts billow in the doorway of the corner store. No passion for make-up: her face does not soften with smiles or fast colour. She is out of balance with semi-rural; ostentation in sheep country is like rhinestones on a barn cat.

Sandra Bell is writing a book, a social history of this area from before the settlers to present day. 'I believe the story of place should ring and resonate,' she told Elizabeth at the church's Lily Tea (pillbox, black Mary Janes, cranberry-coloured wrinkled cheesecloth skirt) in April. Sandra held her cup and saucer high, a shortbread pinched between her fingers and flaunted like a cigarette. 'It's not history in the conventional sense, not the history you've come to trust. Maybe it will take the *form* and *richness* and *complexity* and *imagery* and and and *music* of a long poem; maybe I'll *reenact* time in the form of a journal, one kept secretly by a First Nations woman married to a Royal Engineer – a sapper – or something.'

'What language would you use for that?' Elizabeth asked. The cookies were packaged, the tea weak and only warm. Women who did not like Elizabeth or her dead husband chatted in corners.

'I know what you're saying. I've sper t two months in the archives covering the colonial thing.' And the hat came off, the hair a bright cascade in the dark church hall. 'Now I'm on to James Douglas and the Hudson's Bay Company. Did you know the foundation of his summer house is just down the hill on the beach at the end of Wiltshire Road? Very spooky. Very spooky. But important.' This news of 'the project' gave Elizabeth more faith in Willy, the farm, and fewer misgivings about Sandra. And there's a legitimate reason she doesn't work or mother. 'If I can get more funding – probably Indian Affairs this time – I would consider a collaboration with William for a chapter on early medicinal practices. For example, stinging nettle. Oregon grape. Camas. Did you know all of these have been used to cure serious disease? That whole smallpox fiasco would have turned out much, much worse if not for native plants.'

Elizabeth was telling Nichol about taking the hay off his field. His handsome cowboy's face, his smooth skin, went through abrupt changes – deathly green-white to vivid red, the skin dampening and then drying, his sandy hair appearing combed, then shaken, then combed again. The haying had always been done by Declan. Nichol was complaining about deer in his roses, in his everything, and she told how Declan's tractor customarily overcame three or four fawns in that knee-high field in June, but unable to see them tucked and bedded down, he would run over them and send their brown bodies through the blades. Perhaps, she said, because the hay was left last year, the population had gone up. Every sentence required Nichol to respond with a suitable and painful physical shift, no hidden feelings possible. To end it for him, she said, 'The scraps of deer are food for kettling hawks.'

'You've made a poem, Liz,' he said, his breathing settled down, his eyes gone forsaken and seeking a suitable tide now across the strait. 'I wish I'd made that poem.'

The police investigation of Declan's ditch began. The yellow tape surrounded the scuffed and dragged gravel, fluorescent paint outlined the skid marks that would endure for years, imprints of the night. Last year, before the wet winter, they'd surfaced the new road down the hill and forgot drainage. Declan is a man with many machines and so one Friday morning, after the traffic's rush to the city, he climbed into his excavator and in an hour had dug a wide and deep trench at the roadside. A proper culvert was called for, but this would do. For Declan, bigger is better, wider is stronger. The deeper it is, the longer it lasts. The squad cars come and go with their tape measures and spray paint. They have spoken with Declan, but he keeps details from his mother and so from her mother.

The morning paper quoted the surviving boy in the new hospital, his hands shattered and kneecap torn away, his hot face awash with ointments, his best friend thrown high into Douglas fir and then hard onto new blacktop, his girlfriend little more than stunned in the back seat, drunk now on trauma and the attention. She weeps by his bedside, prone to a cinematic version of tragedy, bereft of permanent scars. He told the reporter, 'There's nothing to do. There's no programs for teenagers, no places to go. What else are we supposed to do? Why did our parents think this place was going to be any good?' So landscape is to blame, the golden spread of Spanish brome and the deer birthing in hay fields, the ocean's promises, the relentless wind from all ways to underline their ultimate exposure. The adults who refuse the city's bimbo glamour and look to landscape for comfort, order and definition, they are culpable. I suppose, thinks Elizabeth Dixon, we are all to blame.

Danny carries a chair from the kitchen and spends hours at the end of the driveway, watching for police cars and writing down their numbers onto a reporter's ringed notepad. At the end of the day, he is hyper with figures and new colours, and he locomotes around the house shouting, 'Five-oh-six is a good train. Tacked. And the six-twelve, too.' Elizabeth gives him syrup for sleep. For a while, he lies with his face to the wall, humming along with his golden singers, flicking at the webs they construct around his ears. And then sleeps.

Night pulls scent from the stock and nicotiana lining the deck at her end of the house. A tall wall of trellis, clustered with white jasmine, keeps her mother invisible. Still, the mumble of her television through window screens. On these close August nights, Elizabeth Dixon takes her soda water and lime juice onto the high deck and watches for change over the Strait of Juan de Fuca. She is on a hilltop, and looks across her own cropped field and the now fleecy lambs, over Nichol's house, his Beatrix Potter brassicas and long lily bed glowing pink, across Rocky Point Road below with the fast cars of evening – teenagers headed for trouble or a movie – past the concrete plant tucked into a corner of what was once her husband's land, the settlers' best field before Joe Dixon owned it. Out where the sun still haunts the water, a long train of logs runs behind Angus Donaldson's towboat. She knows it's his by the shape, the classic lines formed by a wooden hull, history's imprint on its low sides and stern; his father's, a bequest. This must be high tide.

Sandra Bell's pale blue Austin Cambridge climbs the hill at the pace of vintage cylinders and heritage wheels. Regardless of the slow, her springer spaniel prods the passing air, eager for the fugitive scent of sheep and cougars. She drives at a speed so languorous the dog's long ears don't fly. The evening has dropped into dark, but Mrs Dixon sees the car stop just beyond the end of her driveway. The headlights turned out. She hears a lovely British thunk as the car door slams. Nichol's porch light: he was watching. Roy's bedroom has been dark for an hour and now the porch is the little house's only bright place. The spaniel races from the road to greet Nichol there, races back to Sandra, and back and forth, binding the two with a sloppy trajectory, tighter, until they meet on the porch in silence. One hand to join, Nichol backs through the door, pulls her through with the dog tangling their feet, and the light is extinguished and none are lit. Why drive? She usually walks, or rides an old bicycle. Did she tell her husband the dog needs a run on the beach, or maybe that's where they've been and this is the last stop before home.

Willy grew up on his parents' horse farm down the hill where he and Sandra now live. He drove his father's Ford Mercury pick-up in to the university for six years: philosophy, then engineering, then agriculture for a year over on the mainland, then home again to have a go at medicine. Summers, he worked for Elizabeth Dixon's husband, built fences, loaded bales, and picked apples at harvest time. The pay was bad, but Willy worked. Sandra was a student by then, looking into the history of art, living alone and drinking coffee in a little white-walled apartment off-campus. She'd gone quiet after an affair with a creative writing professor, a young man fresh up from the States: prestigious degree; well-received first novel; a personalized no-thank-you note from the *New Yorker*. He mumbled praise for her poems and suggested a meeting in his office. 'Nice image,' he told her repeatedly, and she took it for the flirt it was meant to be; her poems didn't improve one syllable.

Meanwhile: Willy. Whom Sandra met in two crowd-pleaser English classes, one on 'Medicine and Magic in the Dark Ages', the other on children's literature. He didn't talk in class, but leased two acres adjacent to the campus and grew hard-necked garlic he sold to a co-op in the Fraser Valley. Before class, between and after class, he would drive to the field and weed, plant, break off curling seed heads; on weekends, he'd be in the library at eight in the morning. He left the Mercury loaded with sheep manure in the parking lot, took a break for lunch and dumped it, spread it, and went back to the stacks to consider the ethics and strategies of pediatric care, to compose a style of his own. One year he tried leeks, but they were too low maintenance, not enough for him to do. And irrigation was a problem. So back to garlic which the custodial west coast rain looks after until low-summer harvest.

Women with hopes do not choose farmers. He probably smelled of manure and was – still is – a thin five foot six. Maybe the Mercury. Sandra had no rivals for his diverted attention, apart from the bulbs. Why no children? Spiteful town gossips, those who decry a city girl gone country, suggest she has lost interest in Willy as his garden has grown. Mrs Bowen-Roberts considers the hot-toned gladioli and zinnias growing alongside dusty green broccoli to be only a pretext of cooperation. The pretty Austin waiting at the end of Elizabeth's driveway was a gift on their last anniversary – number five? – and must have cost many crops; it is seen by some here as pathetic bribe.

* * *

At midnight, Danny arrived in her room – she knew he was there before she climbed awake – and told his mother the express train was boarding and could he ride in the caboose, his hands wild and his pajamas sagged with wet. 'I did a swim last stop,' he told her defensively, tucking scraps of air beneath his arms. There is no need for him to feel shame.

Sandra's Austin is gone, and the waver of women singing lonely songs rises from Nichol's wide-open back door. Some religions – entire cultures – are premised on the rule that if you don't like someone's behaviour, or the way they look, their attitude, their tone, you can persuade the whole tribe, community, family, to shun them. Eschew communication and the badly behaved will learn. Just cut them off. Elizabeth can still feel the wide silence of her husband's shuns: undercooked beans, cold dinner plates, unmade beds, Danny's night wandering, all her fault and punishable by days or weeks of shunning. Declan now uses similar tactics, though his are honed and subtle from a generation of anger: unreturned phone calls, missed appointments with lawyers, a cardboard box of barn kittens left on her deck. And her mother goes for days without a word if guests arrive and she's left out. As if silence fixes everything, a prolonged and vicious spank, a 'Don't you *ever* do that again.'

From here, Elizabeth feels shame on behalf of Nichol, she absorbs the mortification for his indecent acts with Willy's only wife. Elizabeth endures a long moment of silence, dues paid to the tribe so that she may carry on in her fondness for Nichol and for Roy and for their ghost whom she has grown to think of as her own lost daughter; he has described Arden so well.

Elizabeth cannot break the habit of late summer preserves and so her counters are lined with jars, filled and empty. The kitchen is humid, viscous with the savour of cloves and dill. Chutney, cordials, piccalillis and jams will journey to Declan's

cupboards to dwell and darken until he trashes them all or
has a yard sale. Declan is innocent in the death of the
teenager, his ditch a contributing factor along with beer and
wholesale drugs and fanatical speed. Still, the boy who
survived and blamed them all writes letters to tolerant editors
to say the ditch was the cause, that there has been a cover-up
– bogus absolution – due to old-time community ties. 'A rural
community is a lot like the government of the United States,'
he wrote, confusing generations of readers. Arms trade? Junk
food? Extramarital sex? Massacres in dusty villages?

Her mother rushed into the kitchen, opera glasses hanging
around her puckered neck, bare feet and arms, some sort of
cotton African dress swirling well above her knees. 'Liz, the
young man needs help in the field. I've been watching for an
hour and he hasn't moved.' Between the stirring, chopping,
squeezing through the pinkened cheesecloth, Elizabeth has
tried to persuade Danny to put on coveralls. Today, he says,
he's not going to walk the line and so *this* – he slaps his chest
with both hands – will be fine. Naked, he is the ballooning
physique of any other forty-five-year-old man. Wearing only
his father's huge untied, fur-lined air force boots, he followed
the two women through the gate, into the hot grass of Nichol's
field. Because of an errant and determined ram and a too-low
fence, the lambing is taking place in autumn and not in
February. Alfalfa and mash for the winter will cost. The
frequent long walk to the small barn in the night will tire him
and make him short with the boy.

Roy was saying quietly, 'Dad. Dad. Dad. It's supposed to
happen here,' speaking low as if to a drug addict or suicide.
Nichol was paying attention, sitting cross-legged, looking into
the little boy's chest for consolation. Arranged in front of
them were three small bodies, one-time triplets, lambs
aborted with three weeks to go. Now, they were black,
mummified, their birth sacks swaddling tight, stockings on
burglars, and dried hard. The ewe paced close by, bleating

and nickering grief, licking the air, her milk bags bright and full. A length of blood and matter dangled from her rear, a further shame. Wasps grumbled, frantic with the disaster.

Elizabeth tried documentary to rescue Nichol from the nets of his past. Her mother scampered back to the house, unable to endorse intimacy, the crowd. 'That's just the vibriosis, Nichol. A certain amount spreads every year. Ravens carry it. If they don't peck the eyes out of the lambs, or the tongues, they fly in the virus that makes the ewes abort. This is how it is.' He still peered into the chest of his son, either ignoring her or absorbing through radical senses. 'You'll need to watch that ewe, dose her up with a broad spectrum antibiotic. And keep checking for mastitis or you'll lose her as well. Now's a good time to milk her off, in case you get more triplets and one of the other lambs needs a start. Stick it in the freezer; it'll keep. Get up now, Nichol, and carry on with your work.'

'Hi, Danny,' says Roy. 'You going for a swim?'

Danny says, 'I wish this would never happen. I wish those babies could just be alive. But I have a train to catch.' So does Nichol. He stands and slaps grass from his jeans, pulls both hands hard through his hair and asks, 'Bury them where, Liz?'

'My husband used the perimeter of your vegetable garden. That fenceline is planted with every one of our pets and mishaps. Dig deep and the dogs won't find them.' Danny is already on his way back up to the house, lifting his father's boots with short, white legs, the most effort Elizabeth has seen him expend in months.

On these warm evenings, Nichol stays outside until early dusk, kicking a soccer ball with Roy and burning brassicas to forestall the broadcast of disease and pests. Circling the garden and diagonally across the field, perforated pipes are buried three feet deep and await the chance to transport any water the old field can't manage: into Dixon Creek, down to

Sherwood Pond and the bird sanctuary, and out into the length and breadth of Juan de Fuca Strait.

Each night after dark, Elizabeth and Nichol meet in the little barn where they have confined the last of the ewes. In the warm light of a hanging storm lantern, they drink tea and wait together and watch for the signs: the ewe's concentration, her nose shoved up to the stars, the ballooning water bag emerging, the getting up and down and up and down and then the unmistakable contractions. Last night they helped. Kneeling in the clean hay of the far stall, Nichol shoved his arm deep inside and up. He felt blind, Elizabeth coaching, and found too many legs and their big knees tangled. A head and two legs and another two legs and head, all trying to get out at once. The ewe was exhausted. He needed arm and shoulder power to push one lamb back down the canal, back into the already closing gaps. He grunted and looked terrified and Elizabeth gave orders as if to a young soldier. 'Can you find the other head now? Can you feel the two front feet? Pull. Too gentle, Nichol, really pull. Okay, that one's dead. Go back in and get the one you pushed. Get in there and tidy it up, Nichol, leave the dead one now. Leave it alone and find the other one.'

'It's going to be fucking dead, too.' He was giving in.

She thought she might have to do it herself, a role her husband had rarely allowed. But Nichol took a long look at the ewe's now placid and exhausted eyes, inserted his arm high, found the two front feet and hauled on them like a real farmer. 'Wipe that mouth off,' Elizabeth shouted, and when he did, the wriggling and snuffling began. 'Let the mother lick it now, get them together. Now leave them alone.' Of course, he couldn't. He brought a bucket of molasses water, even cleaner hay, iodine for the cord, stapled an infrared lamp onto the stall boards for extra heat. 'It's not that cold, Nichol. They're sheep, they have wool.' She put the dead lamb – abortion sickness this time – into a burlap sack.

'Do you think she has enough milk?' He was looking for reasons to panic. 'Is that the right smell? What are these things on the placenta?'

'Leave them alone, Nichol. All's well.' The red light warmed the ewe's wool and shadowed and softened and warmed his cowboy face, and Elizabeth saw Nichol's mother there, Margaret, on a good day, a happy day, watching her strong boy swim, watching him send his little boats down the creek, happy.

IV

Louisa

9. Do Fishes Close Their Eyes and Sleep under Water?

Every living creature has its time of rest. Even microbes rest, and plants, and certainly fishes. The answer, then, is yes. But fishes, which are poor feeble things, do not sleep very soundly. They do not shut their eyes.

The Book of Wonder, Vol. IX (1932)

We scooped with pantyhose nets and bare hands and coffee cans and juice bottles, and tried to rescue the strangled trout from Brunette Creek. This is the third time in four years we have restocked only to have phantom poisons leach into the groundwater. Somewhere upstream, deeper into Sapperton or as far as New Westminster, a novice – summer student, new citizen, divorcee distracted by personal problems – tips a vessel, disposes of waste that seems only possibly harmful, and spoils the water.

I suspect the new Portuguese dry cleaner on Columbia Street and his eye-sting toxins. He ruined my winter white linen jacket in January and would not compensate. The Dry Cleaners Board of Excellence tribuned over who was responsible for the million permanent wrinkles; the cleaners – is vested interest a pun in this case? – say I washed the jacket, defied the label: DRY CLEAN ONLY. They say I brought the garment in to see if a professional could undo my damage, that the pink stains under the arms made the jacket unwearable so I had nothing to lose. Do people go to such trouble over clean clothes? If Nu-Way would blame me for my desecrated Pat Boone linen, they would contaminate a fish stream. Possible motives: profit, to save time and unnecessary expense, too long to wait for the one day every three months when the city collects all toxins and takes them to a secret lethal site, like Mexican criminals dumping bodies at wasteland's dusty edge.

The fish could not be saved, the potent substance already disintegrating their gills, eyes and fragile scales. Several women and one elderly man – Captain Prosnick from Kelly Street – wept on the bank of the creek where last fall we planted native species for stability, the refuge of diversity, to hold back the sticky silt that plugs those barely evolved gills, clogs those perfect eyes.

The bodies thrashed and appeared to spawn, but let's skip the rock star sex-and-death paradox, filling teenage bodies with gothic possibilities. We gave up, kneeled and watched, shoving cold hands up our sleeves, shunning our hands for their inadequacy. A row of white and wispy caterpillar tents high in the alders upstream, saved from last year's aerial spray, dangle empty now like settlers' huts.

I did not cry. I grew deeply angered, blamed Nu-Way Cleaners, wanted to drink many beers in a darker-than-day bar, and instead hiked the hill home to escort Nanette, my mother, to church. Sunday morning traffic is no different from any other day in fast times: flatbeds, chip trucks, tankers emptied and filled, climbing up from the river, riding the time-widened road to many somewheres and their human counterparts. Gravel trucks tacked together like toy trains, heavy enough to move the sidewalk under my feet, hence, no doubt, the million cracks, the ruptures clover and chickweed scramble to fill. We expect fish to live inside this corrupt pharmacy; the residue of leaded gas leaches deeper into the roots of deciduous trees. Our group of volunteers will have the water tested, but who knows what fish can tolerate one season to the next? We bred weaklings, misled them through our ridiculous day-in-day-out sustenance.

Nanette waits at the window. She sees the anxious possibility of missing church in the way the laurel hedge needs pruning.

And the grass is thick with moss, there's another sign. This week, her gloves are mauve kid, the shoes to match, the purse off-white, though she'd prefer it, too, to be mauve. The hat will not budge in the wind driving up off the river; six bobby pins per side. 'Do I remove this in church?' She can't picture last week, what she wore. She thinks she is working her way through the closet, the wardrobe, impressing the congregation with her taste and tidy figure. But each week she chooses the same spring suit from her closet, same accessories, even the same clip earrings she'll endure all morning. My sister Arden drove herself off a cliff five years ago, and Nanette is stuck at that moment, suspended, watching the swans maintain their composure below, pumping the brake on Arden's behalf, assessing depth in the richness of blue. Are those small fish wrinkling the surface or a breeze up from Idaho? Before that, she locked up at my other sister's long decline and inevitable passing. I'm the last sister.

Sunday mornings, I will miss my mother, picture her in the front pew at St Mary's, hanging on the minister's every word, her painted mouth and kid gloves pursed and tangled. Always my day off and not one spent without her. No luncheon dates, no sporty getaways. After church, we'll have a big lunch with fresh veg from my cold frames, roast bird, and spend the rest of the afternoon cleaning up after ourselves. Look at the news while knitting a few simple rows, a little reading, early bed. There are those in our neighbourhood and down the many highways into Vancouver, who ride wide-wheeled bicycles on the seawall while exchanging topical words, who meet equally handsome friends and strangers for small, delightful meals. Maybe a cold beer in a sunny bistro. A side order of cilantro. Some plan a concert or an avant-garde play or a suddenly chic hockey game and have booked a reliable sitter for the children, someone who can tuck them in and have them asleep by seven since it is a school night and clear heads are important for a decent education. 'Could you possibly press

Gillian's jumper for the morning?' Some watch televised golf, those able will play, the city now strung out along ultra-green space, nuked by their potent fertilizers. Stores are open, bills add up in a pleasant, unmanageable way. I am in Sapperton. It is not that I can't inhabit downtown, uptown, high life, with its hot music and waste. I drank heavily, I had my luxuries, I knew the tunes.

I was born in Sapperton. My mother's dearest friends considered this the lousy part of town: river, penitentiary, beer factory, hospital; the rough bar that changed its name for every season; the oldest church. The neighbourhood slides to the river below, but the house is small, pretty, wood floors, wood-trimmed windows and a deeply tilled garden. With only two of us – Arden gone to Vancouver by the time I was eight – it was the right size.

'They all died, Mom. We tried but nothing helped.' She turns from the window and begins to cry and twitch. One side of her face has slipped low into neck and her eyes lack purpose, direction. The fingers of one hand dangle in their lovely glove, the other still holds tight the straps of her purse. Why didn't I notice this from outside? It is as if one whole part of her life, a large aspect, has decided to stay behind: it isn't worth it, can't carry on, don't wait for me. Her fish mouth tries to say 'Who?' but only part of her lips forms a word. She thinks, maybe, I am referring to dead people, a war, innocent civilians. 'The trout we started last year,' I elaborate and lift her loose arm to check for breaks, lead her to the couch, shoving at the leg she drags with my muddy boot. 'Someone let poison into the creek again and they've died. We'll try again.' Much can be done in the first few minutes to minimize lasting symptoms of stroke. How long was I gone, did we talk this morning, how long has she been this way, drifting and dragged?

I tell her she's probably had a stroke and that we'll go to the hospital now, just to see. The Royal Columbian is two blocks south, a straight line. I pinball around the house for keys, glasses, call Dr Chippendale and leave a message with his service: here's where we are now, here's where we'll be soon. I turn off the coffeepot. There is a tap running somewhere and I hunt it down, the upstairs bathroom sink drains away what Nanette has let happen. Back to what she calls the front room, but she's gone.

She is making good time down the sidewalk for someone with only one side going for her. On foot will take longer, but I cannot argue, never could. The morning is westcoast high realism, the sky low against too much evergreen, the fragrant and tightly tied gardens an insult to botanical ethnicity. As always, the suggestion of downpour. We slide up the street. I take baby steps, my hand at her useless elbow, her shuffle I must push. I drape a tartan blanket over her shoulders and we are the Indians with their secondhand smallpox, climbing out of the river to persist here, at last asking the migrant sappers – whose accents float the truth, who fuck the squaws and marry some – for strong medicine, relief, care. On either side of the street, neighbours watch and figure it out, telephone the news to others, my mother's community, the old-timers and their lingering and deadbeat children. Heathens digging early weeds from gardens start to wave, put the pieces together, and stand and watch, lumps rising in rusty throats. We are almost hit by Mrs Swanson and her son as their 1960s lilac Impala reverses – vrooooom – down their driveway, almost late for the service. Ida Swanson looks puzzled, then brings an apricot cotton glove not quite to her apricot lipstick. She feigns a crumple, then her eyes brighten with the promise of a story for church. She'll be the first to tell, the originator. 'I was the first to notice,' she'll boast. Big assumptions considering this must be a minor stroke. She sees me look and transforms her hands into prayer position. 'Fuck you and your larcenous progeny,' I say out loud, a saying Nanette loves.

Most people think I lack an erotic component. They think I have grown hard and sexless because of the jobs I've worked, because I live with Nanette. And because I do some very physical jobs and am able to because of my size – I am six feet – they believe I am more masculine than feminine. My mother was poor. An Indian deckhand off my father's first boat, the *Gipsy*, brought oolichan grease to the shop for her to eat, for the vitamins. Putrid taste, she said, and the smell overcame the lavender scent of the silk slips and rubber of girdles. But she tolerated it. She says my smooth skin and unprecedented height originate in the candlefish gifts from Henry Isaac.

At the little wool shop in town, the women who work there are made uncomfortable by my browsing. I bend low along their narrow store, folded in half by their tables and textured displays. They suggest tweeds, Aran and chunky, show me 1960s patterns from *Patons Sweaters for Men*, unisex vests and Perry Como cardigans with cables and deep pockets and faux-leather buttons. I knit pastel lambswool sweater sets for Nanette instead.

These long arms catch Nanette as she ricochets through the next stroke, lift her, careful to conceal her lingerie, and carry her for the next block. I am biblical: my arms do not tire; my legs stay strong. The mud from my boots continues to sprinkle the sidewalk. As in all dreams, the torture is the inability to run.

Nanette worked at a lingerie shop – owned by the Anglican minister's wife – on Columbia Street, downtown, after her daughter died. We took the bus from Sapperton when I was too young for school and I'd play in the back of the shop, sleep on a cot piled with marked-down flannelette. Arden picked me up when she was done at school, angered by my company, the hardship of responsibility even then. My mother lasted at the shop until she was fifty-eight. She was supposed to stock items she couldn't help customers fit: underwire and strapless, one-piece body suits with no support; the resurging garter belt and its attendant silk. In 1974, according to my mother's version, a young man and young lady on big motorcycles rode into the shop, took everything they could stuff into their studded saddlebags, and the young man urinated, one hand still holding the Jack Daniels bottle, onto her cash register. The young lady, meantime, had opened her shirt and was trying to wrap herself in a black satin demi-bra that was far too small to fit such full breasts. She was partly successful; one breast stayed inside, the other was exposed as the two revved their unmuffled engines and left the store, tire marks on the new carpeting Nanette had been asking the owner to install for six months, 'so customers will feel we have a clean shop.' Next morning, the *Columbian* newspaper screamed, DEVIL'S BIKERS RAMPAGE, COST WIDOW JOB!

So starting at eighteen, I worked at everything I could: for my twenties, bass player in the house band down the hill at the Moodyville Inn; thirties, instructor at Centennial Pool; barmaid at the OK Corral across Fourth Street, after it was Toby Foshay's, but before it was Diamond Lil's; I read Faulkner out loud to a Japanese exchange student at Columbia College; I volunteered for the crew rehabilitating Brunette Creek; landscaper for the municipality, topping up the bark mulch around dogwoods and their blasts and blight and picking up garbage in the Fraser View Cemetery; weekdays I dispatch for Rivtow, to keep the family working the river. Sundays, I vibrate with fatigue, walk with Mom down Fourth and along Columbia to St Mary's and have tea with the ladies in the church hall.

Murky relentless mouth harp and a bass line bareback riding boogie woogie. Diamond Lil's hires roadhouse bands on weekends, and the parks crew ends up there when Saturday darkens and falls. We all dance, in our regulation shorts and steel-toed boots, covered in bark mulch, well-rotted manure and topsoil muck, our hands scraped from pruning and shoulders sore from transplanting flats of pumped-up bedding plants. We have tidied society's skidmarks in Moody Park – needles, rubbers, vials – raked them from beneath heritage rhododendrons and marvelled at their numbers. We are gentrified in another generation. Every slow dance, we massage each other's backs and necks, trying to squeeze more time out of our bodies. I'm dry, but after one draft, we are drunk and pleased, our sun-dried copper faces loose and mute, distracted. Timothy goes for my lower back as the band slinks through dirty Delbert McClinton.

> *I got dreams,*
> *Dreams to remember*

He comes close behind and places his huge hands around my waist, starts at my spine, moving both thumbs out toward my hips; he is slightly taller than I am and so his chin rests on my shoulder. I move only my knees and my hips, my arms wrap tenderly around myself, head against his head. The bristles are close, his breath sweetened by those straight white teeth. Timothy has taught me: epsom salts for roses, kelp tea for late blight, filthy sheep wool dags dug deep for clematis. He loves the soil in our yard, marvels at its depth, the organic matter, the looseness of it: ancient. He works his thumbs down to my tailbone and his chest moves close against my back; my arms come loose and reach back to hold his neck, I wait for his hands to come around front, to explore the muscles of my stomach, the brick hard of my thighs, to acupress the bone spur in my neck. End of tune, and Timothy returns to a close circle of boys at the back of the bar. They fold around him, hand him more beer, touch his shoulder blade. We stay till closing, cabaret hours, having squandered our overtime on shooters and jugs of pale ale. That music is close to gospel. If

St Mary's had a gospel choir, instead of the pierce of wobbly old ladies, I'd be High Anglican and spreading the word. I am influenced by that energy, the passion of it. If I could sing, I'd sing like that.

Timothy escorts me the one block home, and we walk the garden lit by the blasting street light. My sister Arden and I lived with the genetic material passed on from my father. We drank and could not stop and could not stay happy when drinking. Brood, fume and lash out, this was our routine. Sometimes others were our victims, but most times we lashed at ourselves, found faults, created worst-case scenarios for the moment-to-moment. And other women were more beautiful, more talented, fulfilled, intelligent, qualified, well-adjusted, wealthier, sexier. We never measured up. The dead sister always the best. Arden never got to quit drinking and see the world; I have been dry for eight years, it gets harder each year, but I would never go back to the wallowing. I am not asking for bliss, but I want nothing to have control of me. Timothy says, 'That house is funny without Nanette in it waiting for you. Are you afraid to go in? I could walk you in, check.'

Perfectly sober, 'I want you in,' I say, 'but not out again.' I have waited too many Saturday nights to say this and so it is too quiet, practically a shy whisper. I am not even sure he heard me, his face too riddled with shadows to tell.

'Princess Louisa,' he says and tiptoes to kiss my scalp. Walks out the gate, turns to latch it, pinches a spent bloom from the rambling rose. Five gallons of water per week and pick off the aphids as they appear. I do not spray Nanette's roses, aware of nearby water courses and the subtleties of contamination, the magnetic grates of storm drains.

I am not her first visitor today. Timothy has delivered Nanette an enormous bouquet of snapdragons, peach and orange and pale pink spikes. The card reads, 'Love and Care to Nanette and Louisa' and I wonder what illness the asshole believes I am recovering from. Take it back: he is kind, knows I suffer and to what extent. Still, there is an implicit condolence and I blush. The bouquet is huge and suspended in a goldfish bowl. I come with current issues of *Canadian Living* and *Chatelaine* for snappy articles, women their major component. She is awake, but a hostage, her eyes search the walls and high windows for clues to what I am reading.

No one's interested in women like us any more. Television and books and movies are all about city boys, their habits and their foul language, their revolutionary fleecing of the world, the chiselled-out girls who need their company and believe they are complete when they acquire a cashmere job. You have to be a slim and suited university grad – the Sorbonne – to make it into glossy. Women like my mother are beyond invention, too dull. I, of course, fit no versions, no expectations. Mother will die five years after Arden, unable to grasp what happened, but smart enough to know her spirit should not recover from the death of a child, let alone two, even one as doomed and distant as Arden. I demand Nanette's release from the burden of responsibility. If it has to be this incremental death, I accept.

Anyone without regret lies. Nanette should have had more children. Families need to be large to compensate for occasional tragedies and assholes. And maybe if she'd had more, I would have learned procedure, created a circumstance and had some myself. I regret that Arden and I lost touch, but take no responsibility for her choice to kill herself. I feel anger, and nothing more. ('50 Dos and Don'ts for Healthy Living': *Chatelaine* says anger is the appropriate response to the suicide of a loved one, right after they say periodontal disease is a 'big beauty bummer'. These, I accept.) You have to be selfish with too much free time to pull a trick like that, especially with a family started and up and running. No one has a right to suicide, but when you sign up as a mother, certain restrictions apply. I worry that the boy Roy now considers it an option, that it will occur to him those times he is mixed up. Some souvenir. Nanette, the doctor reports, has had two subsequent small strokes, and there is no way to tell how many more may occur. The world swallows a few brain cells from her at a time, like thoughts fleeting, bad memories escaping, trout strangling.

Nanette referred to me as Princess Louisa, named me that to honour my father, disappeared by the time I was born. He was a towboater, started as a kid – sixteen in 1922 – working for Royal City Saw Mills in New Westminster, 'Largest lumber mill in the British Empire' he wrote under its picture in my scrapbook. He started out deckhand, assisting unloaded ships, hauling lumber and booms, shunting scows from mill to shipside, tending dredges and piledrivers, ferrying passengers across the inlet. By 1929, he was shipmaster – captain – of the *Gipsy* but the stock market crashed and the need for lumber all but disappeared. Especially American markets. My father took small jobs until the mid-thirties. He met Nanette in 1937 – she was twenty-one, he was thirty-one – and with the intention of raising a family, he bought his own tug – *Louise* – and started a small outfit. The bigger coastal tugs, belonging to forest companies or mills, brought booms into the mouth of the Fraser, where smaller river tugs, like my father's, assisted up through the bridges. He denounced coastal towboaters with their fancy instruments and depth sounders and lighthouses.

For two weeks last year, I dated the young son of Rivtow's owner. At twenty-five, his knees were shot, his hands too stiff to hold a pike pole, so he was off the booms. My dispatch shift would end at nightfall, and for ten nights, Trent walked me along the docks, smoking and extolling, kneeling to get a better sense of boats' beauty, donating smokes to live-aboard drunks with scabby pasts, trying to impress me with the depth of his commitment to commercial ships, the waterfront. My own knowledge disappeared, overwhelmed by the bluster of a boy with family connections. Ten years his senior and no knowledge, no authority. Only when we'd covered the whole breakwater did we go back to the company office.

The light comes in from the piling lamps and textures the dirty office with ripples, gasoline, creosote. I try to respond like an older woman, use some force, maintain composure and think: do not shriek and pant like a teenager but do not tolerate rug burns on your elbows. My fascination is with his weakened points, the vulnerable joints, the labour history his body wears. I spend too much time on his knees, his swelled and yellowed premenstrual hands; my fingers map an S-curve along his spine. Caresses piss him off. 'Can't you just fuck?' and I did for the last few times, but then the point had been made. We are strangers again. When I take my print-outs to his office at the end of the day, I memorize the display of fifty maritime knots that hangs like a sixties art project behind his head, his father's hobby, the ropes too clean to be working. Trent criticizes my records, their clarity. 'Can't you just get it down?' he bosses, and once, 'Sentences are not necessary here.'

The depth and speed of river water varies with the tide, the season, the year, the wind. Bottom shifts and distorts, sandbars and islands form and disappear from spring to summer. One year, the freshets ran so strong in June they shoved barges into rusting railway bridges. There are no aids to navigation; the channels change and accurate records cannot be kept. A useless depth sounder: by the time it flashed shallow water, the boat or its tow would aleady be tilted aground. The way to navigate my father's river is to read the water, largely instinct, but I have picked up some skill. I watch surfaces and map the colours and trajectories of the ripples, eddies. Other subtle movements.

What lies beneath the muddy water is revealed by the complexity of my memories. I read: Nanette's face and each day's new shadows, the freshets that course from her eyes, dips left in the cheek where the muscle beneath shifts. I read: Timothy's hands along my back finding the high ground, the spurs, the muscle taut or slack, the ebb and flow; Trent's long and angry spine, his knees more fluid than bone.

When I was conceived, in 1956, I guess my father panicked, on the verge of an actual family with too many women. One child already on the decline. The big companies wanted to suck up the small boats – to tidy things – so he sold the *Louise* and the next day bought an east coast lobster boat to salvage logs, to make the real money, he told Nanette. And he disappeared near Cape Flattery where he shouldn't even have been, without the skills and knowledge of the ocean, without the education.

No boat, no body. And so the wreckage that threw my mother.

To honour my father, I have planted a bonsai spruce I keep on a maple burl in the glassed-in porch off my bedroom. I clip it and shape it and will never let it grow to full size. Get it young and make it conform to a perverted aesthetic vision. Trim the roots; limit fruit.

After two weeks of visiting Nanette, bringing my dinner in plastic containers, reading Robert Frost poems out loud and sharing the evening news with her on the miniature television, consulting four times with a doughy social worker who wants me to consider as soon as possible an extended care facility which the government would not finance, after seeing my mother's face conflate one cell at a time, I get a phone call at midnight from a nurse to tell me 'The old dear has passed on'.

'What is that supposed to mean,' I snarl.

'Louisa, your mother is dead now.' She tightens and suggests I come visit.

'Right now?'

'In our experience, Louisa, this works best for everyone.'

'You need the bed, is that it?'

'Well, Louisa, you could say goodbye to her in the basement corridor tomorrow morning, but the effect might astonish you. The hallway is floor-to-ceiling brick. It is the old part of the hospital. It is like being confined in a wall.' So now we're in Edgar Allan Poe's nightmare imagination. The word 'impunity'. The phrase *In pace requiescat*. The masons and their ambiguous trowels.

'Will you be working in fifteen minutes?'

'I'm just going off shift. Let's see. Who, who, who? Oh. Hazel will be here for you.'

When Timothy comes, he stands on the back porch and does not move to come in. 'Let's look at the garden,' he says walking down the steps. His hand reaches up and back and I'm meant to take it, but don't. The neighbours next door are shrieking at their little boys, two sets of twins, all under four years old. 'You're stupid, you little asshole, you've done a very stupid thing,' screams Fritz, and one of the four look-alikes reaches a small handful of blue columbines to his father, six stems at the most. The plants are volunteers from my side bed, and there are many more blossoms lining Fritz's back fence. 'You are a shitty little wuss. Mom is going to be very mad.' He grabs the flowers and spikes them into the lawn at the boy's feet. The three brothers try to pick a winning team.

'I think you should move,' says Timothy. 'You have an opportunity for freedom you've never known, Louisa. I can't stand people who give advice to the bereaved, but I'll risk it.' I have neglected the borders while Nanette has been in hospital. Aphids suck the sweet from every new shoot. Grass shoots infest horse manure I bought cheap from rehab convicts on the river; Timothy warned of chickweed. 'You will combust here. Your jobs pay shit, this neighbourhood has no depth.'

'Why don't you want to come in the house?' It has been three weeks of excuses and quick goodbyes.

'I think you know the reason, Louisa.' And maybe I do, and maybe I don't. 'Sell the house and have some fun.'

I would build a boathouse at the mouth of the Fraser River, around Steveston, near the delta. The roof would be reinforced so I could garden veggies in boxes up there, full sun. The dreaded tomato blight would pass us by, ride the west wind from Idaho, hit the Island's distant fields, their ersatz heritage neighbourhoods, turn black and cling to rotted fruit. I would put dwarf apple trees – St Edmund's Pippins and Liberty as pollinator – in terra cotta pots on each corner and have an orchard. This would not be west coast hippie style. No shakes, no shingles, no crappy stained glass depicting rufous hummingbirds sipping hibiscus. I am not opposed to steel and clean lines. I want it to look slightly more boat than house, the emphasis should be nautical, yet functional. Timothy would say considerations of form and function are no longer discussed, dated terms, but those make sense to me. The form will be an ironic statement as to its own former function on the river. Except, no brass, or bells, or sails or wheelhouse. Float, work.

When Nichol finds me – we have never met, another of Arden's 'no service by request' decisions – I am relaxing on the veranda, bare and bruised and callused feet on the rotting rail, watching the river glint down the long hill, drinking tonic and lime, admiring my hanging baskets, living off my mother's meagre savings in a house I have sold to off-shore investors. I am a tenant in my mother's house. I wear a loose mohair sweater the colour of salmon eggs, men's Levi's, not the straight-leg, tight-ass type. At thirty-five, I am tired. I have worked.

I know who they are as they come up the walk. Nichol is a sad and handsome cowboy, a rider of some complex imagined range. I offer Roy – seven years old and wee for that age – half of my Popsicle as he climbs the stairs and looks hard at my face, swallows the magic resemblance to his ex-mom. He struggles with the drips his father repeatedly wipes with a white cotton handkerchief.

Nichol says I seem tall, I say six feet. I must look sultry, or capable, or enough like my sister that Nichol finds me suitable. We flirt but in a flat, past-prime way, and an hour later, I promise to visit Primavera.

10. Is It Good to Have to Work?

Work is a thing we all tire of at times, and we all enjoy the hour
when we can stop working. Yet, if we have any sense at all, we
know in our hearts that our work is good for us. Human beings
must have occupation and a purpose in life or their lives are worth
less than nothing, both to themselves and to other people.

The Book of Wonder, Vol. XVII (1932)

The silvered scar that curls around my left knee: anterior
cruciate, snapped on the fire escape of the Moodyville Hotel. I
chronically knead a ridged bone spur at the base of my skull,
souvenir of a 1963 Precision bass hung across my small frame,
night on night. This chipped tooth is thanks to a bartender
and his stripper date to whom I was out of line. My body
wears its labour history. Now Nichol wants me to do more
around the property – 'You mean you didn't even clean the
coop, Louise?' – assuming the jobs are his to assign. Come
these tender moments, I miss my booze.

Last week's purloin: broad daylight predators left a carcass
in the clearing by the lower pond, where a trio of willows
poses and weeps. 'Look at those beauties,' Roy – my nephew
– said, and I boosted him over the primordial barbed wire to
inspect what looked like white pine mushrooms. Delicacy.
Closer, they are breast feathers. Closer, and there she is. Bare
lungs, empty where the heart used to be, eggs still crimping
along her useless tract. It would be a lesson to complete the
dissection, count ova and measure their increments. 'Let's
bury it,' says Roy, who at eight years old likes ritual.

This morning I took hard pancakes and rotting tomatoes to
their compound. The chickens trundled back from the ponds
in a line of only five, their brown bellies low, wattles flipping. I
found the sixth bird between the driftwood risers, under the

coop, nesting in a hole scratched from dry, safe dirt. There were feathers missing from her neck. She stumbled out for the scraps – one scaled leg wrenched or rodent-gnawed – lowered her beak to feed and the rest of her flopped. The flock will not tolerate vulnerability; they will henpeck her head until they kill her. Nichol has the axes at work and I'm not sure how to wring a neck. Why do I even live here? I should do something rural, competent, but an act of mercy is beyond me.

This is the living he makes. Muscles soothed by the flat line of sleep, Nichol leaves Primavera at dawn with a can of Millionaires sardines, two whole grapefruit, deer sausage, a metal thermos of black tea. In the chill and panic of late October, the city scrounges dry firewood from these outskirts. Nichol cuts three cords a day off his woodlot and mixes wet with dry, punky balsam with dense oak. He fills out loads with arbutus that won't be dry for three years, calls it madrone and himself woodcutter, and cold-blind clientele feel part of something fancy. The dollars per cord climb as temperatures drop.

At dusk, bats drip like autumn fruit from vine maples out back. The chainsaws rattle in the box of the Hilux as he slides down the driveway, out of the truck while the emergency brake engages. A walk like he's been breaking horses or punching cows. In the dark hall, wood chips sprinkle from his eyebrows and big socks onto the muddied wood floor. He avoids eye contact and any conversation that would let us in on the day's work or where his mind has been. This seems old-fashioned. As does the dry-rot loneliness that cheapens my role here, like fish-net stockings on the chaste: asking for it. 'Can I have a bath with you, Nichol?' The child is oblivious to chainsaw stink, eager to share the potbellied tub and see dirt float from his father's arms. As daylight slinks off through fir branches and widowmakers, Nichol and the boy Roy linger in the tub; their cat, Crabby Tabby, watches from the toilet seat. My late-season turnips simmer and steam our cold windows. Flashlight inside my jacket, bare feet sliding inside gumboots, I go out to lock the coop against fugitive coons. The cat shoots through my feet. The wind is up and the night shouts with waves.

The coop sits above coastline on a flat bank that served last century as midden for the T'Sou-ke tribe. Each morning, Roy scatters good seed, and the chickens excavate oyster shells and argillite arrowheads and beach rocks that could have been mortar and pestle, or just rocks. Roy anticipates dinosaur bones, though I have explained history's tight schedule. Tonight, the tide closes in and waves rattle rocks I can't see. My bone spur aches in wind like this.

Lit in the capsule of my flashlight's beam, the coop resembles a dollhouse without the whimsy; the cedar shingles are a neglected shade of pewter from years of salt and lichen. When I clean it out – every three months – the decaying woodchips and mounds of shit fill a fertile trench around my garden. But I am putting off this chore. I am reluctant to count more springs and their fickle crops.

The wounded bird stands at the bottom of the ladder, unable to negotiate those few rungs. Did she try and give up, or, knowing there was no point, give up before she tried? My voice searches the tonic chicken scale and I find her pitch, cluck and gurgle melodically for comfort. I lift her to my side, stroke the ravaged neck, and though I place her gently in sawdust on the coop floor, she stumbles; her clipped wings flap and flutter just short of an all-out careen. The others roost, chuckling in their yet feathered throats. I point the light at each and count, just the feet of the two in back. 'Be nice,' I remind those who still have their health.

Nichol folds twenty-dollar bills under my glasses, on top of my shoulder bag. This spring, he cut hay for McConnells – heaved three thousand bales in six days without a drop of rain. He gave me fifties then, and for a week we prospered: new dish towels, strong coffee.

Regardless of these naive physics of domestic science, Nichol won't call us family; we are 'this house'. For example, 'Your moods are a terrible burden for *this house* to bear'; and '*This house* needs to pay more attention to the state of the floors.' The inside perimeter of Primavera is lined with white powder, borax I set out to stick to the feet of carpenter ants. They seem canny to me, but if they clean their feet, their stomachs explode; they die. So our home is encircled by a perpetual fuse, drop a match in any room and the whole works blows. Nichol abhors mess.

At dinner, he says, 'I'm not about to kill it tonight. I'll do it tomorrow, when I get back. Do you think he should watch? It's not so much the blood as all the flapping once the head's off. She's in shock, that bird. She can't feel it.' Many calories burned in three cords. I make enormous meals that can't fill him. Portions are too small, cuts too lean; I have forgotten the importance of carbohydrates and the Canada Food Guide. I just got good at low everything and now this: doughnuts on the premises at all times. 'When did everything stop being funny with us?' Nichol says, off-topic.

I have also held legitimate jobs here. I assisted an early childhood educator at a cooperative preschool: 'If other parents continue to bring licorice for snacktime, my husband and I will have to withdraw Jeremy from the program.' Taught folk guitar to lesbians: 'Why do all these songs only have three chords?'

Last year, before Nichol's work, before he wanted me at home, I taught swimming to four-year-olds at the Juan de Fuca Recreation Complex:

'*The sharks the sharks the sharks,*' he screams and devolves into the smallest creature possible, skinny arms around bony and bruised knees. His thighs – stupid and long – do not permit him to ball up. He shivers, cries redundant poolside tears. Their heads are too big at this age. To put their face in water is an unnatural return to the now fetid womb.

'Look at my feet,' I shout. 'You can see my feet. There are no fish in this pool.'

This happens, kids like him. Their alert torsos corrugate at the float prospect. Like cats, they know what happens when everything gets wet; the tongue and its cleaning, rinsing, cleaning. Girls forget the risks. They minnow and sputter; hair stabs gaping eyeballs while bums inch out via the flutter kick. 'I don't see the big deal,' remarks some form of mother – tattoos, ankle bracelet. 'Barbie's ass looks just like theirs, no wonder they like her.'

He won't release his body and I will have to come back to him. The meter runs in the minds of tightwad parents. They look up at the Olympian clock, whisper among themselves, crouch athletically to wipe the noses of those submerged and coping. On the middle bench, his mother sits alone, her white hands and matching face around a thermos; flesh-tone pantyhose soak her tiny feet. To her credit, she has offered no support, no interference. Few are so willing to forgo their notions of comfort. I am not supposed to say to the boy, 'Look you, the girls are doing it, what's the hold-up.' No point in shame: bare shoulders enough for one day. But the third time through the class order, her kid no closer to competence, his mother sobs and balls a borrowed Kleenex. If my supervisor spots her theatrics I'm gone.

A hand on each small hip, I haul him off the edge and drag him through shark-infested waters, where Captain Hook awaits with one good eye and the snapping crocodiles, where a rogue wave could carry us out and the bottom is where he'll go and he knows I will forget to help (many pupils, only two eyes). Zoom back to the wall, lift him out. 'Now glide, mister,' and I back away to five feet. The kid makes it, scratches down both sides of my neck with nails too short to dig in. His feet flail and try to connect with the solid ground of my bent knees. 'You did it,' the mother yells and claps and jumps on sopping feet which point inward: she makes a triangle. I peel him off and turn him, point his skinny chest at the edge. 'Go,' and I follow his manic kicks. While he recovers with sordid English Channel gasps, I touch the boy's scabby knee. His mother beams and cries further. I hear her tell someone that's the first time, no one's *ever* got him that far before. I'm ready to say just the right thing, but his four-year-old finger flies. 'You weren't even close to me. I – could – 've – *died!*' The last word echoes off a million cheap tiles and their human counterparts.

An end to all local horseplay.

'I'm not going to let you …' but I am not contractually permitted to say 'drown'.

He cuts in, goes on. 'Some kids are magical and they will never ever die.' The mother covers her face with his towel. 'I must be watched,' he instructs.

It isn't a towel. She wraps him in a ridiculous hooded bathrobe; even his huge eyes shiver. She hugs him and then comes at me sideways, her mouth curled into a dwarf's smile. 'He's lost his back fat. That's the problem. He's cold all the time.' No make-up. Smooth pale lips. Her dark skirt, the white blouse. Waitress?

'You did great.' I touch his head.

A new mother arrives chatty and announces, 'And now . want to do Piaf. I'll find a way. I *must* do Piaf.' The next bunch is younger. They fear, but can't put together a sentence to tell the whole world. No sharp dorsal fins to imagine; no muscle memory.

Gyppo loggers are scavenging the outskirts of Nichol's land. I walked the property line at dusk, watching for cougar shit and black bears. A skidder has scraped its perverted message inside the property line; the raw slab of an eighteen-inch Douglas fir stump flashes in what's left of sun. His tree – as if.

There are four gone, their useless limbs still scattered, evidence of human predation. This is the economy of the bush.

In the morning, Nichol let the chickens out into half-light on his way to work in the woods. I took the curve of crust from his son's toast and found the wounded bird looking better, more red. She'd made it down from the coop and over to the leaking water cannister to sip, raise her head to drench her throat. Sip and lift, sip and lift, stumble, sip, stumble, lift. The rest of the flock ignored her. Do chicken legs heal? She couldn't make it to the crust. Roy tossed seed, but she didn't bother. Noon: no eggs.

The healthy ones have started to roam past the top pond and I will have to search the thick ivy for hidden nests and rotting eggs. Every time I go out – compost, parsley – I note any change in her condition. All morning, I have not seen her eat but her feathers are full. The air is cool and she is slightly ruffed against it. Surely a bird in shock wouldn't think to do that? She is free to stumble around the compound. If she'd eat, I'd hope.

It rained hard and Nichol is home to change wet clothes and switch to caulk boots. He will work as deckhand on our neighbour Angus's towboat until late tonight. These tows are infrequent, a break in our routine. Clean air through smoke. 'Gary's off on a tear in the bush and this came out of the blue. Some barge needs a push through the harbour.' The boat is stocked with jumbo jars of Cheez Whiz, Dad's chocolate chip cookies and freeze-dried coffee. There is always something to say about the work: whales, wrecks, log booms ripped apart by hysteric tides. They once abandoned a million dollars of logs to net a drifting soccer ball.

He has time to kick it around with the little boy.

Gone again, and the house smells of wet denim and cedar and spilled fuel. The outskirts and it's only noon. Roy watches the Hilux taillights flicker. He lingers around the wood pile, kicking dirt, singing a mournful Gregorian ditty to those who inhabit his invisible realm.

This is not an uncommonly wise child, not overactive or defiant. I have some experience with this age, and he doesn't remind me of any clean slate on which I made my indelible mark. He is a hard, smooth surface that beads the stain of my influence. Roy and I climb past the ponds, past Nichol's sheep and their untimely inseminations, into interrupted forest.

We walk the dissolved railway line heading inland, counting ties. It is the phantom of commerce, and yet a line we walk, nowhere near holding hands. There is nothing to say, but if we're quiet, white-tailed deer and quail may allow us a glimpse and at those times, I'm full of living here, coming to the terms of my agreements by witnessing tame-ish wildlife. I point out twin flower, salal, Oregon grape and purple foxgloves, trying to establish a code Roy will draw on whenever he needs my secret support. He drags a sharp stick and carves ditches deep enough for the train rails he plans to collect and replant. Every day after school we do this.

When we get back to Primavera, a white delivery van idles. The driver looks mean, but also relieved to see us coming. He is out of the cab and muscling open the sliding door; two large boxes teeter on the van's lip, the labels written in a woman's flourish, addressed to the house in New Westminster where Roy and Nichol and Arden used to live. 'Sign and then print your name. That's an interesting driveway you've got.'

'Sorry,' I say, but he won't let me finish and describes the two Rottweilers and three German shepherds owned by neighbours down the road. 'No mystery what they've got to hide,' he says, and chuckles in that service-industry-insider way. He heaves the two boxes onto the back porch and touches Roy's hair on his way back to the van.

'These are addressed to you,' I say.

'Let's open them up,' Roy says. 'Maybe it's toys. I'll get

Grandpa's jackknife.' He's back in an eight-year-old's flash. 'You better cut,' and he hands me the mother-of-pearl knife, blade in and safe. The forwarding addresses are Timeless Books in Victoria, and a small town I have never heard of, and Vancouver, and Prince Rupert, and Blackpool Entertainment. I start to get it, the pieces match up and form a picture I am reluctant to look at.

The books are from my sister, sent to Roy on her last road trip, a final bequest to the little boy she was about to leave behind. It has taken seven mysterious, ludicrous years for them to track him down, but here they are. We each take one volume and look inside the heavy pages.

Each box holds twelve volumes of *The Book of Wonder*, circa 1932, in mint condition and stabilized by crumpled newsprint (her hands did that?). It is a child's encyclopedia and she must have been taken with the colour plates and their old-fashioned tints. 'The Daily Life of the Camel'; 'Where Ores Are Smelted and Ground'; 'The Life-Story of a Piece of Seaweed.' In each volume, a list of children's questions from the time: Why does water find its own level? Why does a lump rise in my throat when I cry? What becomes of the stars in daytime? How does the seed make the colours of the plant? and the airy, articulate answers provided by some scholar, a man who understands the perspective of a child, the non-stop wondering and need to know everything.

'Who sent us these?'

Nichol has told me to be direct, to answer the questions factually and without artifice or interpretation or metaphor. 'Your mother sent them to you before she died.' I know what Nichol wants, but sometimes feel I betray Roy's real self, the one that sees his mother flying on the ceiling, out over the water, the woman who tells him to climb the trees to Sapperton.

'The Marvelous River.'

'The Great Cereals.'

'Alloys: Teamwork among the Metals.'

Mother and *died* should never coexist in the same explanation.

'Why?' he says, and is already flipping through to find the intermittent shiny pages, the ones with colours.

'Why do *you* think?'

'Let's see. They were too heavy for her to carry?'

'Good reason.'

'She didn't want them any more?'

'Possibility.'

'She's coming back?'

'Nope. They just took a really long time to find you.' Would Nichol object to personification? Fuck him and his larcenous progeny. 'They've been trying to find you for years, Roy. They went to three different houses trying to find you and finally, finally, they're here.'

'Egypt's Fascinating Story.'

'The Beautiful Parthenon.'

'Lamps through the Ages.'

'Where will you go when she comes back, Louise?'

'Your mother's dead, Roy.'

'Are the books her ghost? I'm afraid of her ghost.'

'Call it a "spirit" and it's not too bad, not too scary. The books are just a present for you to keep so you can think of her sometimes. She thought you'd like to read these books, maybe not yet, but someday. I like these questions, don't you? I'd like to find out the answers to these questions. Look at this: "The Wonderful Story of Wheat." "Toronto as It Is Today." "Learning to be a Radio Amateur." "Canals and How They Work." "How to See through a Brick." '

'Can I watch a program?'

'Do it, but get three cookies first,' I say, although Nichol forbids television at this hour, during the week, and cookies are for after dinner. Nichol believes I can find other activities, that my role here is similar to the perfect nanny with a million devious no-fail ways to create a math genius, a Michelangelo.

'Lizards – A Queer and Ancient Tribe.'

'Little Problems for Clever People.'

How does this change my opinion of her? Do I hate her more, less? There is no note. There is no inscription and by the time I've hunted futilely through the boxes for these, I am so angry I am down the bank and onto the beach scooping the ocean in my shaking hands, up to my face and over my head, and up my arms so Nichol will not know I have been sobbing and moaning and missing my sister and the question and answer she might be with her boy Roy. *Could the earth support all the things that are born? Cannot we bleed unless a hole is made in our veins?*

I believe I've woken up to help his son clear lingering mucus or monsters, that Roy has finally called out to me and I'm up to sprint to his room, to donate a tight hug at last. Nichol sits at the end of the bed with a beer and stops me with his foot. This is standard; a version of tender. It is deep night, the sky involved in its change from late night to early morning. Nichol wants talk.

'There I am, on top of this absolutely huge concrete barge – just an enormous slab of grey cement floating on the water – and there's the harbour and the city lights and colours and people walking the breakwater, waving to us, still pissed. And then we just slide – the tug's gone off ahead to pull us by this time – and then we just slide under the Johnstone Street bridge. And there's the rubbies in their tents, and that slimeball politician's houseboat. I'm just standing on this bed of concrete, thinking about waving back. And the city's right there. All I can think is, How the hell did I get here? What is *this* all about?'

Again, I bring up the chicken. I was late going out to lock up. The wounded bird huddled in her hole under the coop and I couldn't reach her. I did my ersatz chicken tune. I tempted her with crusts, gourmet seed and clean water, but she chose to stay buried. The dark too much, the risk of the flock. Nichol drains his beer. 'This bed is rocking,' he says, and stumbles off down the hall.

When he comes back, naked, his mouth drawn down, climbing beneath the covers, arms and legs only managing the basics, he says, 'So, do I need to do something about this bird tonight?'

The boy and his mother huddle on the middle bench, squeezing their own limbs, enduring the shivers. Our mouths hold chlorine. He discourses on magic and suggests she reject the myth of predators in these waters. 'You're safe, Mom. This water is definitely safe.' She gets up and comes at me – sideways again – drawling one leg or just trying not to startle me. She speaks slowly compared to the fastforward prattle of the swarming beginners making their way to the edge. 'I appreciate what you've done. I have this kind of what's called some sort of spatial disability: I never did sports because I can't judge distance or tell where I am in relation to anything else. Say something is two feet ahead of me? I cannot process that information. It's no use to me. The difference between here and there has always been a problem.'

Our chickens, if they sense threat, if they catch a shadow cross the arbutus out of the corner of a beady eye, will freeze. They don't just stop moving, they turn lifeless and statuesque; even the eyes don't move. They resist shaking with fear since turkey vultures consider this a flirt. Cats will raise their hackles, hiss and spit. Dogs bark. Frogs will scream as they enter the swallow of a snake, their vocal cords loose from all that night chat. Chickens freeze.

The small, perfect feathers are tangled in the clean hole, a trail of them along the bank of the run-off stream, towards the beach. Probably a raccoon got to her way under the coop, maybe several surrounded her. I suppose they washed her first.

His son will cope. Roy is by now accustomed to the story of how we arrive, make the most of it, and go. The newborn kitten smothered by skintight placenta. My sister Arden – his real mother – of course.

Nichol shouts at him to eat more breakfast. 'Three spoons, I'm telling you, or no rowboat.' He talks to him like an equal, but an equal for whom he has no time. As if the boy is in violation of the fundamentals. Up early, it was Nichol who let the chickens out and he noticed the sad debris. I suppose he feels some sorrow or guilt or just one more thing on top of everything else. He has plans by now to redesign the coop, to construct a suitable safe place to isolate wounded birds, has the gauge of wire in mind, knows where he can score the wood, and worries he won't get to it till spring. What became of poetry?

The mother is not on the bench and yet here he is, bobbing with fellow Maroon Starfish, shoulder blades defined, confident and sharp as dorsals. It might be this simple: he fears what mother identifies. He tells me, know what? last night his cat had kittens right on his bed, and the lesson starts. All is forgiven.

She walks along the wet deck as if inclement weather may dump her overboard, wearing a Jantzen suit riveted and reinforced in a long-ago time when breasts were dangerous cargo and packed tight. The suit is off-pink, little contrast to break skin tone on skin tone. While I teach the children to kick and reach, she practises her glide in the deep end, diagonally, from one wall to the other, with no one watching. Her body is a hum on the water, the acuteness of the angle adjusted to conform to new increments of ability and risk. She doesn't know how to swim and works the tides: pushed by flood, pulled by ebb, calm in the high water slack that lingers, temporarily, between them. The children are quiet today, the mood aquatic and focused on spatial perception, the naive physics of reaching the one wall and then the next. Another class, more advanced than mine, has lifted a blue canoe from the wall. Two kids in complicated life jackets paddle slowly – faces so serious – mid-pool, a river, a protected bay. When they reach the deep end, their instructor approaches underwater and tips their vessel. Parents gasp, and the students scramble to link arms across the boat's upturned bottom. Lesson learned.

We all hear her choke – big grown-up coughs and disgusting heaves. Her little boy turns his back on all of us, even her. He holds the wall and pushes himself under, crouching on the bottom, still, holding every gasp of his air. When she slaps the water with her open hands, mad, crying and trying not to, he rises, blowing a million bubbles, the water around his golden head at a boil.

We hike the barbed-wire fence line and follow a game trail to the rise behind Primavera. A mucky patch of skunk cabbage, a peculiar stand of ponderosa pines – they shouldn't grow so near water – mark the spot to cut left, down toward the bay. Through the trees, we watch the towboat make a long arc out towards Race Rocks, guiding the short line of boom sticks around demon reefs and into the Strait of Juan de Fuca. Sixteen hours: Jordan River to Esquimalt and then home. Why does such a big engine move that slow?

This morning, Roy stormed into the bathroom to show me a sparrow's nest he'd found at the base of the shattered balsam. I was wiping Crabby Tabby's muddy prints from the white porcelain, rubber-gloving the grey squirrel stomach bag and tail she spat out in the big tub. The ants persist beneath the sink. I sit on the toilet while the boy picks out strands of his own hair, blond and soft, woven deep through dry grass and spirea seed pods and lichen. 'Where'd they find all this?' he whispers. Deeper, and we find bits of the grey mohair I used for Nichol's scarf last winter; I hung scraps on the clothesline for the birds, artifacts to mark my new territory. Roy straddles the bathtub's high edge, sneaker toes for balance, and peels the nest apart, hyper for details, oblivious to mess.

He says, 'Louise, I've figured out how to walk all the way to New Westminster on trees. I'll tell you. I could climb the big cedar out there and jump into that maple and then, I've checked it, you can do it, all the way to the road, the branches of the trees overlap and I could make it.'

'Tell me,' I say, sitting on the floor. 'What are you going to do when you hit water?'

'That's where my dad can do something about it. What'll happen is this. He'll bring a log boom up really close to the beach – the tide will have to be really up – and I'll jump from that small fir tree down there way down low on the bank, and float a little in the air kind of like squirrels, and land on the log boom. I might have to roll with the fall. I never said the trees had to be standing up with branches on them. I never did. My dad will tow me up the river all the way back to New Westminster so we can visit where we lived with your sister. If I get cold, I'll lie down. That's how you can walk in the trees to New Westminster. After that, there aren't any trees except for the parks they have there.'

She stands at the curb, a straight-haired girl, a girl clutching her diary so she can turn and write it all down as soon as it happens. The Queen is coming along this four-lane stretch of back-country road, any minute, and this girl – I see her look off, up the highway, enormous pleading eyes of someone waiting for a late bus, a connection missed – is one of only a handful stationed outside Juan de Fuca Recreation Centre. The woman who sold me cat food this morning suggested,

'People out here don't really go for that Royals crap.'

Many cops in sporty orange waistcoats camouflage the real security: coverts with the technology, the infrared, the common sense, to thwart the actions of those who did not get enough attention as children. They lurk on the third tee – medieval castle, deluxe turrets – of Majestic Mini Golf. There's one arranging to test-drive a '72 Skylark on the lot of Runnymede Used Vehicles. The floodtide of empire.

The way her thin black skirt billows just below her knees, or the flat heel of the shoes makes me think she will stomp one foot in another minute, unable to cope with the wait. The bright rush of a gobbled chocolate bar – Don't let the Queen see me eat! – waxing and waning, then waning even more, only just the dark stain of pleasure by now.

It is that kid's mother. Don't tell me she's crying again.

There's another one, lurking behind the ponderosa pine, scaring little kids. Terrorists. Maybe the tight security is for the mother. The world fires on vulnerability and will take advantage or take responsibility. She is not armed; a doll's waist.

Angus is at the door at 6 a.m. It is light out and the birds are frantic. Nichol and the boy are still sleeping so I cinch my bathrobe and follow Angus to his truck. It always idles. Conversations vibrate with the toxicity of air, but without the engine, Angus cannot make conversation.

'We slaughtered the young bull this morning. Thought you folks would like some of his liver,' and hands me a platter heaped with organ jelly, rich burgundy, without odour, practically still involved in cleansing the system of the beast from which it has been ripped. I take the plate and control my face while the talking carries on.

There are no scars on Angus's hands, no visible calluses, no rough shelter in the texture of their polished nails. But wrists like oar blades. He is round, overweight; his face is

reddened by rollercoaster blood pressure, not hard labour.
The jeans hang in that unpleasant way: men who cannot
conceive of women watching them walk. He stands a certain
distance from me to minimize the steep upward angle he
makes to meet my eyes. 'Chimney sweep's coming tomorrow,
I'll send him over here when he's done.' This is our talk, the
extent of it. 'Dog brought me a Canada goose baby this
morning.' He looks out toward where his tug is moored.
'Know how I'd always said I'd wring the neck if I ever caught
one? Ha. Took it back to the mother, nesting on the bank
down to the dock. Pissed the dog off.' End of conversation.
The truck rumbles off, takes a while to climb the drive, in no
hurry. I am reminded of John Wayne and the walk, the tilt of
the hat, the white scarf concealing the wrinkled brown throat.
I skirt the garden twice, watching for slugs, the scarce
improvements in this impossible midden of soil. The soles of
my boots are thick with clay and my legs feel even longer.

They are up when I come in. Nichol keeps the coffee mug
close to his mouth and has stationed the pot on the arm of the
couch. Roy, still in his Toronto Maple Leafs flannel pajamas,
has a full glass of water balancing on the flat of his right
knee. The expression on his face: are those tears or sleep face?
Does his mouth go that way with concentration, or upset?
'You guys doing something?' I ask without pressing. A
kingfisher screams territory on the water.

'Dad's making me do this so I calm down.' A look from the
boy, quick, so he can go back to the glass.

'He came into the bedroom so worked up, completely
unable to contain the energy, asked me a million questions,
asked me to do a million things, never waited for an answer,
so he's doing this. My father made me do it when I was a kid.
It made me learn to calm down.'

'How old were you when your father made you do this?' I
am soft-spoken, a weak smiler, I carry liver.

'I was twelve, hyper for my age, too worked up about

everything. I'm glad he made me do it because it taught me self-control, a work ethic. It's meditation.'

'Or water torture. He's eight. His tribe has no word for calm.' The surface of the water is rippled, the glass resonates sympathetically with the boy's nerves. He hasn't eaten. I move to take the glass and rescue him from further humiliation.

'I can do it,' Roy says, challenging me, unwilling to lose face or his father's regard. He moves his knee away from me but Nichol was waiting for the moment, catches the glass, and hands it to me. 'My father's coming tomorrow. That meat should be refrigerated,' he instructs, but I don't see the connection.

In the kitchen, trying to think through the steps of making more coffee, I swell with this: that man killed a big animal this morning. I have to sit down. The water in the bay is still; a skin of diesel surrounds the dock; nine otters on the raft where the compressor is moored; a heron stretches prehistoric wings, oblivious to the threat of evolution and fossil fuel. Don't tell me this is where I'm headed. Into that bog of lust, sucked down by combustion so dark. Just because he made something live and then made it die.

11. What Does the Pattern in a Brick Wall Mean?

Mortar is not a strength to the brick-work, but a weakness, and because the mortar joint is a weak point the bricklayer avoids arranging his bricks so that one joint comes directly over another.

The Book of Wonder, Vol. XI (1932)

Roy's grandfather, Nichol's father, Tom, comes to stay with us and he comes with history. He lives in Vancouver with a leathery woman he knew years ago from bridge club and its serial gin and tonics, but she has stayed behind in their little townhouse to look after the Siamese cats, tuberous begonias likely the colour of bad lipstick. Tom and I don't converse. I am a waitress he gets a kick cut of, maybe even his favourite one, but only a couple times a week and only when he's really thirsty. And Arden was his type? I doubt it. But she is the real mother, the first wife, and Tom has loyalties. He must have a timeline of questions – What happens when I sleep with Nichol? Why am I dressed like a man? What did I not do to keep my sister from suicide? Do I want legal rights to this property? Will I run off with the family fortune? So Tom talks to Roy. It's legacy time. What passes to Roy, along with non-stop Scotch mints and a teakwood croquet set, is details of who was here before. Primavera is Tom's lost love and he wants to woo her with how much he knows, what he remembers, the details.

At four o'clock, we sit out on the shaded veranda and watch for the towboat's return. Tom bundles himself into what has always been his armchair, though Nichol has had it restuffed and recovered. I bring him the first drink, and the tall and brightly limed gin and tonic teeters where Margaret probably delivered it years ago, near the end of the overstuffed arm. His favourite tumbler, its heavy bottom. Roy has set up the wooden tracks of his trains to run in and around Grandpa's legs, across the sloping floor to my own legs, my bare feet, and under the little table that holds my basket of wool. We are Roy's terrain, landmarks, flora and fauna. Dutifully, I say, 'Tell us a story about this place, Tom. Give us some past to think about.' I am working up the front of an Aran knit for Roy. Some kind of winter, of course, will come and I won't be here to intervene on his behalf, to dress him warm enough. The colour is heather green and the yet-lanolined yarn is softened with 10 percent alpaca. As always, the love – yes, that sentimental – is in every stitch, every twist and cable and careful rib. Another three weeks, at this pace, I should be done.

'Really? You want to hear an old man's blabbering?' He's asking Roy now.

'Ya ya ya ya,' says Roy, but that could be the train's engine rounding the pass and heading into the first of five tunnels he's built from opened-out cereal boxes. Or early Beatles, his mother's long thin shadow.

'Stop me when it's boring,' says Tom. He plays to two audiences: for Roy, innocent and half-attentive, the vocabulary is hard but, given enough strong nouns and active verbs, he'll remember. And for Louise: I am supposed to interpret, absorb significance, learn that I have no history here and no real future. So it feels. I can't see the boat yet, and the wind has whipped a light chop into the bay. Kingfishers. Cormorants. Turkey vultures speckle the stratosphere, kettling, waiting for the right updraft to support their outward-bound soar. 'Your grandma, Nichol's mother, was Margaret.'

'I already know this story,' Roy says. 'Ch-ch-ch-ch. Ch-ch-ch-ch.' Tom looks at me to make the boy stop interrupting, but I squeeze the little bent cable needle between my lips, knit.

'Margaret's Great-Aunt Cassie – your great-great-aunt, Katherine Whitney – sailed across from New Westminster the January she came seventeen to wed a widowed British colonel and farmed property here for forty years more, till she died young. Stripes, they called him; it's possible he was only captain, something to do with the Hudson's Bay Company and all that. They found two hundred waterfront and wooded acres with a massive log home; imagine the age of those trees, Roy. They cleared stubborn Douglas fir stumps with woolly horses and wooden wheels and made fields; they scratched back scrub alders and planted pedigreed apples – Pippins and Kings – and made a massive orchard, some of the trees still stand, down there behind the chicken coop.'

'Some apples give me diarrhoea. Shh. Tunnel. Man oh man, it's dark in here.'

'Roy, these people built their dirt from hay and seaweed and sheep manure and more dirt. At thirty, no children yet or ever, Cassie wanted a willowed pond in the lower field but when they dug, their shovels hit red bricks, already chipped and crumbling. Three inches down to plant crocuses, brick. Six inches for Dutch tulips, more brick, darker brown. The British hedging – boxwood and yew – stood rigid, supported by a deep and dense circle of them. Insects and parasites and worms worked, swallowed, expelled.'

Roy runs his little cars gently across my instep. He pretends oblivion but he's doing something rough. I may be landscape, but I have tender parts and he knows it.

'Now in places,' says Tom, 'the bricks resembled a mystery road or vast spoked whorl. One afternoon – Stripes off in the south field burning spent brassicas – Cassie took her spade up behind the barn, beyond the slaughter pit and began excavating. She meant to unearth the bricks. She had been reading of other cultures in mail-order books from an American university, you see. And she processed these diggings, stacked a line along one border of the property, making her way to the stormed beach. They were not the desiccated castings of a lazy and ancient wheel cult, or meant to form a road; there was no ambition in their tumbled rest. So many, and heading to the beach.

'At the end of each hot hour, she drank from her Mason jar of warm well water and stopped to smell the ocean coming at her. The Indians arrived off-shore to watch and laugh their laugh. The Sokes and their communal canoes still plugged this shipping route with confounded quiet, close enough for the wave of a hand or a bargain.'

'Nichol calls them "Sookes",' Roy says.

His blond head is wedged under my chair. 'Quit poking, Roy.'

'The cargo is shifting, Louise. Your patience is appreciated.'

'Yes, just up on that knoll, behind that totalled Garry oak, Emily Carr later went nutsy bingo. Her long hours of painting, the lead, breathing her spectacle, she absorbed through fat fingers the toxins and poisoned resins from those firs, ponderosa pines, Western red cedars, name your conifer. Distilled oleoresin, turpentine: brain cell thinner. Yet another chicken and egg paradox.'

I haven't heard or read this theory before, but it works. Tom has gone lyrical in his 'History of Art: British Columbia' lecture. The cynical students look at each other sideways, wanting him to get back to the point and wondering how to paraphrase for the midterm; the class is almost over and the seats are hard, but they will recall him, years later as they hike the West Coast Trail in February with their first real lover, for those passages of lovely digression. Here's Crabby Tabby come to clean a paw, to pull burr from fur.

'*Puss*-puss-puss-puss. *Puss*-puss-puss-puss,' Roy improvises. The sun is still hard on our faces.

'Back to Cassie. Salal and Oregon grape vine thickly, conceal the toppling bank of bricks that begins and ends at the sand, up to Cassie's knees. Walking is difficult and each step pushes edge on edge and corner over rough corner. She is a rock slide, the last straw. Stark above the tide line, behind the last fat yellow cedar denuded and planted horizontally, she finds grey and ivory and shell-pink bones. These vulgar pick-up sticks, flung and some stacked beneath foliage and in winter concealed by blankets of kelp the Oregon storms and waxing tides send up. Some of the larger bones – something's thigh – are freckled with seaweed and have the look of beginner's melanoma.'

Roy has stopped the perilous train trip at the cat's flicking tail – she is elongated in a choice sunbeam – and he wants to know: 'Who made those bricks be there?'

'That's what Cassie wanted to know, Roy my boy. Stripes told her, "It was a brick quarry, Catherine." He smelled of rotting produce and incineration. Tired and hot, Cassie listed the possibilities: slaughters, murders, cults, battles, evidence of genocide. He told her, "Well, they had to eat something, Catherine. Perhaps a variety of local sheep. Or an exceptional season for elk."

'The bricks, it turns out, were born there. The clay was dug by hand along the drying creek bed in the highest heat of summer. Another generation's horses hitched to turn the mixing paddles, their cracking hooves wearing a circle of hard crust into the lower field as they became the spokes in the wheel. The women – Cassie's mother and aunts – pressed the clay, softened to pug by horsepower, into wooden moulds lined with old-country tin and arranged the green bricks in row after row in the lower field. Like crops. Baking in August, drying quickly with the prevailing winds and sun off Juan de Fuca Strait. Meanwhile: build fire. Blowdown and windfall, the twisted limbs of oak and madrone gathered and stacked; the children sent to collect smaller sticks for the scove kiln to layer with straw between the criss-crossed strata of bricks. This task was hijacked by what else there was: the flicker of alder leaves, their roots slurping artesian water by the creek; a rope swing; snakes dancing, and the red-tailed hawks and vultures kettling and carving sky circles. Also, berries.'

'Those berries give me a rash. *Puss*-puss-puss-puss.'

'A slow fire was set and left to burn for all of August and part of September, a smudge between shore and the house. Pulling their canoes up the beach, Soke Indians gathered in families at dusk, impressed by the shapes, the heat, the longevity of this pale ceremony. Wary, even then, of common ground, or what appeared to be respect for the elements. When cooled and upended from their moulds, the bricks were scarred.'

'Nichol calls them "Sookes".'

'When your Aunt Cassie died, Roy, she owned seven thousand bricks from all over the world. There were all sorts of shapes and sizes and colours. She used to stroke them, apparently. Brick isn't always brick, if you know what I mean.'

'There's your dad, Roy,' I say while Tom finishes his drink. 'I see the boat out there, see it?' Feel it, more like. It is a long way off and impossibly slow. Regardless of the distance now growing between us, I thrill when I know he's headed this way. The cave of my chest vibrates.

Roy gets up and leans his small body against the veranda rail, puts his hand above his brow like a sailor's wife and regards his father's progress. 'That's another week away,' he says, increments nonsensical, therein his wisdom.

'Good,' pipes in Tom. 'I'll give you another part of that story. This one has cats in it.' I place another drink in its allotted position at the end of the arm.

'I'm desperate for a dog some day,' Roy says, and runs his cars fast over the end of Crabby Tabby's tail. She screams and shoots off into the salal and down the bank. Roy's head is under my chair again, banging me. I know Roy wants my intervention but those days are behind us. The cat will live. The boy will survive.

Tom lifts his hand in thanks for the drink, has a contorted frown at my bare feet and continues: 'Dusk began its shroud in the high field. Spring lambs bobbed and dipped. Aunt Cassie saw the tail of the cat, sloped and pendulous; each tear and growl sent it swaying. It is the soft brown she would like for a suit, a collar the colour of the tail's tip. The cougar looked at her face, eyes fired and rich: communication. They had lost two lambs already and this would be the third, a favourite with a black face. Women knew guns then and Cassie carried hers.'

Roy wants to know, 'Wait. Does the lamb die in this?'

'When Aunt Cassie died, she had collected over one hundred cougar kills, a reputation in the community, an identity founded on extermination of predators. She could do bears, too, but people counted cougars. In late August, young males spurned by their mothers –'

'What does "spurned" mean?'

'Rejected, turned away, ignored,' I translate, and Roy looks out at his father.

'Yes,' clips Tom, low on patience. 'Young rejected males roamed riparian zones, looking to establish a territory. Cassie spread sand from down the beach on game trails through her woods. At the edge of alder groves, she cast the sand and raked it smooth, went a hundred feet further and did it again. The periphery of her land was a flat ring and the next day she would check the sand for prints, the autographs of cougars intent on roughing up her flock, her dogs. Like tapping nature's phone line.

'When big-toed prints appeared, she knew the cat was close, but it would do no good to stake out that trail. She had to find a thread, a connecting path by which she could predict and determine the cat's next move. So she would move on, the next day and the next, tracking the path of the cougar and by the third day, sometimes the fourth if weather was foul, she would wait at the spot the cougar would be next, and kill it.

That done, she'd bring the horse – her husband overseas or fly-fishing the Elk River – and drag the cat home, call the newspaper. A house can have too many skins: on the walls, couches, chairs, on the ends of beds; as rugs, even in the bathroom. One big *homo sapiens* flaunt.'

'Are cougars here right now?' asked Roy, still looking out to sea, his hand exploring the territory beneath the waistband of his shorts.

'Likely. Get your hand out of there, Roy. One August we had a cougar visit. I was reading to your father at bedtime and your grandma Maggie came to get us, to take us out for a look. I knew a fella in school who studied – just watched them for a long time, really – he knew cougars and claimed they were not so unpredictable as people thought.

'We stood apart, Maggie holding Nichol, me away to the right, closer to the door. Two deer fences and a dry and narrow creek between us and him. The cat had a long look at me, thinking it over. Eye contact. They know where to look. He began to move slowly in the direction of Margaret and the boy – my family, you see – and your grandmother started to belt out Johnny Mathis, "Chances Are", in defence of any impulse that animal had to chew them up. Her falsetto, I regret, was never steady; the cat bounded off anyway.' Tom is chuckling and drinking at the same time.

I am fixed on the distant past, its elements, while Nichol tiptoes closer. I will always associate the smell of diesel with rejection, I will look down at my breasts and wonder, Who would want those? I will look at the deep lines between my thumb and forefinger and think, No wonder he didn't want me. Whenever I smell diesel, I will want to hit the road and I'll miss Roy wherever, whatever I am. 'What happened to the other couple, Cassie and her husband?'

Tom smiles at me, right at me, for the first time since he got here. 'When Cassie finally couldn't stand to live with Stripes any more, they divided the property in two – Cassie got the orchard, or course – and converted a large chicken coop for Stripes, since they could not come to terms over the log house. The coop was comfortable enough, once they sterilized it; Cassie's job, no doubt. Half an acre across hay field, Stripes lived in his outbuilding; Cassie stayed in the big house while she had this house, which she called Primavera, built. But Stripes was not happy and degenerated into territorial provocation. He'd rise in the morning and sing a chesty "Battle Hymn of the Republic" – every morning. Cowbells were then rung for no livestock-related chore. After two years of this – two! – Cassie took to keeping her gun loaded every morning and shot out from the back of the house, toward the chicken coop. Two shots. When this made no difference to the singing, she aimed closer. Still no difference, but she kept it up; this was their relationship. And when he finally stopped singing one morning, feeling the effects of a nasty strep throat, and she fired anyway, he fired back: another ritual born. For three years more, they shot at each other for no reason every morning. The animals got used to it; raccoons watched, robbing kitchen scraps at their feet.'

'I'm a cougar skin,' says Roy, and he drapes himself across my back. One paw dangles between my breasts. He is warm and smells like blackberries and paste.

'When she was only in her fifties, skin red-brown and a narrow swath of hair across the top, Cassie was asked what it was about firing a gun that made such a difference, what was it that made them keep it up, with no regard for danger, or boredom, or bad taste. "Well," she coughed and feigned frailty, "I suppose we never had children."

'Stripes died of a stroke in the night; Cassie stayed here at Primavera, oblivious to the shrubby renters who erected the cedar cross on the lawn in front of the big log house and painted it white, who gathered her bricks and built a four-foot wall around the house and another around the chicken coop. A fortress of some kind, later all that was left when their stupid fire took the big house and all nearby greenery.'

'I'm a dead cat,' Roy says, twirls and then doubles himself over the railing, first taking a look at where Nichol might be closer.

'The log house had been constructed as a fort. The settlers planted spreading elms and laurel and hawthorn, erected beehives and two three-pound bore guns on a conical rock in front, facing the Pacific Ocean, the Strait of Juan de Fuca, Angels' Gap, the Hudson's Bay steamships, the Sokes and their canoes sifting inland waters. The Indians were warriors, their part of the island also a fort, or a fortress to protect an identity on the downslope, and all the rest of it. They fought only other Indians though – the Cowichans, the Clallams from Puget Sound, the Nit-i-nats – and Aunt Cassie, at seventeen, received many scalps and small white skulls, gifts from the Sokes after these battles, who for some undocumented reason, considered her blessed and worthy of their best loot. She was a healer, a trained nurse and the daughter of a Royal Engineer doctor, but that wasn't it; they had their own. They just liked her, thought her worthy. They threw other people's hair at her feet and she knew enough to say thank you.

'Listen to this, Roy my boy. Picture it: they slide into this bay, pull their long boats onto the round rocks, looking sideways at what remains of the bore guns, wanting them and not wanting them. Some sort of chant to ward off what still may be inside, powder burns on history. Listen here: *During her last illness, the Indians called daily at the home, bringing some little gift of fish, or pretty baskets, or herbs, or wild game. And when she died they all gathered to her funeral, forming a procession of mourners more than a mile long.* More than a mile long, Roy. That's how much they loved her. A hundred years before, the Sokes were almost wiped out when other tribes got together and ganged up on them. Imagine a mile of Indians, lost in battle.'

'Is that the end?' Roys asks, standing up and trying to keep his legs from hurtling off the veranda. 'Can I go down to the dock now?'

The question was meant for me, but I am minus all status. 'Off you go, son,' says Tom. To me, 'I hope I haven't said the wrong thing,' and holds out his once again empty glass. 'That was just a story.'

Even this far away, I see Nichol standing tall on the tug. He tosses the bow line onto the dock. He misses, reclaims the now wet line, and throws again. His arms must be tired. During dinner and then after Roy is in bed, he will try to rid his head of the engine throb and Angus's prattle. Tom will go to bed, and Nichol will manage to say only 'Goodnight, Dad.' And then when I propose a conversation, when I say to him, quietly, 'This waterfront is alive with enemy memory,' he will sigh, rub his eyes with one hand, shake his head and stumble like a sailor down the hall.

Timothy has found me a house two blocks from Kelly Street. The yard, he says, needs 'a fundamental reworking', but there's nothing a load of goat manure can't fix. The little house is immaculate, sweet, comes with sunporch, rambling roses, all the concepts that make Timothy happy. And from the attic window, the Fraser River is visible, my one stipulation.

'Are you aware, Louisa, of the changes in this city since you've been rural?' Timothy asks. I go upstairs for our after-midnight phone calls – Nichol towing round the tides – so I can watch the water for lights and watch Roy's sleeping face. Timothy makes me laugh and his voice is smooth, urbane, sexy but not like liver on a plate.

'You're still living there, Tim, it can't be so bad.'

'It's bad, but I like bad, it excites me. Drugs, constant crime – don't buy a car, for example, you'll lose it to baby thugs.'

'I like bad. The house is not in the core. Sapperton's always been outskirts. What have they done with Toby Foshay's?'

'I can't tell you.'

'Tell me.'

'I can't tell you.'

'Just tell me.'

'Laundromat cyberbar.'

'I don't know what that means.'

'You still off booze?'

'So far. Barely. It's stalking me.'

'Then you'll probably be okay there.'

'It's now called?'

'I can't tell you.'

'Tell me.'

'Moodyville.'

'I like it.'

'You do not. No no no no. It's a pornographic co-opting of colonial history for the purposes of capitalism's degenerate profits.'

'Yes, I do, I do. Who are you seeing anyway?'

'Come on, Louise.'

'Tim.'

'I need to know you are not coming back to – to – I can't say it, but it has to do with the last time we went to the bar. I need to know you are not coming home to – to – be with me in any but the horticultural sense.'

I ask, 'What's another word for "crush", a word that is sophisticated and detached, yet unthreatening and friendly?'

'Aphid? Louise, there is no such word. Stop it.'

'I see lights. I need to be asleep.'

'You've told him.'

'He knows time's up. He knows I'm going. He's not going to care. He is all work and no play and he is a dull boy with a hard heart. Roy, though. Roy could use another word for father.'

* * *

For Roy, I leave a black-and-white photograph of three little girls running toward the camera – my mother, Nanette, was the photographer – on a grass-tufted summer beach near the British Columbia/Washington border. A whitewashed cottage tidy in the background. Movement. Blur. Sisters.

The little one – maybe two years old – is out front with long and chubby legs and bare feet, gleefully running at the camera or her mother and the water behind them, and away from her older sisters. Her grin is full of wile: the escape is both trickery and enticement. Come and get me.

The girl in the middle – she is then nine – seems calm and thin in her white running shoes. Her black hair is neatly cut and swings out behind because she is a good runner. The train-tracked braces are concealed behind her smirk; her open smiles do not show up until after the braces are gone. Her body is bent, her hands reach for her little sister, but she does not appear doomed to die from cancer. She is a girl chasing her little sister, saving me from the water's edge and my urge to freestyle for the distant shore.

The tall one at the back is eleven and she is angry. Her legs are so long she could catch me in a second, but her hands are on her hips. She would rather be listening to Bobby Darin or the Shirelles in the cabin on the record player she takes everywhere, pretending to flirt with a dance partner, pretending to be the singer on stage. She would rather be reading Daphne Du Maurier.

I am two, and my sister Arden did not want the responsibility of me, and so I am running to make her care. On the back of the photograph, in faint pencil I write, *How Do Our Bodies Stay Afloat?*

V

Della

12. What Do the Poets Mean By Arcady?

Arcady, an independent little kingdom of long ago, was inhabited by merry people who boasted that they lived before the moon, and saw its birth. They were known for their rural ways, their love of music, songs and poetry, and for their enjoyment of tranquil happiness. Poets of the Greek time always pictured the Arcadians as fortunate beings, so that nowadays Arcady means to our writers the place of purity, of faith, of love, the imaginary land where rural pleasures make everyone happy.

The Book of Wonder, Vol. x (1932)

Some houses beg to be built. Nichol contacted Plumb Line Construction on the advice of a friend, a poet he cycles with, and called Della for an estimate, a consult. She ventured out to Primavera from the city in her pickup, negotiated the steep and stippled driveway and they talked for three hours on a wintry windy Sunday afternoon. Fir cones clattered on the shake roof. The weather over the water out in the bay was Shakespearean – brood, clear, brood darker, whip, brood – but the woodstove ticked and crackled; there was white wine and ginger cookies. Roy, nine years old, sat upright and cross-legged in a huge armchair reading an encyclopedia, several volumes stacked at his feet, two draped open on his lap, one upside down on the puffy chair arm. 'Why leave this?' she asked.

'Enemy memory,' Nichol said. 'Or I need to start something myself. And then also finish.'

Nichol liked her reading of his plans and Della convinced him she could cover the budget and keep him happy during the process. Immediately obvious: this will not be subdivision purgatory. Nichol's skin-thin drawings – months of erasing and revising – depicted a home from another era, a happier time. He started with Primavera's good bones and then rifled his Great Aunt's 1910 subscription to *The Craftsman* magazine and found the Platonic ideal, or at least a dwelling to please him. Della recognized William Morris and his ilk in the design: form, function, art. Nichol scored a two-acre waterfront lot on an island in Juan de Fuca Strait notable for squatters and Esalen dropouts – why that island? – and hired a neighbour with a skidder to select-log half of it. He made some good money off the old-growth fir, scaled the best logs to use on the house: six-by-six cedar posts, a dying maple for tongue and groove flooring; tight-grained fir for the upstairs. He wanted to garden, and his drawings showed hawthorn and English box hedges, pin oak and apple trees with old names under them – St Edmund's Pippin and Liberty – and pinkish fruit tattooed on with Roy's felt pens. The weeping willows, he said, will suck up the muck at the low point, where winter stays too long for early vegetables, where any other tree would suffer root rot. And he wants a Lombardy poplar wind break, though she'll talk him out of those: they'll screw the foundation and septic field. Close to the house, he'd drawn a Victorian-style greenhouse, and noted below, 'The Romans grew cucumbers under mica,' to place himself on some agrarian continuum. Amazing detail for amateur preliminary.

The two dormers were high and pointed. 'I want shingles all over and I've got the shake bolts cut already.' Driftwood scavenge and endowments from the back of neighbouring properties, a small mill on the back side of the little island is cutting them into Number One Red Cedar bundles. He didn't have the patience to draw the shingles evenly, but he was right about the look: a quaint splice of imperial power and New World swagger. In violation of conventional wisdom, he'll keep the shingles natural, inviting weather and rain forest damp to mildew and pockmark his dream, but Della knows original vision is immovable. White window trim is his only concession.

Despite what he said about shingles everywhere, the red bricks appear all around the foundation and the porch, leading down a path, and a short wall of them surrounds a kitchen garden at the back for the best sun. He wants heat for sauce tomatoes and an espaliered peach, and crevices for woolly thyme. 'Mortar and brick – the two substances,' he says, 'are used like the threads of a fabric and are interwoven with reference to a general colour scheme. These colours grow more beautiful with age as the bricks take on "bloom" – a fungus that adheres to rough surfaces. We look into these walls, not at them, their surfaces make a textured, unified whole. In looking at it the eyesight goes sprawling over the surface like a dog on slippery ice.' It's uncommon to find a man of his age – mid-forties? – with such sensitivities, yearnings.

The house will be small, by today's ballooned standards of opulence and excess. But he borrowed features from his mother's era that made sense to him. Back then, they had built-ins for economy, so no one would have to buy furniture. Now the labour and materials will put the cost way up, but he has to have the bookcases and window seats, an inglenook around the woodstove. He has some source for distressed bricks.

He remembers Primavera as it felt when he was a child – all build-their-owns do this, complicated when childhoods were unhappy and the shit cannot be reno'd. But Nichol remembers Primavera as a place of air, light and golden space. Maybe, maybe not.

His mother gave up the whole top floor, his bedroom led to an open-plan playroom which led to a summer sleeping porch, screened when August heat deepened, which overlooked the lush path lined with massed rhodos and sword ferns to the ocean. The yellow ceilings were angled and some walls only four feet high, since the sharp roof peaks eliminated the notion of adult-size ceilings. The floors were six-inch fir, shiny and slightly sour. Outsize windows, window seats with storage for dress-up clothes and extra blankets with the family initials stitched by mother with blue silk thread. Toys she knitted and Aran sweaters on chairbacks. Built-in bookcases for Doulton spaniels, mollusc collections, and a hedge of stuffed animals along the top. Why not stay here? Della shouldn't ask again.

He tells her, unnecessarily, he wants similar comfort for Roy, the little boy. A world map on the ceiling above his bed, a good easel placed always at the window with the best light. A music stand. A fluttery tulip tree just beyond the bedroom, visible from teddy bear on pillow. Truth, as Roy understands it, everywhere. This is not guilt, but an acknowledgement that the boy is now the focus; subtle neglect or misplaced attentions – small regrets – will be corrected by these new walls.

Nichol says, 'I have been present as a father in the minimum way a boy will accept,' and Della wonders where he read that one, or what fed-up step-female put it that way as she packed her bags and went back home. Nichol longs to be a new man and the house he builds will prove he can do it. He will forgo examining his unexamined life and build a new one instead, a hundred bucks a square foot if she keeps her eye on the budget, cuts corners he'll never notice.

The community he has chosen is on an island cut off by miles of water from Mainland slime and excess, from prefab neighbourhoods and crime stats. Also miles of strait between his island home and Primavera. He will be buffered. There is peculiar wealth there. The tiny ferry – more Tom Sawyer raft than sea-going vessel – runs several times a day, but Nichol has a line on a converted herring skiff he'll moor in front of the house and have the convenience of joining some nautical rush hour when necessary. A few thousand citizens support a local economy: grocer with bank machine, video rentals, import produce, charge accounts; a bakery with hard-crusted weighty bread and other health foods; drug store with penny candy and video rentals; travel agent; a small café (lentils, beets, tofu, etc.); post office with government liquor store in back and video rentals; small hardware store, walls lined dense with everything in many sizes. That's just downtown. Every house, it seems, has a home-based business breaking even and spread over several green and gentle acres: accountant, yarns, seamstress, barrister, hay, Cornish game hen, résumé writing, Cavalier King Charles spaniels; electrolysis; family counselling. No one does nothing.

Primavera has been rented. Roy will stay with his grandpa in Vancouver for the first month or so of construction. Nichol has his father's stinking mildewed war-issue canvas tent set up in a waterfront clearing next to the house site. He will bathe in the ocean and shit and piss in the tradesmen's fluorescent green Porta-Loo. Meanwhile: build house.

When the tide changes, these days around noon, the wind shrieks through the site and Della's shoulders get cold and stay that way until evening in the deep bath in the Swallow Hill Cottage room she rents. If she wants to stay on the island until the house is done, she'll need a sweater. 'Down the road and up the curved hill, the pretty little house on the right,' directs Swallow Hill's melodious hostess and there, in a tarted-up hippie shack – whitewash done wonders – is a woman whose hair smells and appears rinsed in lavender. Her face, too, bleached by something. She sells yarn. Duck through the calendula bundles and garlic braids slung from the living-room ceiling; try to ignore the tug of garlicked vegetable soup on the oil stove, the fresh sourdough bread. The back room is lined with good oak pieces – a Stickley desk and leather armchair and footstool – and cubed pine shelves hold a big-city array of colours and textures. Italian merino, local grey and camel-coloured alpaca, 126 jewelled shades of

Greek cotton, a four-ply originating in Russia that an American company imports and sells as a relic of peacetime. (It seems stiff.) Her sample sweaters, hung on angular metal modern art, floor-to-ceiling hangers, are couture – no layettes and booties or old-lady dishcloths – these are deep, oversized sweaters that shimmer with design, Adrienne Vittadini and her consideration of the body's place in fibre, the ethics and husbandry of textile on skin. The room seems huge. Needles, fashioned from antique musical instruments in cherrywood and mahogany, dangle like some tribe's curtains in front of a small window. The light is beautiful in this room.

'I don't know you,' the woman says, after a suitable period of silence.

'I'm contracting that house on Water Street. I'm building it.' No eye contact in a wool store, too much textile. 'I'm here for another couple of months and I'm cold in the afternoon. Maybe a vest; something fast and warm.' Despite the arty style of this room, its compliance with trend, there is the webby shawl around the woman's shoulders built from something just off the back of a sheep and sprinkle-dyed, probably, in a steaming vat of shrubbery and piss, brown coreopsis or yellow loosestrife. Mordant. There would have been some tinkly midnight pagan ceremony to make the neighbours fret. Like it or not, the sixties persist. 'Do you have a pattern for a man's vest, something long and baggy; this tweed would be good.' Della can smell the lanolin after all this time, her fingertips softer already.

The woman opens a magic drawer in the desk and conjures a pattern that depicts delighted people – three kids, a handsome young man, three grown women – sporting down a hillside, carrying each other in a French wheelbarrow, laughing and helping the children to remember this day forever. It is early autumn, the sky is dull and the greens of the field and trees flirt with dormancy. Their sweaters are purple and ochre and shell pink and knit from mohair, a fuzz

Della's own mother judged 'far too obvious'. The woman at
the helm of the wheelbarrow, tilting the two smallest children
and their wide faces, wears a long vest of deep blue, the blue
the sky was for her that blurred and dwindling summer. Her
hair is labyrinthine, her strong throat shows in the low
V-neck. That could be the south of France or a tidy park in
upstate New York, or someone's castle grounds in Scotland.
'Do you sell this stuff?' Della asks, but the wool woman
knows how to adjust expectations and change lives.

Her sentences are one long exhalation. 'Why not try the
yarns from our island. This is from our own animals, we
process and card it and dye it ourselves. This one's a blend of
alpaca and mohair. The colour's good for you, your eyes.
You'll need fives so it'll go fast.' A little breath left. 'You'll
never be cold again.' Someone's hands made this from
something rough and thick and plugged with shit. Someone
twisted and pulled and then soaked and lifted and created
this tapestry of heather blue and purple and flecks of deep
green. How do they do this?

'You're probably keen on bamboo, but no one here uses
bamboo any more.' Again the magic drawer opens. 'These are
Turbos. Nickel-plated, faster than shit; they cost but you'll fly.
Get the wood if you're set on them, but they'll catch on a
hairy yarn. These are so smooth. You'll find the tension is
very cool.' She covets those symphonic needles.

And so in the evenings, after Nichol has kept her deep into
dusk with his final debriefing – *Here's today, here's tomorrow,
here's the budget, here's the timeline* – Della removes her
overalls and in the black spandex bike shorts and sloppy
sleeveless T-shirt underneath, rides her bicycle along the
edges of the hot dirt road back to Swallow Hill. She greets the
silver-toned hostess on the porch – 'The bathroom's all yours,
Della, the towels are nice and fresh. And I put a bowl of
raspberries in the sunroom for you.' After the impossible
bath, its rosemary oil and white towels, she settles into the

darkening sunroom, the pot of strong tea and sugared berries the hostess's bewitchery, and hugged by headphones, she listens to early and wavering Emmylou and devises the turbo-charged mohair sweater – *So come on wheels, take me home today.*

Windows arrive first ferry tomorrow. The fine craft of a four-man joinery in the city, they are framed in edge-grain fir, the lights true-divided using the heritage profile of a long-ago Brit. Nichol's house will take thirty-five and this order has tested the production capacity of the little joinery. Within weeks, though, the company will expand: bid on and buy a pricey precision router; win a contract to export old-growth window frames for the closets given workers in Japan; fire and hire a chorus line of dope-smoking tradesmen. George the framer has called his two sons in Vancouver to come help him install the windows, to make sure they all go in, truck to house, within hours of delivery. That's how it should be, says George, windows should never touch ground.

Gypsy drywallers have shown up on site since the day the windows went in, each recovering from last night's drug. It feels like the Depression, a more materialistic Steinbeck novel. They arrive three crews per ferry in two-hundred-dollar vans, hand-lettered business cards ready, or some lame excuse as to why there is no business card: 'Shit, I gave the last one to that computer mogul building out on the spit.' Blonde girlfriends do Raymond Chandler, smoke and scowl and slouch in the passenger seat, dissatisfied with the relationship. For drywallers, there is a tightly constructed hard-luck story. No one, it seems, chooses a career in drywall; like waitressing, the sanctuary exists. Most of these guys are too skinny to be waitresses, let alone boarders. 'We're willing to do a measure at no cost to you, ma'am, and I'll just quickly work up an estimate – is there a pub of some kind on this island? – I'll work something out for you by say three o'clock today. May I ask what you paid for that roofing job? My cousin here was a roofer for five years and he says something's fucked with those shingles. They shouldn't sit up like that.'

Della chose a company she uses for smaller jobs, but management has changed. The four boarders show up sleepy off the first ferry, smoking Player's, their bellies and meaty backs drift out over bad jeans. Hungarian brothers, bona fide gypsy newcomers to this plentiful land, they are just off the boat and seem dark and vulnerable and astonished, off a boat again so soon. They are terribly young, and she builds a life for them back there, one that demeans them and then presses on each this opportunity: to carry heavy walls up steep stairs, to mud them in place, to inhale lime and sawdust six days a week. How did that truck make it up the ferry ramp?

Nichol is agitated by the volume of their 1960s acid rock – Jefferson Airplane, Janis Joplin, Country Joe – but Della explains the nature of boarders and so he does not impose noise bylaws. He is working on the wall around his garden. Della offers her own headphones and he tries them. She gives him Emmylou, but within a minute he's down on the shore, skipping rocks across the water, with what she reads as too much force. His throws punish something.

Last week, she came back in the late evening to check the wiring again before the windows and doors arrived, and he was here, walking from room to room, levitating through what will soon be walls. 'This is the last time I'll be here in this way,' he said, and she imagined a bad poem constructing itself each time he crossed a threshold. For Nichol, everything carries weight and the potential to amend mundane existence with metaphor.

'They're just walls, Nick. Division – separation – they are not just bad. There will be windows, big windows. Thirty-five big windows. That's a lot of light.'

'No. A window is a mirror,' he said and they climbed the

ladder to Roy's floor, stood together and looked out invisible frames, through walls, at the water's still surface. She understands his regret: how we limit transparency, make it impermeable and then name it shelter. Why not let him know the compassion she feels, why the hard mouth? His blue eyes, the long legs, the now longer and greying hair above his ears, and the way his hands smooth and wander his own face and neck; his forearms and wrists tightened and built by the hammering he says he has to do (plywood, now, layered into all bathroom walls where towel racks will hang). Each night in her Swallow Hill rosemary bath, for no more than a minute, she imagines his army tent, storm lantern flickering amber light across his probably bare chest (she saw it last week when he climbed up to check trusses, their perfect fit). What's he reading? Or is he writing poems:

> *The air of the country is not so*
> *Surcharged*
> *With men's ideas that they must*
> *Perforce*
> *Be absorbed,*
> *As is the case in*
> *The city.*

That night last week, with him at the window which was not a window, she resisted the feeling she often has at this euphoric stage of building: we are married, you and I, and we are raising this house to celebrate intimacy. That surge makes her pay attention to finishing details: skewed tile grout, nail holes not countersunk and filled. She turned from Nichol's contemplation and said, 'Fuck off, Nick. Cheer it up. Your stupid moods distract me.'

Introducing the Flying Wallendas. They average seven minutes a room. They shout and curse and dance with each heave of wide board and drink gallons of root beer; they work

to the rhythm of the radio pushed by the flatout now of a
newer, cleaner era, of Creedence Clearwater – 'Proud Mary';
cigarettes dangle and threaten to ignite inflammables. They
squeeze minutes for a break and sit outside high atop
excavated dirt. Their translucent singlets reveal dark furry
bodies. Each man scribbles complex math problems on a
piece of paper; they smoke and compute, drink more root
beer, and relax in this way.

Okay, back at it.

The only English they speak all morning is 'Tapers coming
tomorrow' as they tumble wearily into the truck to catch the
one o'clock boat, back to civilization and who knows what
accommodations and fiscal arrangements with the
government of Canada.

Footprints of cheap runners are etched into every grey
panel in every room. Della had taped plastic over the bathtub
up on Roy's floor, but they have torn that and deposited all
garbage – gum wrappers, pop bottles, Ritz cracker box,
cigarette packages, a used condom (?!) – in the new tub.
Custom demands boarders shit in new fixtures, but these boys
are new here, not yet assimilated to local customs. Let's not
rush it. Nichol looked shell-shocked and Della opened a beer
from his cooler. 'Here, Nick,' she said and laughed at his
brick-broken hands. 'So much for your career as a glove
model.'

They sat on piles of dirt and drank. A small-scale dairy
farmer from up the road a couple of properties – an old-timer
– arrived for all the bits and big pieces of drywall. He drives a
Ford pick-up, a round model, and he poked and puttered,
scavenged and picked it all up, full boards as well, and
offered to pay. The finishing carpenters were too polite to ask
what for. But Nichol, glad to be washed of evidence of 'those
boarder assholes', shook his hand and said, 'What the hell do
you want with that toxic crap?' Out in the Strait of Juan de
Fuca, Nichol said, ghost barges dump phantom walls beyond

the hundred-mile limit. Some disposal crews, dodging fuel costs, will skirt Race Rocks and sneak and tuck behind Frazer Island, out of radar's sticky reach, and tip the load onto shallow and shingled reefs temporarily teeming with life. The old man said, 'That's just the paper, for Chrissakes. Rip that off and you've got something.'

She stops her bicycle beside the farmer's fields on the way back to Swallow Hill the next evening. Hereford cows like nuggets of wisdom are scattered between wiser Garry oak and manzanita. Around the bathtub water troughs, he has laid the drywall, one layer thick, like snow on the ground in summer. Since yesterday, his cattle have considered this their lavatory. They have pissed and shit and stomped over it, the lime has begun to crumble already, to leach into starving and soured soil, mixed now with crucial and bountiful elements, trace and otherwise, to alter pH. They climb the walls. His fields, celtic in their green, shimmer between adjacent ones that have lost their vernal youth to hot wind, insufficient well water, pounds of prefab fertilizer.

Always one for a good image, for transformation, Nichol wants to know a cheap way to truck Mainland drywall to supply the farmer, and now himself, with fertilizer by the board foot. 'I need to get this soil more neutral,' is his latest project. The two finishers are always present, trimming and sanding and sawing little shelves for tiny nooks. A bookcase is miraculously embedded in the space under the staircase leading to Roy's floor, another behind the main floor toilet, a linen cupboard tucks into the hallway outside the master bedroom. The windows are framed with a tidy wood trim, plenty of angles and clean lines and subtle reveals. The house now looks solid, old, the beginnings of home and its implied comforts. Della considers taking a bottle of wine back to Nichol's tent but gets on the bike and rides to Swallow Hill.

* * *

The evenings will still require the sweater, though Della's taken longer than planned. She has been back to the yarn shop and its lavender lady for advice about sewing the pieces together. 'You come back when you're ready, I'll show you invisible. It will revolutionize the way you finish.' One half of one sleeve, then the neck border and she'll be done. Della thinks of Perry Como, of her father crooning *Catch a falling star*, their cardigan sweaters in her garden.

The day before she came to the island to build Nichol's house, on June seventeenth at three-thirty on a bright afternoon in the city, Della spied on Jeff, the husband of her friend Becky who keeps the roadside veggies stand: 'Don't Steel: Ask If You Need Food.' Watch this: in the broad window of a back-street bistro, with two fingers of one hand, Becky's husband Jeff places an already perfect wisp of hair behind the ear of Ms Batten (grade three: Enriched *and* Special Needs). Then Jeff touches the ear, both fingertips. Ms Batten reaches across the little iron table, picks up Jeff's cigarette from the ashtray, and performs a fellatious act on it, then a long and squinty exhale over his shoulder, maybe into his ear. Ms Batten uncrosses her knees and then stretches out her shimmer-hosed legs like an on-ramp. Ms Batten's olden-days schoolmarm lips.

Smoking?

Handsome Jeff turned to look out at Della staring in at him. She thought of the yellowed polar bears at the zoo every birthday party until she was thirteen, how appalled those bears seemed when she pulled out the harmonica her father gave her that morning. Their hard and heavy heads swung as she played the intro to 'Wichita Lineman', the one-note staccato urgent part. She remembered the man who leaned into her eight-girl party crowd, pushed her against the railing, shoved his Kodak Instamatic up her little kilt, groaning as he got off his shot. How she didn't tell because it was her birthday.

Her friend's husband: National Geographic and the empty, open tundra. Della didn't tell.

In 1972, at eighteen, she spent a prickly afternoon in bed with a racquetball star from her father's tennis club because he resembled Derek Sanderson of the Boston Bruins. The Turk: his poke check a lazy lovely sweep, the white skates, the hard eyes and their end-of-career puff, the sideburns' expanse and the rock-star shag of hair; the perverse post-game locker-room cigarettes. Unwilling to fight, but he never backed down or out of a scrap, the scars accumulating like paint chips on a car door. For her father, the princely Jean Béliveau. And so the dining-table fallout regarding the incoherent racquetball player who said to her, 'I'm trouble, every girl in high school knew that. Who'd you know in high school? Did you know Chris Ferry? Doug Derkson? Did you know Sylvia Washburn? What's your dad's income?' – son of a real estate baron.

Parents, her deadbeat brother, screwed-up golden cocker spaniel, Della: hostages to the stuffed beef hearts and scalloped potatoes, to the absence of a crystal chandelier, to the television news still cranking out of the living room. A break in the action and her father said, 'The locker room was all about you today, Della.' The space between them expanded, a regulation-sized rink of ice. Just before Mother could enforce the family-wide shunning of the naughty daughter, her father cleared his throat and took a long drink from the evening's second of four Scotch-and-waters, looked at Della's hands, her face, her hands. 'Jean Béliveau,' he smiled at the dog, 'is a gentleman. As I've always said.'

Single men do not arouse her. Visible hunger and easy satiation disgust her. In those who are spoken for, though, Della finds an appealing distance, appetites satisfied, no room for dessert, that's plenty, thank you – and yet, room for her. These relationships have been bubbling since she was sixteen when a thirty-year-old restaurant manager – Michael Landon as Little Joe – claimed he didn't know what love was until pubescent Della clarified it for him. Of course, he discovered he was in love with his sterile wife, but thereafter kept in touch, called occasionally. Della's mother, who did not sympathize as Della thought she would, called a lawyer to check on the viability of the alienation of affection law. The dear family friend lawyer had begun to carry a small Chanel handbag and to frost his hair. He told Della's mother, 'That one went out with the sixteen-hundreds. The wife isn't gonna sue you. This is not a legal matter, even. At nut-crunching time, he'll pick up where he left off – torqued up for a while – and sweet Della will swallow a bottle of aspirins having bussed downtown to see Zeffirelli's *Romeo and Juliet*.' He spoke like television.

'What about disowning her, can I?'

'She's fucking somebody, for fucksakes. Everybody's fucking somebody. That's the part you don't like, you keep seeing your little girl licking some guy not of her own era. What are you afraid of? That she'll like it? That people will think she's a slut? We're all sluts, right circumstance.'

Women who frequent men not datable are, typically, bereft of love from parents. Fishing with Dad, shopping sprees with Mom, these are the little time-consumers that keep girls from breaking more fortunate homes. So, Della stayed off guys with kids. She picked established relationships in which young men had grown bewildered with adulthood. At forty-two, though, she has never had a relationship with anyone who did not belong to someone else. She did not want to burgle hearts. She only occasionally visualized the wife as crumpled roadkill beside a back road. These relationships proved something and disproved something else. Evidence of her value and its opposite.

The erotics, however, were always off. Della is a lovely forty-two. Her hair is still youthful and dark and tumbly. She does not dye the swatch of Emmylou grey on the right side.

The small lines at her eyes endorse her attractive humour.
Her body is brown and hard and she moves with precision
both on and off the job. Her breasts are still upright without
the *Sturm und Drang* of childbirth. Each of the infidels,
though, right back to number one at sixteen, has grown
sexually passive. There is a point when the fruity brunches
and seaside beers continue, but the cunnilingus in their wake
does not. Pointless to shave her legs when even the talk lacks
fumes of arousal. Della has blamed: pornography, wives, body
odour, cellulite, Plumb Line Construction, feminism, her
vocabulary. The men remain blameless, in tune with
microchips of desire.

There have been phases of her life. For each of them, Della
was surrounded by a community of men she could arouse. In
university she was one of only three female architecture stars;
a lineup formed that she could not get through by exam time.
In the first firm she worked at, again a token skirt, the sexual
tension in the little brick office was both good and bad for
business: even married men sulk when dismissed, contracts
are broken. The year she took off from building and saw
Wyoming and Montana, the runaway boys on the buses were
all would-be writers, looking for the right character, the long
enough legs to work into their cowboy novels.

But something arrived and then left town. Why do men
now ignore her in any but the most practical ways? Until
now, flirtation was the top note of her conversations.
Although men still populate her realm – drywallers,
plumbers, finishing carpenters and their short shorts, their
nice fingernails – Della does not sense heat. She has passed
through some sexual riparian zone and now dwells in a land
of little contact, no sustainable erotics. They do not look at
her that way, and if she thinks hard, she has also lost the will
to thigh slide, hair toss, lip purse, calf flex. She dwelt once in
a verdant land and now watches for changes in the dry and
the beige, for an ecosystem to emerge and diversify.

Nichol has left the little island to retrieve his boy. There has been some trouble in Vancouver, but Della isn't clear on details. The list of instructions, directions, requests and promises Nichol left her lacks emotion. What made poetman get so cold?

13. Why Is Concrete Used for Building Purposes?

As soon as concrete has been mixed, if left undisturbed, it begins to harden, and soon becomes like stone. The hardening, which is a chemical change, continues for a long time. Concrete grows stronger with age. This increase in strength is the quality in which concrete differs from all other materials. Concrete is low in cost, sanitary, proof against rats, fireproof and water-tight.

The Book of Wonder, Vol. XVI (1932)

The boy says, 'I like your sweater.'

Della holds out a hand to shake his and says, 'Thanks. I made it.' The boy and his father – a tired and tense Nichol – look at each other and then out to the water, away from her and her trespasses. So knitting is now obscene?

'Put your stuff in the tent and wait for me in there, Roy.' The suitcase is heavy and oversized; the boy is slight, blond, and carries his beautiful shoulders straight.

'You sound like Mr Bad Cop, Nick. Is it that nasty? Is the boy wanted in this province?'

'Did the plumber show, Della? Do we have toilets? What's the septic status?'

She touches his forearm to transport him back to Arcady. He won't look at her. 'Everything's fine, Mister Boss. Nothing is overdue, or past due, or undue. You have flushable toilets, you have sinks in cabinets, you have tubs that fill and drain. You've got spurs that jingle jangle jingle. In fact, you have hot water. In fact, your plumbing is caulked.'

'Is that how slow the shingles are going on? Is the guy getting hourly or a flat fee? Who's the kid with the stupid pants?'

There is a point in all contracts when the homebuilder

achieves the apex of efficiency and then explodes with details and the threat of the end. He is done building and now wants to live again but doesn't know how to let go of the courtship, the process. This is the time permanent arguments happen and bills don't get paid. Della is adept at negotiating this smooth-over; it is like good sex, she believes. 'Yes, he is slow, but you will have magnificent corners and on this house, less than magnificent corners would be disaster. This many corners makes it slow. That's his son, eighteen years old; he's a trumpet player, favourite radio station Seattle FM jazz. They're both getting hourly, so this would be a good time for you to apprentice and learn to shingle. It's soothing. It's like knitting – one row follows the next and it goes on and on. Or it's a poem – line after perfect line. The pants are fashionable in Vancouver, where these guys hail from, and they will not fall down, no matter what it looks like. The pants, I mean. Your fencer came by and dropped off the posts and rolls of wire. I told him the sheep come Wednesday and he said, "perfect", so he obviously thinks he can get the job done in time. By the way, Mr Fence Man once played solo trumpet in high school when Vic Damone came to sing with their band. His thighs are so big he can't get jeans to fit. When his kids grow up, he's moving to the Queen Charlotte Islands, with or without the wife he worships, who washes her ceilings three times a year. The good news is, he's also a sheep-shearer, has a degree in agriculture from a university in Ireland, and he makes his own beer, which, I can attest, is awfully good. Also, he loves your house, and asked that I pass on his compliment.'

'So you're fucking the contractors now, Della?' Nichol walks away and bends into the tent.

The finishing carpenters are clicking the clamps on their metal boxes and unzipping their tidy overalls, folding them, placing them in easy-access piles in the back of the van, ready to zip on in the morning. They comb their hair and reapply sunscreen to their chiselled faces, over their ears, along the back rise of their necks.

Della has wheels and she's not afraid to ride.

Nichol bursts out of the tent like it's full of bees and places his hands along the handlebars of her bike, then places his hands on top of hers. 'I am incredibly sorry I said that to you. Please come back tomorrow.' They're not usually so close, their faces.

Della speaks slowly, trying to see through the dense fog of her outrage. Are you in there, Nick? His hands are so heavy on hers, like layers of blankets in winter. 'If it was your business, if I thought it meant anything important to you, Nick, I'd say you're psychic, I did indeed fuck the fencer last night, by moonlight out in the middle of what will soon be your sheep paddock. Not fucking likely.' Nichol removes his hands; she is untouchable. 'If it was my business? You'd now tell me what happened with Roy, because you are a mess and I hate mess.'

He hasn't looked at her. The flock of crows that appears each evening at this time, rises above them and each member takes cover at the top of a Douglas fir. 'He helped another kid burn down an empty preschool. He brought his grandpa's kerosene.'

'Who told?'

'He called his Aunt Louise – she's in Sapperton – and asked her to take him to jail. She called me, etc.'

'Get him a dog.'

'Pardon me?'

'A dog. He needs a big dog.' She has pulled away from his hands and loops figure eights around Nichol with her bicycle. The crows natter. 'We need to discuss decks, Nick. You can't have fir boards in this climate, they'll rot out in five years. You're opposed to treated, so I'm suggesting concrete with an aggregate finish. I've got a guy bringing samples tomorrow and I left an article on the process on the counter in the kitchen. Yes, you have a counter in the kitchen. Appliances Tuesday, painters Wednesday, provided the finishers can give it up and let it go. Ten days at the most, then I'm gone.'

'The man and his boy are here for you, Della,' sings the Swallow Hill hostess, 'So I've brought your coffee in a thermos – creamed and sugared – and I tucked a half dozen blackberry muffins into a little backpack, and you'll find a small tub of soft goat cheese, some flatbread, and a jar of greengage jam as well in the cooler bag. Oh. There's an extra tube of sunscreen in the bathroom cabinet if you're running low. The day looks hot. Anything else you'll need?'

Della is still in bed. Today is varnish on wood floors, and they need to stay away. Too much air circulation plus too much dust equals shitty finish. She planned a day at Swallow Hill to knit Roy's sweater (denim blue Egyptian cotton bum-covering rolled-neck drop-shouldered guernsey), drink coffee, phone and harangue the contractors for the job she starts in the city next week, drink more coffee, knit, sleep through the heat of afternoon with thin curtains drawn, then in the cool, cool, cool of the evening, look for the sheep shearer, a bottle of red wine, just to see. The hostess, her yellow skirt fluttery, stands in Della's doorway. 'How long have they been waiting?' She can't find her other sock, she can't find a clean T-shirt. Laundry, too, pencilled onto the day's overruled blueprint.

'Five minutes, give or take. I'll let the men know you're on your way down. I'll leave clean socks on the hall table outside the bathroom. Oh. Let me pop a bottle of lemon water in that pack, and a few Scotch mints and a couple of yellow plums for the little boy. I've clamped my wicker basket onto the front of your bike so you won't have all of this loaded on your back. There's a beach towel at the bottom, just in case.'

Five minutes?

'I've found the perfect woman for you, Nick,' Della says as

she mounts the bicycle. 'She knows magic.'

'I know,' says Roy. 'She already gave me a chocolate chip cookie.' Its remnants shape his perfect lips and the teeth they cannot conceal. 'My dad got a gigantic cup of coffee with cinnamon and whipping cream on top, or something.'

'Let's move,' says Nichol.

'Move to where?' Della asks, circling, warming up, still sleeping and wanting to proceed with her original plans. Roy is in high spirits, though, and Nichol – perhaps the hostess's brew gets credit – seems perky and delighted by the surprise they have screwed her up with. His face is shining and dark brown. For the first time in three months, he's wearing shorts, his legs clad in the whiteness of many years. Why so pale? Nichol can't keep still on Hiawatha. The legs kick and flex and twirl the huge pedals. The bike is a relic. He rides the good times. It must be eight o'clock and the morning is broad and hot, the birds suffering the heat in silence amid the leafier trees.

'Picnic, Georgina Point,' Nichol says and they are off up the hill on the curving road, beyond Swallow Hill Cottage.

'They've got a deserted lighthouse and probably some shipwrecks,' shouts Roy, but he's in the lead and flying, a zigzagging maniac on the now dirt road, no gears high enough for what he feels, the pure torque.

So he is kind of married, but does that qualify him for Della? By mid-morning, Della and Nichol recline in sand and tufts of crumbling August grass, in lighthouse shade, the Strait of Georgia spangled and wanton before them. Roy: climb high barnacled rock, plummet to small clear spot of beach, roundhouse arms and shriek simultaneously. *Encore!*

Nichol pours sand from both fists onto his knees. Naturopathy. 'His mother died when he was two. He got imaginary friends: Steve, Ricky, Helga.' He looks at her and almost laughs. That was close.

'Helga?' Maybe if she laughs he will. Nope. The coffee is freighted with maple syrup and light cream. The muffins have dark speckles of mint leaves and orange zest. How do people learn to make life like this?

'I have no idea. Maybe from a book. Maybe Helga's someone his mother knew; they spent the first two years together, travelled together. See him yakkety-yakking up there?' Roy has his long arms out, pretending to be either a fighter pilot or a seagull, hard to figure allegiances at ten years old. 'He's daring Helga to jump even though she's scared. He's telling her she can do it, there's nothing to worry about. He always terrorizes Helga, makes her do bad stuff.' Helga jumps, tries to fly, can't. Flap, flap, flap, thunk. 'Ricky is the one who makes the bed and hangs up his towels.'

'And Steve?'

'Redneck. Racist. Foul mouth.'

'This all seems normal, right? You've done a good job with him, Nick, considering you did most of it alone.'

Nichol takes a last theatrical gulp of coffee and flings the rest behind them into brown grass. 'I've never lived alone more than a month since Arden died. Everything good about Roy, I owe to my absence. Everything bad, likewise. Hear the sea lions out there?'

'That's bullshit. So what have you heard about the school here, Nick?' The sea lions sound trapped or very happy.

'Small. Small. And small. I've heard four boys and six girls on top of Roy. That's a pretty nice student/teacher ratio if you ask me. He'll be fine. He's a reading fiend, several grades ahead, his last teacher told me.'

'And social skills with so few?'

He dusts off his knees, sits up and crosses his legs chief-style, tidies up persona for the keynote address. 'I believe that schools are, at best, a slick and publicly funded system of incarceration. As we know, prison relationships mimic the violence and aggression and misused power of the outside world. If anything, prisons reinforce deviance, they do not teach love, grace, respect, passion, and never art. Here, on this island and in a country school, Roy has at least a slim chance of acquiring those virtues.'

Della is trying to put her finger on Nichol's tone. Smarmy preacher? Esteemed colleague? Last-call barfly? An asshole with excess complete sentences? She screwed a professor once who resembled Richard Burton or Joe Namath, she can't remember. After sex at his glassy little condo, sipping white wine in the living room, he made her put on his black nylon trouser socks because the white shag carpet would absorb oils from her feet and so be a magnet for dirt. There she was: floozy underwear and socks like her father's. The encounter brought down her grade, she assumes. Della hates professors.

'I spent some time with gypsies in Wales when I was younger,' Nichol goes on. 'Sure, those dark children were scoundrels and thieves, but they were also passionate, full of joy and enthusiasm for their work and for their relatives. I never saw a child cry.'

She cuts in, breaks his stride, shuffles the deck. 'Isn't gypsy culture also run on a macho system that says – and I'm translating here – "Crying is for dickless wussies?"' But Nichol does not go along with her tease. He brushes now absent sand from his knees, irritated suddenly with its presence, its grit. Roy leans against the lighthouse window behind them, his hands cupped around his face, muttering, trying to see the abandonment in there. She could touch his leg if she tried to fly.

'Okay. All I know is, I have never felt more full of my own essence – call it masculinity if you want – as when I lived with those people. I think what I learned – about duty, and obligation, and family dynamic – is very healthy. You, of course, Della, might consider me – what did you call that slimeball electrician we fired? – a "chick-fascist".'

Della kissed his cheek quickly, one firm hand on his

shoulder. 'I like you, Nick. And I like Helga,' she said, 'I worry for her in such a culture,' and tiptoed and pranced down to the shore, her feet still hot, her legs requiring the first aid of sea salt. Many minutes later, she can smell the hiking trail, the coffee, the mint, the lowered tide on her skin. She pulls the shorts higher up her thighs, then lifts the hot dark hair from the back of her neck, turns to the beach, and watches Nichol: writing. Roy has a long stick now, and points it like a rifle at every bird he spies or makes up.

They are all too cranky for proper goodbyes. Roy takes off down the road, confident of destination. 'You all look pooped!' chirps the hostess from her veranda.

'Thank you for the goodies,' Nichol calls to her as he wheels into the late afternoon. 'See you tomorrow morning, Della. It was good to talk.'

'Great legs, Nick,' she makes a final effort at intimacy but knows it is not enough for that kind of man. She is neither gypsy nor ghost.

In the sunroom, showered and fed arugula salad and Roma tomatoes with cilantro, fancy beer, she is at last a citizen of the Everly Brothers' ancient nation built on the paradox of skittish fraternity and tight harmony, the pump and fucking groove of a Roy Orbison cover: *My brand new baby is my brand new wife*: *Claudette*. The volume she's at spears the snare drum's slap into her top vertebrae. Albert Lee solos sexy waterfalls, rock slides, the mortar of Telecaster grace notes.

She finds the poem from Nichol tucked into the front pocket of her backpack.

Many Uses for Concrete

churches, squash courts,
barns, sundials, dog kennels,
greenhouses, water-towers, chicken-houses, cisterns,

clothes-poles, garden-rollers, jetties, dams, pontoons, monument:
balustrades, bridges,
swimming-pools, piggeries, drinking-troughs,
mangers, reservoirs,
masts.

More uses for concrete:

piers, walls, houses, pipes, belfries,
motor pits,
tennis courts, staircases, roofs,
harbours,
blackboards, lighthouses, canals, pergolas, platforms, caissons,
  cow-stalls, barges,
signal towers,
telegraph poles.

Now what's all that supposed to mean? *So sad to watch good love go bad.*

She wants to be on site when the concrete is poured. The small cement truck, its beehive drum ready to roll on top, arrived on the last ferry last night. The clutch of men knocked together the plywood forms for Nichol's many decks, finished off by lantern light, vamoosed for the little hotel and its beer-heavy pub. Crack of dawn: we pour.

Finches are up and at it in the lush hedgerows on the road to Nichol's house. Hunched rabbits stay put in the weeds, oblivious to Della's bicycle at that hour. Her legs, she notes, have gone dark brown from the summer's evening rides, yesterday's beach. Her hands: is that called leathery? At this age?

She has brought Swallow Hill blackberry scones, goat cheese and a tall thermos of Ceylon tea to share with Nichol. The schedule ticks on and these mornings will be few. He still has his heart set on wooden decks and it will take all her skill to smooth him through this morning of thick batter scooped into rigid forms. She has shown him photographs of rural craftsy Olmsted, Morris, and described their use of concrete, its necessary permanence, its friendliness to lichens. Pre-plan cracks, she counselled, woolly thyme will thrive and carpet. 'What about more bricks?' Nichol had countered with his own layers of romance, but Della explained they would have to be new ones, manufactured for weight and weather, crumble resistant. 'You can get distressed ones, but kiss good-bye to many thousands of dollars. And they're a nightmare to set.' And they would not resemble those he has corrupted and trowelled into his low wall around the huge garden and its extension to the beach. He accepts concrete.

The skiff is not tied to the tilting and tumbly dock: they must be fishing. Outings, two days in a row? Della regrets the absent family, but feels the promise of friendly tired faces, salt and sea burned, climbing the sand to greet her with the morning's catch in the morning's climbing sun. She will offer to fillet, marinate and barbecue. She will save the scones for that.

But here comes Nichol to greet her. That looks like fondness around his eyes, perhaps the first light of a more meaningful flirt. 'Hey,' he shouts and seems happy, 'I'm glad you're here.' He calls for Roy, bellows the boy's name into the trees and towards the beach. 'Breakfast!' he hollers. It is the trucks that give him energy. The day the site was packed two deep with contractors' vehicles, he'd grabbed Della's shoulders, kissed her forehead and said, 'This is so great. They're really going at it.'

'Where's the boat, Nick?' she says quietly and puts her hand on his forearm to underline it. She is accustomed to details, the way they fit together, knows how one thing must lead to the next in construction, the fraction-of-an-inch discrepancy of a window's frame will screw the mechanism that opens it, its hinges. One wall off-plumb and the whole house binds and buckles. She pays attention to a million things at once and links them in her mind. Missing boat plus missing boy equals – ?

In the morning when the winds are the strongest through the Strait of Georgia (and at their lightest in Juan de Fuca Strait), northwest winds will move across the northern Gulf Islands shortly after dawn.

Heavy freshets from the Fraser River increase the rate of south-going tidal stream.

On strong flood tides, violent rips, dangerous to boats, occur over an area extending from mid-channel, south of Mary Anne Point, to Georgina Point.

The wind came all ways.

He is off Helen Point or Mary Anne Point or Georgina Point in a tangled mess of current and wind, the clouds low puffs coming fresh and fast across the morning sky. First plan: row to the Mainland and surprise Louise. Second plan: row around the island back to Georgina Point and surprise Nichol. Final plan: stay in the boat, stay close to shore, do not get wrecked on the rocks.

The letter Della received from Nichol in September thanked her for her calm and support on that tortured day they thought Roy battered and lost. 'I handled the whole thing badly,' Nichol wrote, 'and I owe you so much for so many things you have done for us. I yelled too much. I hardly said goodbye, so wrapped up in my boy and his fuck-up. I hope it is not goodbye.'

October's letter detailed the litany of manures he had

added to the kitchen garden, the sand, the peat, the compost, all the fertile amendments, the purple sprouting broccoli planted and coming up already, the promise of broad beans in the early spring, given the heat of the brick wall, Cowichan Valley lathyrus. 'Yes, Della! There is thyme in the concrete cracks!' Roy was settled at school. 'Roy says thanks for the sweater. He looks great!' Nichol dropped the prison metaphor and said he was spending time in the classroom himself, teaching poetry some days, bricklaying the next, weather pattern lore. 'So you're fucking the schoolteacher now, Nick?' she wanted to say. And he was. Debbie moved into the new house in November: no letter that month, but a quick note to say the seal on the big window overlooking the bay had broken and the panes were a messy fog of condensation. 'Will this be how it goes? Who is responsible?' he wrote in what sounded like a schoolteacher's superior bluster.

December, the ewes began to lamb on Christmas Eve and produced into the New Year. Nichol and Roy and apparently Debbie took turns at night, every two hours, gumbooting out to the new shelter to check progress. By January 11, twelve lambs – seven of them healthy ewes. 'Hey,' he wrote, 'your sheep-shearer knows his anatomy. He was a big help with middle of the night panic situations. His wife remains, by the way.' He wrote too poetically about the language and energy and smells of lambing. 'No deaths this year!' he bragged. The only mention of Roy: Debbie gave him a three-volume history of the Canadian Pacific Railway for Christmas and he's on number three already. Is he bragging about the boy, or his taste in women?

March, things begin to crumble. 'I came across a Turkish proverb: "When the house is finished, death enters."' They have lost four lambs to island dogs – an Alsatian and a lovely, happy Bouvier de Flandres – and their feral appetites. Roy found two, their throats and bellies ripped out, the dogs lurking, ecstatic for more blood, more panic. One the next morning, the last the night Nichol wrote his letter. 'Roy is taking everything hard. School doesn't please him, I don't please him. He is eleven now and critical and correcting and he whistles twenty-four hours a day. He wants to move back to Primavera and seems to think he has a legion of friends there, though I know nothing about them. We certainly haven't met. Debbie says he's trouble at school, joining the tough-guy trio like a practising hooligan.'

Island friends would not come over to play. Roy had his mother's Fender ReVerb amplifier set up on his floor, her Shure microphone plugged into it. He liked the violence of feedback and turned the volume to 10 and pointed himself at the glittery speaker, its beer-glass tattoo on top. A rock star's shrieked 'Are you in there?' would expand and mutate into a hundred thousand decibels. Black cardboard now covered Roy's windows. Nichol grew tired of intervention.

April. 'Dear Della: What do you make of this story, written by Roy and handed in to his teacher, Debbie, yes, the woman I love':

The Hundred Thousand Squirrels

This is a story that begins on the banks of the Nimpkish River, in Cascadia. There are villages on the banks of the Nimpkish, and in one of them a little boy called Henry lived in a wooden shack with his father and mother. It was his business to make bread for his father and mother while they were busy outdoors, fishing for the great salmon returning to the mighty Nimpkish River.

But one day Henry found it hot and also dull in the shack where he was busy with the bread, kneading it, pushing and pulling it. The sun was hotter still outside, but when he went to the door and looked out, Henry saw cool shadows under the cedar tree, cooler than the dark of the shack because of the breeze that was lifting the big boughs and letting them flop softly back again. So Henry went and lay in the shadow of the tree.

Presently his father and mother came back hungry for their bread, and when they found that Henry had forgotten all about it, that it had risen and spilled over the edges of its dish, the mother beat him till he was very sore, and then made heavy bread and sweet cakes and raisin buns for herself.

Henry ran away, along the river for a while, and then turned away, into the forest.

There were ravens in the forest, black and strong and shiny, and they shrieked loudly as they flew from the tall cedars to the Douglas firs, and to the feathery hemlocks. There were bald eagles soaring high above the trees and the ravens saw and chased them higher still. There were snakes, spotted and shiny ones, brown and yellow ones, and black ones and they slid away into the long grass and bracken. There were swarming anthills and there were bright green tree frogs and there were bigger things, too. Cougars and black bears.

Henry heard the young alders crack and the branches break, and saw the high ferns wave where the big beasts were stepping. He also heard them roar. He thought they would probably claw him and then eat him. But he did not mind, because his body was sore. And then a grey squirrel dropped to the ground in front of him. The squirrel had been still on the bough of a tree watching Henry for some time.

'What is the matter with you?' asked the squirrel.

'I have been beaten,' said Henry.

'No, no, that is not what is the matter with you,' said the squirrel.

'What is it, then?' said Henry.

'Why, your beating is over, and your skin is already not so sore as it was. The matter with you is that you want to tell a hundred thousand people about it, and there's no one to listen to you.'

'Yes,' sobbed Henry, 'that is quite true. They are eating bread and cakes and buns at home, and if I try to tell them about it my mother will only beat me again and make me more sore.'

'Come with me,' said the squirrel, 'and you shall tell a hundred thousand people, and they shall weep for your sore body, and you will feel better.'

Henry ran through the undergrowth of the forest, following the huge tail of the squirrel. Henry ran with him for a long time. He was too busy dodging branches, and jumping over fallen logs or puddles of mud to notice how they went; so he was not surprised when the trees came to an end and the forest opened into a white city lying in white brick ruins. There were fallen temples and wonderful broken pavements, and everything shone dead white in the hot, glaring Cascadia sunshine.

There were no people in the city, but as for squirrels – there seemed to be more than Henry believed there were in all the forests of the world.

'Tell these people,' said the squirrel who had brought him. And when the other squirrels crowded up, this squirrel looked laughingly at Henry, and went away, and sat alone on the brick steps of what had long ago been a temple.

'I have been beaten and my back is sore –' began Henry.

'Aah!' said a hundred thousand serious-faced squirrels, their shiny eyes fixed on his face.

'Because I lay in the sun and neglected the baking while they were working.'

'Aah!' said the hundred thousand squirrels, all looking interested.

'My name is Henry, and I am very miserable.'

'Aah!' said the squirrels.

'My mother has cast me out with a sore skin and no cakes or buns.'

'Aah!' said the squirrels.

'A sore skin and no bread,' said Henry again, for he could not think of anything else to say.

'Aah!' said the squirrels, as if these were only the beginnings of his troubles.

Henry could not think of anything else, and he was very unhappy, because he wanted to complain.

'Aah!' said the squirrels.

'A sore skin,' said Henry miserably.

'Aah!' answered the squirrels impatiently. He heard some of them say, 'Is that all?'

'No bread,' he said once more; and then getting up quickly, he looked for the squirrel who had brought him.

'Please take me back,' he said. 'I am not miserable enough for these people.'

And the squirrel said, 'I thought so,' and laughed a high chatter, and took him back. But he was not beaten again. His mother was glad to see him and gave him a warm bun and put him to bed.

Now, that is the best of all ways to be comforted. If ever you feel miserable, go and tell it to a hundred thousand squirrels, and you will find that you are not miserable enough.

By June, Della is living in Vancouver, converting industrial into domestic and residential, stripping whitewash off brick, taking it back to its original state. Open-plan warehouses, brick roundhouses. Early Canadian wood floors with the wear and tear of labour: she sands them down, but not too clean. Nichol's July postmark is Primavera. 'Roy and I will try again,' Nichol writes. 'The tenants have done considerable damage. But the garden looks lush and happy. You tried to warn me, Della, and now this. Roy and I will rattle in this huge house, but I will stay alone – no more Debbies – stay focused on him, on myself. The island house is empty, maybe doomed. Or maybe he'll want it some day.'

VI

Roy

14. What Does Birthright Mean?

In nearly every part of the world, at one time or another, alike among savages and among civilized people, the eldest son had special rights and privileges over the others. He inherited most or all of his father's property, and had a special right to his father's title and position, whether as chief of a savage tribe or as a duke or king, or as holding some other title or dignity.

The Book of Wonder, Vol. xvii (1932)

Me and two friends went to the lake on Saturday. My dad finally said thirteen is old enough so we were allowed to go on our bikes. We got there around two o'clock. It was Matheson, the really small one that runs along our property and it has good riding trails. But the weather's been pretty hot, so we went to the sandy beach, where people can swim if they want. We wore shorts. Who was there when we got there were:

1. The three of us

2. A lady wearing big shorts and a big hat. She had a little kid, almost a baby but walking and digging with beach toys. The kid – big cheeks, too – had a purple bathing suit and was wearing a hat, too, but hers was smaller and bright yellow. Both had fat legs; you could tell they were related by their legs

3. Two girls our own age (but not from our school), one chubby kind of, one hyper and weird kind of. They kept asking to borrow the yellow-hat-girl's beach toys but the mom said no

4. Those girls' grandmother. She had a hump on her back, just like the sub who comes to our school, the one who tells us to pretend we're in a recording studio to make us be quiet. This one didn't dress like a grandmother. She had on jeans and a pink fluffy sweater. It looked as if she had a softball riding her back.

5. Some Indian kids, one from our school – Chum – who's always in trouble for laughing

6. A whole bunch of rowdies. They had a really tiny baby sleeping in a stroller. A couple of the ladies wore bikinis; also, there were two big black dogs, one tied up, one just running around and yapping at waves. There was lots of beer – two coolers full of it – and they were all smoking what I thought were just cigarettes but my friend said he was positive it was drugs. His real dad smokes drugs, so he knows.

My other friend wanted to leave right away when he saw the rowdies, but I didn't think we needed to. All they were doing was standing around drinking, smoking, and laughing and saying dirty jokes. So what? The beach was crowded, though. It's only as big as a backyard and with all those people it was too small to do much. Even though we brought a frisbee, we cancelled that plan; it would've been too dangerous. The other people seemed all right to me. Kids seemed happy.

My friends' names are

1. Kim, but I and everyone at school except teachers call him Butchy so he's tougher than he's named and

2. Pascal. I call him Pascal because I like the name. I know two guys named Pascal, but the other one's older than us and quite strong.

We were standing in the water and Butchy said, 'Who wants to see who can throw the farthest?' Pascal picked up a rock and said, 'I'm in,' and I said, 'I'm in,' too, like it was going to be a poker game or a bank robbery. We took turns. We watched each other throw out to the white floats that were around the swimming part of the lake, trying to throw past them. They have those things at the pool where I take lessons to mark off the kids' end. Butchy started his throw way down by his ankles, like he was doing the shot put; he muscled off some good throws. Pascal just relaxed and, really cool, wound up like a pitcher would, lifted his leg and put two hands around the rock. He used lots of followthrough. I copied him. We were being careful about other kids. Nobody was close to us. The yellow-hat girl started trying to throw rocks with us, but her mom was there and told her it was dangerous. I tried to show the little girl how to do light throws but she didn't learn, she just wanted to throw hard like us. She'd probably like to have brothers some day.

Then the granny with the hump started screaming at us to stop throwing rocks and to quit scaring everybody. We thought she was being very weird but we stopped for a little while, and just stood around in the water, waiting for her to do something else and be distracted. Throwing rocks was all we felt like doing.

One of the rowdy guys – the skinniest one, who owned the dogs – went up to the lady and gave her a beer. He said, 'Right on, ma'am. I agree a hundred percent. I'd feel bad if I didn't give you a beer,' he said. I thought he was sucking up so he wouldn't get in trouble for the drugs and noise, but Pascal said, 'He's just stoned.'

We waited until the dog-guy was sitting on the blanket with her and then we started throwing rocks again. More people came. We still weren't close to anybody and were being extra careful. Three kids came with their parents and two air mattresses, nice ones. The smallest kid had very white hair. Her bathing suit was too small so you could see almost her whole bum and Butchy said some rude stuff about her, just quietly though. That little girl cried almost the whole time. Her mom said to us, 'She's not very brave. She doesn't like water.'

The chubby girl and her hyper-weird friend asked to use one of the mattresses right away and the mother said okay. I would've said no way. They floated off to the edge of the swimming area and just giggled and kicked their feet, and generally acted weird.

Then the granny hump starts really screaming at us. She

says she's already told us once and she's not gonna tell us again. Pascal turned around and just looked at her and she said, 'And don't give me that kind of look or you'll regret it, mister,' but Pascal always looks like that; he's Estonian. The beer guy yelled, 'You been told, assholes.' It was pretty embarrassing, because everybody looked mad at us. So we stopped. I think Butchy ended up winning.

The mother with the three kids was wearing a bathing suit like they have at the Olympics. She had a flat chest too, like she'd done a lot of athletics. She put on some goggles – first she wet them, then she put them on – and she swam out, under the floats. Her husband said, 'Don't go too far, Pat,' but how could she hear him if she was already swimming? I don't know why he had to say it.

Whenever one of the rowdy ladies went in the water, the rowdy guys hollered and did wolf calls. One guy said, 'Turn around' to one of the ladies walking into the cold water and Butchy told us that meant he wanted to see her nipples get big but me and Pascal already knew what it meant. She didn't turn around. She was a bit fat, too. 'Yuck, beer belly,' Butchy said.

The Indian kids stayed over by the trees, in the water where it was dark and kind of swampy. One of them, a girl with really short hair and long skinny arms, stood around in a T-shirt and really shivered. Her brother (I know him from my class) kept saying, 'You should go in, you should go in' (to the water, he meant) but she never did. She was watching us and smiling at the yellow-hat-girl.

That girl's mom never went more than a couple of feet away from her but didn't tell her not to do stuff and didn't always say, 'Be careful.' When the girl kept saying 'Pickee up pickee up,' the mom wouldn't do it. She kept saying, 'You can do it' and 'You can do it yourself.' I think it's good to talk to little kids like that and treat them with respect. I guess the rocks hurt her feet.

Butchy, Pascal and me were still standing around in the water. We were making bird noises because there was a kind of echo. Even if you were quiet, the lake made it louder. Pascal is a good kingfisher.

When the swimmer finally came back, she asked for the air mattress. The family washed their mattresses off and left. Then four older people wearing really stupid clothes came and stood around and talked about the lake like it was a tourist attraction and took their socks and shoes off and put their feet – very white ones – in the water. The old man had an English accent and said, 'Vera, go and get the towel out of my golf bag, will you?' and all four of them laughed. Not funny. Then they put their shoes back on and walked off. They looked at the puddle on the beach where the yellow-hat-girl was playing and one of the old ladies said, 'Look, everyone, a natural spring,' and they all stood and looked down at the puddle and the little girl put her arms up in the air and yelled, 'Pickee up, Mom. Pickee up.' Her mom gave her juice and a cracker. They sat on their towels with their legs sticking straight out.

The three of us stood in the water up to our knees, balancing cans of pop on our shoulders, first one to spill has bad nerves and no guts. And talked about

1. TV shows we like
2. Hockey players we like
3. Teachers we hate

The rowdies were talking about trucks; one lady laughed really loud all the time and then coughed. Butchy drank his pop, threw a stick and said, 'Yuck. Smoker.'

Then this swan came around the trees, past the Indian kids and right up to the shore. It was very, very big. Its wings were out a little and it looked like pictures in the encyclopedia I have, but I'd never seen a real one and I felt excited. Everyone liked it and started talking about it and coming around to look at it. Pascal got out of the water and warned me not to get near it. One of the rowdy ladies – the beer belly one – came with some bread and she talked to the swan softly: 'Here you go, sweetheart. Oh, you like that do you?' And the swan took the bread from her hand. The skinny dog-guy came and pointed at the swan and said to us, 'See that lump on its beak? That's where it whistles from. That's a whistling swan. That's what's called a whistling swan,' like he was trying to be our dad or teacher or somebody. Pascal said later it wasn't a whistler, it was a trumpeter and they used to be extinct.

Everyone was kind of excited and talking to each other. It was quiet and loud at the same time. The little yellow-hat-girl said, 'Go see it go see it,' but her mom said, 'Not too close, that animal's not for touching, he might snap.' I think that was smart; Pascal said it was possible. 'They are a very mean bird,' he said.

A rowdy with curly hair (I heard him say earlier he didn't show up for a court date that morning) was throwing sticks for the skinny guy's dog. Then he threw one into the water and the swan got scared of the dog; the dog went after the swan, yapping and biting the water, the swan chased the dog and hissed and opened its wings and the dog yelped and tried to fast dog-paddle back to shore and the guy grabbed the dog by the collar and yanked him out of the water. The skinny guy starts yelling and almost crying. 'What the fuck are you doing, man? What the fuck are you doing? Are you fuckin' nuts, man? That's my dog. Are you fuckin' nuts? That goose was after my dog, man. You're fuckin' nuts.'

It was really loud because the water and the trees were so quiet and we were all just silent. The other dog – the tied up one – was yelping now and jumping in circles and getting tangled. Everybody tried to calm down the skinny guy. The hump lady brought him a beer from his own cooler. One of the rowdy ladies rubbed his bare back. The curly-haired guy came up to him and said, 'Listen. Bottom line? The goose wasn't going to get the dog and the dog wasn't going to get the goose.' He said it like a slow song or something. The swan disappeared around the trees. I don't know why they didn't just call it a swan.

Pascal said, 'They're really wasted' and we left. The mom was getting the girl ready to go, taking off her purple bathing suit and putting on a dry diaper. It was really quiet again. The skinny guy said to everybody, 'I just want to say I'm sorry. I want to say to everyone that I'm sorry about the shouting and the language.'

But everybody was mostly gone. Butchy wanted to stay and talk about it, he was really excited about the swearing and the bird. But Pascal just said, 'They were so wasted,' and we started walking up to the parking lot.

We had to walk a long way on the path to get our bikes, through the trees. Their branches overlap and you could probably walk all the way to the road up there. I heard, 'Pickee up, Mom? Pickee up?' and the mom saying, 'You can walk yourself. Let's get going.' The parking lot was full of cars so a lot of people must've been on the trails because the beach was too small for that many cars. Pascal says there's deer in the parking lot when the cars are gone.

15. What Makes the Fire Change Colour?

The fire changes colour partly because of variations in its air supply and partly because of the escape of different gases from the coal. It must be remembered that different substances and gases have their own colours when burning. The flames from different woods show differences in colour.

The Book of Wonder, Vol. xviii (1932)

I packed my grandfather's corroded jackknife and the down vest Louise sent for my last birthday. I put a dozen stick matches in a plastic film canister I got from my dad's middle desk drawer. A half-roll of cheap toilet paper from out in the barn. I packed a hatchet because no one else would think of it. CDs: Janis Joplin's *Pearl* and some Celtic. No one reads: no books. Dried apricots and banana chips, packaged everything, one can of beans, pepperoni sticks from the freezer. Dad made it out of the big old Suffolk ewe in the spring and it is revolting, truly, but we'll get hungry enough.

We will follow the rail grade – easy on mountain bikes – north and up into the mountain to a clearing on the lake Butchy knows about, around three hours. The logging road there is totally grown over, but he knows where it is, where it goes. Butchy says we can bushwhack – his favourite word – in to the lake where we'll make camp, completely gone and invisible. There are trout. Chum is rigging us up some special Indian lines and hooks. Beer's too heavy, a twenty-sixer of whisky each, tequila for Butchy and about a pound of Butchy's dad's dope is lighter. Butchy said he could score harder stuff, so we could all be ready for next year, but I wasn't enthusiastic. I am a loser, but not totally. Pascal agreed.

I want this weekend to be the opposite of when school

starts next week. Grade twelve will mean the end of our time, pushing hard to win the district cross-country, skipping weekends to cram for provincials, jamming new tunes so we get picked to play the dance. Yes, I am a loser, but it won't last.

Good grades plus good money equals out of town and into the city to study, to work: I don't care. Dad's okay with it, but the expense is all mine. Also no problem. We took three cuts of hay off the fields this summer. First time in ten years, the old guys said. I saved many thousands working farms. When the weather was right and the rain held, we baled and hauled hay for twelve hours. We used floodlights in the barn to unload and stack. Our neighbour Isabel would run the tractor, baby on her chest, and I'd follow behind and throw the bales onto the deck. My arms are huge. My neck is black from sun. But the weather cooperated and the fields are clean and smooth. Every barn in the valley is loaded with dry hay and Isabel has sold two fields worth to farms up-island. Between crops, I helped Dad fence the side paddock so the rams don't get out again; in June we planted the chick peas he says will be his retirement fund (as if) and last week harvested everything we could find.

Also, he paid me to type up four new chapters of his book. If he stays up drafting all night, I can't read his handwriting and then he has to read it to me, dictation. He has tapes of really old-timers – the guy with the gravel pit, the cougar lady on Mount Matheson – they all know Dad and feel okay talking to him – and I transcribed some of these for him, too. My lightning hands. Also, I cleaned about a ton of those old bricks from around the property and sold them for twenty-five cents apiece. My lightning hands are gouged to shit. I split twenty-two cords in ten days – fir, mostly and some alder – off the lot at the back. It's piled, some stacked. I can deliver loads to the city all winter. The money gets put away for after school, so I will have choices. There's nothing I want to buy right now anyway. When you list it all like that, no wonder my arms are huge.

They ride like four cowboys, high in the saddle, pumping hard and firm, respectful of the mount and yet fully in charge. There are saddlebags with supplies, rations, a teenager's version of what survival entails. The rail grade is, indeed, flat, a 3 percent incline the most old trains could negotiate. The surface is a soft and historic ochre mix of needles and leaves. The cherry trees – hundred-year-old litter from a passing child, a child on his way to somewhere via rail – are loaded and the young men stop often to feast and stockpile for a future feast at the lake. Apples, too, from an abandoned orchard that has metastasized up the slight slope and onto the shoulder.

'They should make this for trains again,' Roy says without judgement, a glad shout that echoes along the tunnel of mixed forest. The maples show the heat of summer. Their massive bodies are weighted with dust, the yellow of autumn already creeping from the top down. 'I'd like to bring a skidder in here for some of these cottonwoods,' he says. He is alert to the possibilities of commerce, his role in it. Ten thousand wasps persist at his mouth. There's another dormant anthill and Roy wonders if the others recognize the contours.

Butchy rides beneath headphones he put on in the parking lot and wears them still, two hours later. He leads the pack, propelled by some very new and very mean music, smoking thin and tidy joints and not passing them. He speeds up and yanks his front wheel into the sky, slows down and takes it easy, zooms and yanks again. He loves what his bike will do, how it makes him look. His pants are wide and black and must be hot on a day like this. His head is shaved in honour of this trip and the scalp beneath is white, scars crosshatch where hair does not grow. Even in kindergarten – the graceless tumbles from one tree, fence, barn after another –

he was tough. His chest and arms harken back to that era; he is tiny and white and set on trouble, bare feet on pedals merely one of a million safety violations. *'You're a fucking lesbian,'* he screams along to someone's hit parade.

Chum is behind them all, calmly pumping his loose body and laughing at every cowboy quip, every outlaw squirrel that makes a dash beneath his wheels, every useless slug he smears with his fat front tire. He does not ride the centre, but zigags. How does he manage to keep up at all? Chum is magic, and Butchy would be shouting, 'Shut the fuck up, squaw-butt,' if not for that other nasty realm, where the beat throbs on and on and past the present into a violent and dispossessed future. Chum hates that music. He shaved, too. 'I wanted to resemble you, Butchy,' he said in the parking lot and laughed and looked at Roy, 'I like your white-boy style. You want to feel my head, white boy?' Butchy spat into the bushes, applied his headphones and shouted, 'Wagons, ho.'

Pascal has returned from summer's cut block with a revised posture. He is upright, his back broad and moral; he wears a clean straw hat and his dark hair hangs in a ponytail straight between his shoulder blades. He steers with his wrists, letting his battered hands dangle in front of the handlebars, a hint of planter's claw sometimes in the right one; or they rest on his dark brown thighs and pick at persistent insect bites. His legs and arms and face are riddled with such summer scars, his shins a mangle of bruise and indentation. Whenever Chum laughs, Pascal looks pleased, amused by the good will and merriment, but he does not talk as he did three months ago. He is more serious about something and is reluctant to share – to brag – of some new knowledge he's gained. But his body – his hands and the stained muscles in his legs, the way his hair hangs straight and much longer – expresses some certainty about where Pascal fits in the world. Butchy holds up and falls in beside Pascal, *'You're a fucking lesbian,'* he shrieks into Pascal's calm face and then zooms, pulls up on the wheel and darts into the forefront of some bitter movement. 'Hold on. Here it is.' Butchy slides sideways and the boys dismount, drink water from their diminishing bottles, smoke two joints. Roy passes a length of pepperoni and does not hear a complaint. 'What's this? Fucking mutton?' says Chum and Roy is impressed.

Roy's hatchet bushwhacks. He thinks of Louise and her code, 'salal, Oregon grape, kinnickinnick'. He leads, and Pascal – he who no longer gripes at pain or pleasure and seems unaffected by the smoke or the mosquitoes – follows him, tidies the trail, takes over the lead when Roy's hand is too wet with sweat to hold the handle. They team wordlessly. Whenever Chum gets a blackberry branch in the face, he speaks: 'Hey, asshole,' and Pascal says, 'Sorry, buddy,' and they laugh. Butchy is far behind, balancing his bike and Roy's along the tentative trail, shouting commands and insults; he is the wind at their backs and he comes all ways.

Butchy will not remove his pants at the lake but knows he must get into the water. He cannot swim; he floats for thirty seconds. His pants billow in the weeds around him. It is seven o'clock and the sky is not so blue and the air, far up the mountain, seems thinner and laced with cold. The water pours from Butchy's smooth head and he lumbers out, one long shiver. 'Gotta watch for leeches, I'm warning ya, so don't blame me if you get stuck to one. And don't ask me to get it off.' He inspects his thin arms, slaps his torso, looks between his toes, falls back into the grass and sleeps.

Chum takes a hooked line down the shore to below a tilting cottonwood. He also takes a full tequila bottle and an enormous bag of corn chips. 'Hold up.' Butchy slams upright and awake and digs in his plastic saddlebag. He presents a perfect lime at arm's length up to the sun, takes out a pocket knife from one of the hundred pockets in his black pants, places the lime on the seat of his bike, and slices it into six immaculate wedges. Three of these he takes down the beach to Chum, tears a piece of the chip bag, and places the lime slices there. Not a word. Butchy is back and asleep before Chum's mouth finishes its first pucker, before his throat recovers from the poison's burn. The trout will not approach such potential combustion, but Chum doesn't mind.

Pascal and Roy play hackeysack and wait for night's scrim. They are cowboy clowns, waiting for the next bronc rider to tumble down the chute, playing the crowd, causing women's smiles despite the violence in the sky, the tallest trees. They are dancers, but more like funky Greek gods and the little leather ball stays mostly aloft. Their arms are late summer bronze – part dirt, part tan. Their torsos lack the tone and muscle and bulk of men, but the transformation is starting. The work they do has begun to map them, to contour their visible selves. And yet their faces are so smooth. Their smooth faces reflect life's efflorescence, the flirting girls, the sex in even the curving branch of an arbutus tree: they smile always, because that will win them everything. Their weighty little ball drops onto Butchy's chest – 'You fuckin' stinkin' hippie freaks,' he erupts and spews and wings the ball at Roy's head – misses – and goes back to sleep. Down beach, Chum's deep laugh.

You stoked the fire with thick balsam branches. Your hatchet, your new arms swam through the wood. You were drunk, but not too drunk to cover your friends where they slept, around the blaze now heated with the evening's coals. Pascal's face has gone dark in the summer. In the lost light, its sheen on his high cheeks, his long hair shines full across the damp towel he has folded and now sleeps on. He resembles a gypsy movie star about to wake and change the world, choose the moral good no one else has contemplated, mount the most beautiful horse with the fullest mane. All the women want him and yet feel disgraced by their desire.

You wrapped Pascal's bare feet in his canvas fishing vest after checking for barbs and leaking lighters. Those feet are still sore from his summer planting trees at Prophet River. Before this night's holus-bolus drunken blather, he told of the girls on his crew and the colour of their legs, the length and power of their bare arms, and the space between their collarbones where sweat pools. The sculpture of their calf muscles, he called it. Their hair, he said, was one colour at the start of the season, and gradually bleached to something more brittle and fine. The T-shirt turbans they wore by day to dissuade bugs unravelled as they rode the crummy back to camp: the hair toppled over their strong shoulders. And Pascal, each evening, longed for their release. The women bathed in lakes in only thin underwear, or by the end of summer, nothing at all, brazen to the leer of family. Each evening, they cared for Pascal's dark feet, performed shiatsu massage, stimulated numbed pressure points, smoothed warm cocoa oil into his insteps and rosemary oil into the arches, careful to avoid layers accumulating to callus. The same care on each other. The boys on the crew would try to watch, but were too shattered by the day.

Of course, there was one. Pascal has always focused, always leaves enough for everyone, only enjoys what is his own. Sarah.

'Did you fuck her?' Butchy said. 'Come on, asshole, detail it. Tits and hole: specs, man. Calibrate. We need numbers here.' Butchy rode the crest of the night's demon wave, swaying and turning with the season, rocking with the rhythms of Pascal's summer, sucking smoke and hootch. Peanuts in handfuls. Butchy was born a relic of harder and faster times. With night's fall, the crows had shut up. The bats woke and frisked mosquitoes around their heads.

'I don't want it to seem like just that,' Pascal said.

Chum said quietly, 'What is it, then? You held hands with

a big-titted treeplanter for two months?' Chum laughed and so made you laugh. Across the small lake, your own echoes. You do it again and laugh at yourselves laughing at yourselves. Here and there.

'I might see her again. We might try to hook up on the same crew next year. She might go to film school in Vancouver instead.' Pascal removed the elastic band that held his hair off his handsome face. He lifted, swept his fingers through and then let it settle to just below his shoulders. Are those eyes black now or still a very dark brown?

'You wear it like that when you fuck her, don't you?' said Butchy, outraged now by Pascal's looks. 'Aw, Christ, you're turning into something, Cally. You probably used a fuckin' safe, didn't you?' Butchy spat whisky into the fire. 'Is she rich, at least?'

You said, 'She sounds cool, Pascal. Sarah. That's a cool name.'

'All I need to know is,' Butchy was up on his knees, hands spread across his black thighs, 'Just tell me this one thing then I'll drop it: does she, or does she not, Cally, douche with wolf urine?' Chum's laughter, its tumble and romp, drove them once more to the lake and filled them with howl.

Butchy slept farthest from heat, his white shoulders bony and rounded by summer's TV and bad food. Even in profound unconsciousness, his face expressed the cradle to grave piss-off of malfunctioning lungs. No sports, no stamina. To cover him, the big sweater Della sent your dad last Father's Day. She said the lanolin from the animal still permeates that wool and will insulate other animals. Like you, your friends. 'Never be cold, Nichol,' the card said. You worried the heavy sleeves across Butchy's slim chest. You warned the night air, up there close to the sky: do not invade him, rehash the asthma, ear infections, bronchitis and sinusitus. The dance card of Butchy's summer was full of these. For the trip, he packed skin mags so hardcore you had never imagined their images but would never forget them, and tequila. Also, four limes, one for each camper.

Chum, his hair a shadow, was even then too close to the fire, his big socks inches from flame. You lifted his feet and spun him so that his long body pointed into the woods, his head now a body length from the big fire. Chum was a spoke driving the fire wheel. His chest, you noticed, had thickened, beginning to take the shape of his father. In July, Chum fished his uncle's boat, made twenty grand, flew home from Prince Rupert and spent the wad on a truck for the mud races on the reserve coming up in September. He wants to win, and he has the wheels to do it. Across his bare hill of a chest you arranged your vest, removed the vial of matches first and snugged the collar under Chum's chin. Even then, Chum seemed dead, the booze and weed collecting in the sinkhole of his brain, history's deep caverns. His hand still clutched, the bottle within.

You stoked the fire, Roy. You had never been that drunk, that stoned, that released from a summer that made your arms big, your neck black. Your thighs now filled your jeans. Stars, yes. Shooting and fixed, take your pick. You listened to Joplin's tortured screech again, again, again, alert for heroin's residue, humbled by what the biographies call her dark pain. Your mother's voice has escaped but you encounter her in Joplin's throat, pyrotechnics and the booze, laughs, in the tangle of face on the cover. This is not nostalgia; it is spectre. Joplin, you know, lay for eighteen hours in a heap between the bed and the nightstand at the Landmark Hotel in Los Angeles. Her friends ditched the balloon of smack, covered her tracks.

By the end of grade twelve you will be over her. You will understand your mother's flight over Vaseaux Lake and know she did not leave you but her own circumstance, her fire wheel. By the end of grade twelve you will hate her because she pitted your smooth surface with an ugly option. You will watch for opportunities on every highway, curves to misjudge. And these are just the metaphors. Imagine the reality. You stoked the fire.

When the moon was high, Chum got onto his knees, pissed, emptied his stomach into unwary groundcover and then the remaining half of his bottle of whisky down his opened throat. You fell asleep to the shriek and roar of forever-young Janis insisting, 'Trust Me.'

Your grandfather's knife is too dull to cut away the vest and so you leave the green synthetic shell melting into the bubbling skin of your friend Chum's neck. Butchy will ride for help and do it fast enough, but not before Pascal hits him hard and breaks his right cheekbone to stop the inhuman shrieking, the loud assumption that Butchy's pain is worse than your friend Chum's.

You and Pascal woke together when the smell of Chum's roasting face was pushed by some fortunate downdraft. You each took a leg and, crying already and in the gulps that men do, pulled him from further heat. Chum, trying to get warm. Chum, laughing.

'We fucked up,' sobbed Pascal. 'We left him.'

'Is he breathing?' you asked, but both nose and mouth had melted. It was Pascal who placed the pipe between what were once lips and breathed soft air into Chum. You placed one backpack beside him and elevated the burned arm above his heart, as Pascal directed. The summer had taught him first aid, grace under all circumstances. 'Does he have a heart?' but you meant to say pulse and Pascal understood and nodded.

'I stoked the fire,' you said to Pascal, two hours into the many you waited out, the hours into dawn it took Butchy to posse the motorbikes and their good-guy paramedics, while Chum only breathed.

'That's okay,' said Pascal.

'No. I mean I really stoked it,' you said.

You walk quickly with your god's long legs to the lake and wade to your knees, still in the slouching underwear you slept in far from the flames and safe in the sleeping bag your father donated for this trip. You plunge your hot and thick head under water. Whatever the substance is called on your hands – blood, flesh, meat? – its particles are now suspended in the water around you. Chum is everywhere. You see bubbles, come up for air and go under again. Come up.

'Roy,' Pascal shouts. 'I hear them.' A sound like your father's chainsaws, like inboard motors seeking speckled trout offshore on the wide Prophet River, like Butchy's transistor race car circling and circling the parking lot at Matheson Lake, like Angus and his dozer boat shunting five-thousand-dollar logs in Becher Bay, like all the work our fathers do, comes through the thick shrubs and takes over, takes him away.

16. Is It True That Children Will Rule the World?

All individuals are mortal, and the destiny of the world, the ruling and the being ruled, is all in the hands of the children. Those who rule today were the children of yesterday. That is the law of human life. It means that 'a mother is the holiest thing alive'; that history is made in the nursery, that the bringing up of children is the noblest, the purest and the most necessary work in the world. And it is the most difficult, just because the human being is so wonderful and complicated in the nature of his mind and his body.

The Book of Wonder, Vol. XII (1932)

The river still works. Regardless of commerce's digital hocus-pocus, logs must be towed, fish netted, barges and railcars loaded. From his open kitchen window, the day falls into the dirty water, and Roy watches the towboaters and their tides, onboard DVD and the crass canned laughter, their on-line chess matches and short-wave tough talk to American navy ships. Some evenings, barbecued steak wafts over from their decks, a smell – cooking animals – his stomach can't abide. Fish, maybe; no longer the ruminants. The river is all mud and turbulence, but it locomotes. The narrow banks thrive with slick-furred otters and muskrat. Three long blurts of the whistle: the swing span of the railway bridge. The dusk-driven murder of off-shift crows passes over en route to their secret hideaway.

On hot nights like this, he does not wear a shirt, only loose and long and frayed denim shorts, Tom Sawyer shorts with deep pockets for beetles and dead cats and granite. He is so clean. His chest and face are smooth, his arms smooth and muscled. At this point in the year, his blond hair is close-cropped, a ten-year-old's hair. Almost white, almost transparent against his lovely skull. He repeatedly runs his hands over it and waits for the kettle. Bare feet on varnished wood floors. The Louvin Brothers – their skyscraper harmonies and bittersweet major chords, the mandolin's needling, his mother's album – soar over the river and all pertinent tributaries.

If I could only win your love.

These walls were whitewashed but are now the texture and fabric of brick again, history recovered and splashed with modernity. This huge room – his home – was a section of roundhouse for the rail yard on this river. The building is not round. It is only a section of circle, a chunk of curve, circa 1920. Close out Roy's back door, the original turntable now spans a Japanese water garden, the concrete well is loaded with lily pads and bog plants and shaded by cutleaf maples; its trestle, once the lubed swinging arc of the circle's curve, is now fixed as a footbridge across the pond, painted railroad black. He stands in the middle of the bridge, both hands around his mug of black tea, and looks down into the water, past the blanket of chickenwire, to the huge fluorescent koi. From there, that elevation, he looks back at his home and imagines himself – his chest and wide shoulders, the bright blue and ancient eyes – framed in the curve of its golden storm-lantern light: he's here, he's there.

The childhood houses were deadbeat brothers: they got attention but their allegiance was fleeting, changeable, disruptive. Roy's father was tormented by them. He thought his shattered heart would mend with walls, high ceilings and wood windows. Roy has loved those who wanted to ramble and roam, but they also craved permanence, could only function with home comforts. Louise has her houseboat and that seems a reconciliation. People live in trees – deep in the dressy branches of red cedars – in this rain forest.

Twenty years ago, his grandfather brought him here to see the rail yard as it was: a glossy museum concocted by

American tourist-scammers. They had promised to renew the roundhouse, to make it fully operable again, make it heritage, return it to the nine-cars glory days of the twenties – the smith will forge! the cars will steam! signage will explain it! 'Your father would be appalled,' his grandfather said then. They watched a heritage family of quail beat it into the dust beneath the heritage apple trees. They walked along the grade for hours, right into New Westminster, had soft ice cream on Columbia Street.

Della picked up the building cheap when tourists balked at the cover charge. The trains' home, their circuit of commerce – gypsum, lime, coal, Fraser Valley grain, pulp and paper – once motored through Roy's bedroom. Their steam pumped through the smoke funnel that is now the exhaust vent above his gas stove. They puffed away along the clear and straight stretch, through his front door and out across the whole country. The place is all coming and going. It is huge and open – the ceilings must be twenty feet high – and warmed by hot-water heat beneath hardwood floors laid over original concrete. His neighbours inhabit the car shops, signal house, the blacksmith's forge. Four others occupy homes parallel to his in the roundhouse. Each of the five divisions – separated by brick walls – had two sets of track. The walls are so thick, Roy's music can't be heard.

He is in the end unit, and so lives with a wall of much glass and its divisions. The light is always muted and always bright. At night, he leaves the blinds up so he can see the white lights that mark each side under the span of the highway bridge. At the railway bridge, there is a white light at each end of the centre pier projection of the swing span, and there are red and green lights used for signals. Inside, Della left all the tracks and filled in the deep wells beneath them, their servicemen ghosts, and made the wide Douglas fir planks seem original, had the floorlayers work around the building's form and function. Do not erase the past; inlay it into design. *Because you're mine, I walk the line* and there is an echo beneath the grade.

Roy walks on trees to his mother. An air whistle blows in fog.

His mother kept track. The tea is only warm; for this month, he is off red wine. He leaves the back door open to watch the lights on the river, but the daylight is shot. Diesel, creosote, and distant bivalves: these make his forehead feel tight, but they, too, sing. Each night, nicotiana and stock in a half-barrel beside the door retrieve the comfort of Elizabeth, his love for the brain-addled Danny: 'Boy, that's a lot of books you've got,' is how he'd live this night.

The notebooks surround him on the warm floor, the photographs, details: how can this ever be ordered? He sees her alone on the road, unable to find a friend on her breaks, no one to laugh with, to press for baby wisdom. The jukebox kicks in and the music is harder, louder, newer than hers. The bartender is cold and forgets her name. Regulars ignore her according to custom. So she drinks at a little corner table and writes it down. Or at night when Roy is finally asleep and tucked beside her on the sagging, stinking bed, the tips of her fingers are dented and sore, no telephone or TV in the crummy room and, anyway, no one to call. She wrote it all down. His hand – his man's hand – fits across each cover like a mask. Inside, she has traced or copied and schemed her own trajectory: 'You are here' beside a large and sloppy star on each map. And he is.

He is twenty-two months old. She does not name the bar, but the date is there, and he could trace it on her *Heritage Buildings of New Westminster* calendar: she notes gig fees collected; ovulation, period expected, period length and actual arrival; for three months that year, she calculated the circumference in fractions of inches of her thighs, her waist, her chest; on the last month, no gigs, the last ovulation, the doctor's appointment, no period length or arrival, the enigma:

did she abort that one too? Or did it fly with her over Vaseaux Lake? It is too late to ask his father for more details. Nichol must be allowed privacy, their relationship's history. Roy is proprietor of her words, pictures, documents. He spares his father. But tonight's story took place well before that last month.

She always describes the stage. This one, gummy nylon carpet over a hollow box of plywood, the stage the stripper endures on dayshift. Management – Phil – does not allow Roy's mother to use the brightly gelled spotlights: 'Save those for the real show, sweetie, I got bills to pay.' Each night, she lifts her speakers, the ton-of-bricks Fender ReVerb, the rusted and loosening mike stand, the rhythm machine and bass pedals, down to the floor beside the stage. Next night, she boosts them up, sets the angles, replugs patch cords, tunes up. Two weeks, six nights a week. She could use a hand. It is dark on that stage. Third set, she is rocking up the Everly Brothers – 'Claudette'. She has learned some *Nashville Guitar*, some kindergarten Albert Lee licks, and the Roy Orbison – composer – allusion connects them. Roy is upstairs, this time alone: no-show sitter and unreliably on-call sub. His mother believes she can contact him this way, through the songs, their punch, their drive, through the floor/ceiling paradox. The cradle will rock. *My baby thinks he's a train.* She is happy with her hands' new magic. She has graduated from Chuck Berry. In skinny black tights and a little red T-shirt, wide black patent belt cinching in the waist she cannot fathom, she looks authentic. Her hair – dark blond like his own – is a whirlwind mess and has been since his birth. Only one of us can look good at a time. Anyway, third set. *Pretty little pet, Claudette.* For this tune, his mother wears the Big O's square sunglasses, regardless of ambient light. She is being ironic. One knee turns to the other.

A hippie chick in gauzy, glittery skirts, a string-necked blouse over loose breasts, bangles and beads, brings her lovely long and bare feet onto the ten-by-ten parquet dance floor. She is alone there, in the dark, twirling to his mother's voice, the crunch of her Telecaster, the bass-note throb, the rhythm machine's half-depth tick-thud tick-thuds. The girl's hair flies, too, down to her waist. Then she holds it up, twists, and somehow makes it stay tangled atop her head. The girl dances like a wild horse. She flirts with his mother. Because she is happy, his mother adds another verse and as she starts – *Oh-oh Claudette* – a beer bottle smashes onto the floor at the girl's feet. And then a second round. The dancer is very drunk, could be mushrooms, and she embraces this trigger talk as an aesthetic event. Before his mother can stop the music, remove her shades, the girl has lifted her lovely curved arches and now her barefoot boyfriend is with her, dancing too, dancing on glass to be with his baby.

A foghorn.

He believes: I am the suicide she cannot commit.

He thinks: I walk the trees to my mother but will not fall.

He means: I am here despite her hand-me-down temptations, here for good.

Acknowledgements

Thank you to the BC Arts Council and the Canada Council.

Roy's encyclopedia – its questions, answers, his squirrel story – is adapted from several wonderful volumes of *The Book of Knowledge: The Children's Encyclopedia*, published by the Grolier Society in 1942. Also important (and wonderful) was *The Wind Came All Ways: A Quest to Understand the Winds, Waves and Weather in the Georgia Basin* (Environment Canada 1998) by Owen S. Lange. The title of Lange's book comes from Emily Carr's journals.

Many people – friends, family, editors, students – are asked to say the right things at the right times and do. I'm grateful to them, and in particular to Jack Hodgins, Mark Jarman, Bruce Grierson, John Burns, John Metcalf, Max Jackson and Tom Henry.

And the late Sandra Elder.

TOM HENRY

Lorna Jackson spent nine years as a musician on the bar circuit in British Columbia before settling on Southern Vancouver Island. She has been a columnist for *Quill & Quire* magazine, a contributor to *The Georgia Straight,* and serves on the editorial board of *The Malahat Review.* She is the author of the acclaimed story collection, *Dressing for Hope,* and her writing has appeared in such magazines as *Brick, The Fiddlehead,* and *Canadian Fiction Magazine.* She teaches in the Department of Writing at the University of Victoria and lives in Metchosin.